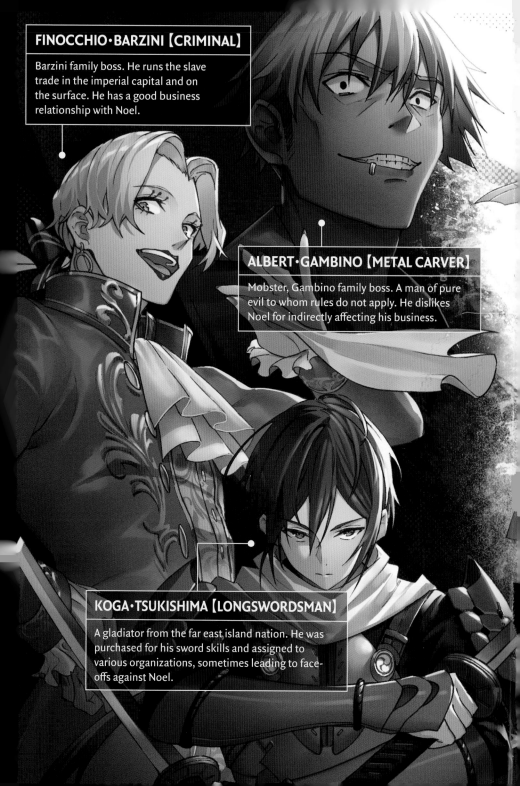

FINOCCHIO·BARZINI 【CRIMINAL】

Barzini family boss. He runs the slave trade in the imperial capital and on the surface. He has a good business relationship with Noel.

ALBERT·GAMBINO 【METAL CARVER】

Mobster, Gambino family boss. A man of pure evil to whom rules do not apply. He dislikes Noel for indirectly affecting his business.

KOGA·TSUKISHIMA 【LONGSWORDSMAN】

A gladiator from the far east island nation. He was purchased for his sword skills and assigned to various organizations, sometimes leading to face-offs against Noel.

LYCIA·MERCEDES [ARCHER]

Member of rival party Lightning Bite. She is a member of the long-lived elven race and has taken a liking to Noel.

ALMA·JUDIKHALI [SCOUT]

Successor to a legendary assassin. Interested in Noel, who intends to become the strongest Talker, and covertly creates an opportunity to meet him.

NOEL·STOLLEN [TALKER]

Member of the up-and-coming Blue Beyond party. Heir to his hero grandfather, he aims to be the strongest Seeker in the world.

I would no longer waver. I would no longer mourn.
There was only one path for me.
"I will conquer the strongest to become the strongest."

CONTENTS

KEYWORDS

SEEKERS

A Seeker is exactly what it sounds like: a person whose profession is searching for missing things. They may seek treasure buried in ancient ruins or hunt criminals, but they make the most money from locating and subduing the beasts that threaten the world. Seekers are managed by the Seekers Association. The minimum age to join is fifteen.

CLAN

A Seeker organization officially recognized by the national government. The national government manages all requests to subdue beasts, and only accepts bids from clans. Seekers who do not belong to a clan can accept subcontracts from clans that cannot fulfill a request for some reason.

TALKER

A rearguard battle-type class that serves a buffer role. Every Talker possesses skills that they can use to buff allies through verbal commands, and without expending mana points (MP), though they cannot benefit from these buffs themselves. As Talkers tend to play support roles, lacking the ability to defend themselves, the class is widely considered a poor one.

THE MOST NOTORIOUS ⟨TALKER⟩ RUNS THE WORLD'S GREATEST CLAN

NOVEL
1

WRITTEN BY
jaki

ILLUSTRATED BY
fame

Airship

Seven Seas Entertainment

The Most Notorious "Talker" Runs the World's Greatest Clan Vol. 1
© 2020 jaki
Illustrated by fame
First published in Japan in 2020 by OVERLAP Inc., Ltd., Tokyo.
English translation rights arranged with OVERLAP Inc., Ltd., Tokyo.

Seven Seas press and purchase enquiries can be sent to
Marketing Manager Lianne Sentar at press@gomanga.com.
Information regarding the distribution and purchase of
digital editions is available from Digital Manager CK Russell
at digital@gomanga.com.

Follow Seven Seas Entertainment online at
sevenseasentertainment.com.

TRANSLATION: Jenn Yamazaki
ADAPTATION: Nick Mamatas
COVER DESIGN: Erika Terriquez
LOGO DESIGN: George Panella
INTERIOR LAYOUT & DESIGN: Clay Gardner
COPY EDITOR: Meg van Huygen
PROOFREADER: Teiko
LIGHT NOVEL EDITOR: Nibedita Sen
PREPRESS TECHNICIAN: Rhiannon Rasmussen-Silverstein
PRODUCTION MANAGER: Lissa Pattillo
MANAGING EDITOR: Julie Davis
ASSOCIATE PUBLISHER: Adam Arnold
PUBLISHER: Jason DeAngelis

ISBN: 978-1-64827-610-1
Printed in Canada
First Printing: October 2021
10 9 8 7 6 5 4 3 2 1

THE MOST NOTORIOUS "TALKER" RUNS THE WORLD'S GREATEST CLAN

Prologue

"**D**ON'T LET ANYONE look down on you."

That was what my grandpa, a Seeker, always used to say.

A Seeker is exactly what it sounds like—a person whose profession is searching for missing things. A Seeker's target may be treasure hidden in ancient ruins, the ruins themselves, perhaps even a fugitive or an unknown creature. But the plunder that brings the greatest profit and most renown has to do with the coveted Abyss.

When a link is established between this world and the Void, ordinary land and buildings grow tainted by the Abyss. Seekers strive to locate these abyssal places and hunt beasts that manifest in these accursed spots. At least, that's what they're most commonly known to do.

If an Abyss is ignored, it will continue to indefinitely corrode the world, so the government encourages and supports the work of Seekers. Beasts, who thrive within Abysses, must be hunted and subdued to purify the land. Further, materials harvested from beasts are essential to produce the many inventions that form the basis of modern civilization.

Modern *magic-engineered* civilization.

Magic-engineered civilization is more prosperous than any that had ever existed. Today, massive airships dot the skies. Seekers, thanks to their wealth, their physical prowess, and their essential role in harvesting the raw materials necessary to keep society running, are superstars, universally hailed and beloved.

"Noel, men can't let anyone look down on them."

My grandpa was once a famous Seeker in the imperial capital of the Velnant Empire, Etrai. He was the toughest of the tough, a true hero.

"Noel, you better become a man whom no one looks down on," he said, stroking my head with a hand rough as stone from the years he was active.

My grandpa had been a Warrior, a class well-suited to his massive stature. Classes are assigned by an appraiser, based on an individual's potential, skills, and limitations. The average person began with a C-Ranked class and could climb the ranks through hard work and talent.

The most common combat-type class was Swordsman, a C-Rank class. The B-Ranks were called Gladiators, while those who achieved A-Rank earned the title of Swordmaster. In very rare cases, people might reach the special EX-Rank.

My grandpa began as a C-Rank Warrior, advanced to B-Rank Vanguard, then achieved the A-Rank level of Berserker. Finally, he was granted the EX-Rank title of Destroyer.

Though promotions don't change a person's class itself, skill compensation improves greatly, and there are new skills to be gained. Take, for example, strength: C-Rank Warriors have ordinary strength, B-Rankers have preternatural strength, and A-Rankers are truly superhuman. EX-Rank fighters have power akin to the gods.

Grandpa was really strong when he was young, rough, and brazen. My grandma, whom he fell desperately in love with and wooed, was beautiful and very kind. But she was weak. Grandpa adored Grandma so much that he quit being a Seeker for her. They moved from the polluted imperial capital to live in the countryside. He used his savings to buy some land, hired some hands, and founded a vineyard. It sounded like an ideal retirement. They were living the slow life.

My grandpa, once the most feared Seeker—nicknamed "Overdeath" by other Seekers—had become a devoted husband and contented retiree. He and my grandma loved each other dearly and supported each other in everything.

However, my grandma died giving birth to my mother. Her frail constitution made childbirth especially risky. Grandpa was grief-stricken, but instead of abandoning himself to despair, he decided to raise his daughter—my mother—on his own.

My mother grew into a wonderful person. She inherited her father's black hair and hazel eyes, rather than her mother's golden hair and green eyes, but she was otherwise the perfect image of my beautiful and beloved grandma. My mother showed potential in a production class, and when she grew up, she started working at a vineyard. She married a childhood friend. They had me, and the household grew to four.

But I have no memories of my parents. My first memory is of my elderly but still-muscular grandpa crying. I remember the warmth of him holding me while he sobbed.

"Noel, you poor child... You got me, kid. You'll never be alone. I... I'll never die, no matter what! I swear it, upon the name of Overdeath!"

My parents died in a carriage accident while I was still too young to understand. The gossipmongers said that the accident was caused by a curse laid on Grandpa by all the beasts he'd killed. They said that every member of Grandpa's family died young due to that curse. My grandpa didn't let them get away with that, of course. Whenever he overheard someone talking like that, he beat them to within an inch of their life with a steel bar he carried with him. And he always told me one thing.

"A man can't let anyone look down on him. He must defend his family's honor."

I remember him saying that after I was bullied and called a cursed child by the neighborhood hoodlums. Grandpa went to their houses and tore them down to their very foundations.

Grandpa often spoke about his time as a Seeker. He and his comrades were my heroes. It was only natural that his stories made me grow up to admire Seekers.

"Noel, you look exactly like your mother," he told me once. "But in you, I see talent as a Seeker that she didn't have."

He was right. When I turned ten, I was assessed for a class. I was told that while I had potential as a Warrior, I was most suited for the class I least wanted.

I was assessed as a Talker—a class specializing in party support.

The Talker's role is to enhance the power of a party's warriors. In other words, it was a supporting role—a buffer.

I'd really wanted to be a Warrior. Not only did I want to follow in Grandpa's footsteps, but also because Warriors develop strong offensive and defensive skills. Buff specialists such as Talkers, by contrast, focus only on support skills. Talkers are the weakest fighters and extremely vulnerable in the field. We have to depend on the rest of our parties to survive.

Even with a tank present to absorb the brunt of the attacks, lacking the ability to protect yourself can be fatal for a Seeker. Even Healers have *some* offensive skills. Talkers, on the other hand, are nearly powerless.

It's common for Seekers to mock Talkers for their weakness. It hurts to hear, but the truth often does.

When I received my assessment, Grandpa laughed gently and stroked my head. I couldn't bring myself to look at him.

"Oh, Noel, don't cry. It doesn't matter how you were assessed. I'll teach you to be the best Seeker the world has ever seen, Talker or not!"

I loved and respected my grandpa. I believed what he said. I knew I could trust him, and so I began training under him. The training was relentless and demanding. My ever-gentle grandpa disappeared during it, leaving only a fiercely strict instructor who was the Seeker leader feared by his brothers in arms, who called him Overdeath.

"On your feet, Noel! Beasts don't rest! No matter how much it hurts, you need to get right back on your feet. Don't just lie there, dummy!"

More than once, I wound up kicked into the middle of next week while I lay hurt and writhing on the ground. I trained harshly from morning to night. In the early days, I was often covered in puke from my exertions, and I bled from my rectum.

But no matter how hard it was, I trusted Grandpa. He was right, after all. I knew that this intense training regime came from a place of love. The beasts would sniff out my weaknesses, if I had any. I dared not neglect my training, or my career as a Talker would be nasty, brutal, and short. Grandpa was doing all he could to teach me to fight, and I did all I could do to learn. I could survive, even as a Talker, if I could just master Grandpa's cruel lessons.

Four years into my training, I was stronger than I'd ever been. Even though I was going to be a Talker, I was developing skills to match any Seeker. Perhaps I'd even achieve EX Rank one day.

However, Seekers must be fifteen years old—legal adults—to be officially certified by the government. So I continued honing my skills under my grandpa for one more year.

It was near my birthday when it happened...

"You stay inside, Noel! You hear me?!"

My grandpa, usually so calm and collected, wore a ghastly

expression as he led me and his hired hands down into an underground shelter.

That night, the town we lived in suddenly became an Abyss.

An Abyss forms when the concentration of mana in the local atmosphere reaches critical mass. In remote villages such as ours, the townspeople occasionally perform rituals to disperse the mana, but for some reason, the most recent ceremony had failed and the mana had continued to build up. Worse, when Grandpa measured this Abyss with a special instrument, its abyssal depth—which determined how dangerous it was—proved to be 12. On a scale of 1 to 13.

A deeper connection with the Void leads to a greater abyssal depth, and to the Abyss manifesting more powerful beasts. Overnight, our small town was swarming with the strongest of abyssal beasts. Though only a Seeker-in-training, even I could feel the power of the great beast within the core of the Abyss. It was mighty enough to compel even Seekers to bow to it and call it Lord.

My beloved town had been consumed by a black-flamed inferno. In the sky was a venomous red full moon. The strange new dimensions through which the Void sunk its tendrils into our world echoed with wild shrieks of bestial delight and the agonizing cries of human prey.

"Don't worry," my grandpa said to me. "I'll protect you with my life."

He wore a confident smile as he donned his armor. Shrugging off my attempts to stop him, he left the shelter, closing the door after him.

The Abyss had already spread as far as we could see. There was no way for Grandpa to cut his way through the horrors with me and the vineyard workers trailing after him. He also couldn't hide with us, since there was no telling when reinforcements might arrive. Our best chance for survival lay in Grandpa taking on the Lord-level beast at the center of the Abyss.

Before long, we heard the death cries of beasts. There must have been hundreds of them. It was proof that my grandpa was still good with a battle-axe, but I was not reassured. How many beasts had this Abyss manifested? I was terrified of the power of the Lord that unified them.

Eventually, the death cries of the beasts faded. Instead, we heard the sounds of an otherworldly battle. The fight between Grandpa and the beast lord had begun.

The sounds continued for hours until, all at once, they stopped. The horrifying Abyss started to fade away.

Certain that Grandpa had won the battle, I ran out of the underground shelter. Outside, the dawn was breaking over scorched plains scattered with the corpses of both men and beasts.

I ran through the wasteland, frantically searching for my grandpa.

Then I found him.

He was covered in blood, and he had lost his right arm and both of his legs.

Grandpa grinned at me as I held him in my arms.

"I guess age is the one unconquerable foe... To think that Overdeath would end up like this..."

I couldn't stop the tears streaming down my face. I cried so much I thought my body would wither and dry. Seeing this, Grandpa stroked my head gently, as he always did.

"You're such a crybaby, Noel. Just like your grandfather," he said, turning his face from me. "I'm but a shadow of the Seeker I once was... Choosing a life of combat means that the god of death is always by your side. Do you still want to be a Seeker, Noel? Will you travel the same path as this old man?"

I sniffed and wiped the tears from my cheeks. I forced myself to smile like Grandpa and nodded confidently.

The truth was that I had never been so scared in my life. All I wanted to do was hold my grandpa close and scream for him not to die and leave me all alone.

But more than that, I didn't want to show him my weakness.

I wanted to tell him that his grandson was strong and reassure him.

I would never be able to repay him for everything he did for me.

"I see..." he said. "Then you must become the greatest Seeker of them all. Do not bring shame to the Stollen name. That is my last wish."

My grandpa looked at me and reached out to stroke my head again with his one remaining arm. "Noel, make your grandpa this promise."

"I promise, Grandpa... I'll become the strongest Seeker ever."

"That's...my boy... Noel...I'm sorry...I couldn't keep...my promise. I'll...always love...you..."

And with that, my hero died in my arms.

It had been two years since a great man passed. I'd lived my life in accordance with his dying wish.

I, Noel Stollen, Talker, was a Seeker living in the imperial capital.

1 The Ruthless Talker

I WANTED TO BECOME as strong a Seeker as my late grandfather. No, stronger—the *strongest* of them all. That was how I could honor his memory.

But strength comes in many forms. Someone who defeated any foe they faced could be called the strongest, but such a person could never exist. We always brought our weaknesses into battle with us. Nobody was so accomplished a fighter as to be impervious to *every* enemy. Even my grandfather, the EX-Ranked Overdeath, exquisitely balanced in both offense and defense, had his limitations.

My class, Talker, meant that I would never develop combat skills of Grandpa's level. It was impossible for me, as an individual, to become the strongest Seeker.

So what could I do? There was only one answer.

"I'll create the strongest clan and become its master."

A clan was an organization of multiple Seekers. Unlike parties, which were formed on a mission-to-mission basis, clans were officially recognized by the government. To put it simply, a clan was a glorified party. Certain conditions had to be met in order to be certified, but once a group became an established clan, they could also accept missions from the government directly. In other words, a clan was a true professional organization.

I could never become the strongest Seeker on my own. People are strongest when they work together, and so I needed to find the strongest individual Seekers to fill every class and forge them into an unstoppable fighting unit—the most powerful clan in the world.

Fueled by that ambition, I started looking for allies as soon as I arrived in the imperial capital. Luckily, I was able to put together a party with three excellent allies.

The slender, red-haired Lloyd was a Swordsman. Walter, a massive man with dark hair, was a Warrior. Our Healer was Tanya, a blonde beauty.

They were all rookies like me and had graduated from formal Seeker-training schools. They were all older than me. The only thing that matters to a Seeker is actual skill, but among rookies, there can be an excessive focus on small age differences. Infuriatingly, I wound up being considered the group's kid brother. Lloyd was our party leader; I was practically a mascot.

It couldn't be helped, at least not at first. I remained calm, bided my time, and took the opportunity to rack up some experience. A party's roles weren't set in stone. I could still rise to a leadership position, and if my comrades balked, I'd quit and find a new crew to run with.

I didn't dislike the rest of the party, and I trusted them, but it wasn't common for parties to stay together for long. I could leave at any time. Basing your decisions on logic, not emotion, was a skill a Seeker had to master.

But for now, I was a member of Blue Beyond. In order to fulfill my role on the team, I put everything I had into my work.

An Abyss could arise anywhere that mana concentration reached critical mass. It didn't matter if the area was populated. That said, it was easiest for mana concentrations to occur in spaces far from human settlements, such as deep in a forest or in a cave, since such remote places weren't routinely cleared of mana.

This time, the four of us had been dispatched to an abandoned mine that was once exploited by dwarves for mithril. The mine was deep and wide, but luckily, the Abyss had progressed slowly and was only affecting a fraction of the space. The abyssal depth was 4, a relatively low danger level. Even the beasts that had manifested, bloodsuckers known as lesser vampires, were ones for which we had established strategies.

Vampire types generally looked like humans, with great physical strength and regenerative abilities. They were onerous beasts with strong magic at their disposal, save for lesser vampires, which were an inferior subset of the species. Lesser vampires were vaguely humanoid, with four arms, a single cyclopean eye, and pure white skin. They were primitive and unintelligent, but could reproduce, and were even capable of parthenogenesis. A single vampire could birth a dozen offspring in a month's time, making them a horrifying menace.

If we took too long to root them out, this cave would be overflowing with lesser vampires, and we'd need to call for major reinforcements. Even incapable of magic, they were still bloodsuckers who could tear apart an ox with their bare hands, and their superior healing powers allowed them to recover from any injury short of decapitation. Even a proficient Seeker would be doomed if surrounded by vampires.

No one in our group had scouting or tracking skills, so we had little knowledge of our surroundings. It would have been convenient to have a Scout or sharp-eyed Archer, but it wasn't easy to find new members who meshed well with the current ones, even in the huge imperial capital. We couldn't recruit just anyone—a member with subpar skills could do us more harm than the beasts we fought.

But Blue Beyond needed the work, so for now, we relied on Tanya's Illuminate skill—a sufficient replacement for a trained Scout. We all kept our eyes open and beheaded lesser vampires as we came across them. We were careful to kill them quickly and quietly, so the great beast in the center of this Abyss wouldn't notice us. We didn't want to trigger a boss battle before we were ready.

A party with more raw combat power might be able to go straight for the boss and win. Eliminating a boss meant destroying the Abyss, causing all the lesser beasts to lose their connection to this world and return to the Void. Unfortunately, our party wasn't that strong yet. In fact, we shouldn't even have qualified for this mission—the minimum requirement was B-Rank, and we were all Cs.

It was up to me, the Talker, to make the impossible possible.

With my skills, I could not only boost the base combat power of the other members, but also increase the rate at which their HP and MP replenished. We wouldn't tire out easily, even when using consecutive attack skills. Unless we were ambushed, we could keep winning. I could also limit depletion, so we didn't need to rush into dangerous battles in the hope of winning them before we exhausted our stamina.

Talkers and other support classes were typically scoffed at as weak links in the chain, but I was no typical Talker. My grandfather had trained me well, and I was able to provide powerful support without burdening the party. It had been a year since Blue Beyond had formed, and our tactics had served us well. Our persistent ambition had gotten us mockingly nicknamed "The Rookie Giant-Slayers."

Though it was still our rookie year, Blue Beyond had surpassed the other parties and was already recognized as the most effective C-Rank party in the capital.

But If I wanted to honor my late grandfather's dying wish, I needed to aim even higher.

We were able to take out all fifteen underlings without attracting the attention of the boss. As the preliminary survey suggested, they had all been immature lesser vampires, ripe for the slaying.

Had we arrived at the site a fortnight later, there would have been twice as many underlings, and they would have gained the knowledge of how to fight as a group. Lesser vampires lacked the intelligence to employ advanced tactics, but in greater numbers, their combat skill improved.

Once that happened, there would be nothing we could do. The rewards for defeating lesser vampires were lucrative. We were working to make sure we got everything we could out of them, when—

"The boss is about to launch a ranged attack! Vanguard, retreat!" I shouted.

Lloyd, the Swordsman, and the Warrior, Walter, obeyed my order and instantly withdrew. A moment later, sharp tentacles flew out from the boss's back. With a sound like breaking glass, it slammed into and then shattered the invisible barrier our Healer, Tanya, had just put up.

The lesser vampire boss was powerful enough to destroy the barrier by touching it. If they had been a second slower to retreat, the barrier wouldn't have gone up in time and our vanguard would have been shredded alive.

But I wasn't concerned. Everything was going according to plan.

"Tanya, put up another barrier for them! Lloyd, Walter, engage!"

"Got it!"

"Roger!"

"On it!"

Though Lloyd was party leader, I called the shots during battle. Why? Because all my orders came with supporting effects.

Tactician was a Talker skill. When I used this skill, giving orders to my party members boosted the efficacy of their actions by an average of 25 percent, according to our appraisers.

And that's not all I had to offer.

Battle Voice is a Talker skill that increases HP and MP by 25 percent and also accelerates recovery rate. I applied this skill at the beginning of the battle, so the rest of Blue Beyond was able to fight at maximum capacity for an extended period. This gave us an advantage in the battle.

Now that we had dodged the boss's tentacle attack—his last resort—all he could do was delay the inevitable. Lloyd closed in with his sword, Walter with his battle-axe. I could feel the panic rising in the heart of the beast.

But there was a problem none of us had foreseen.

"Ambush!"

Tanya realized it first. When I heard her scream and looked up, I saw three lesser vampires hanging from the ceiling, baring their snaggleteeth. They'd been lurking in the one place we'd failed to check.

We were on the verge of victory, but these beasts could turn the tide. The two fighters heard Tanya's scream and froze in place, unsure of what to do.

I decided for them.

"Stay calm! Keep fighting!" I said, invoking Talker skill: *Peer Support*. This stabilized the target's mental state and reinforced their willpower. My order renewed my team's fighting spirit and eliminated fear from their hearts.

Naturally, I didn't order them to press on just so we could all die in battle. I had quickly calculated the odds of victory. Rearguard positions—Healer and Talker—tended to be held by the more intelligent members of a party. Talkers were generally the smartest of all. And *I* was among the most intelligent and quick-witted of Talkers.

"So, eighteen seconds," I muttered to myself, verifying the strategy I'd put together in my mind. We couldn't lose. Victory was guaranteed. We just needed eighteen seconds.

I pushed the button on my stopwatch and relayed new orders.

"I'll take care of the riffraff! You three concentrate on the boss! Tanya, keep throwing barriers up! Lloyd and Walter, concentrate on feints and dodging. Prepare to activate your limit breaks!"

I was using Talker skill: *Tactician* again. And one more, *Marking*. This skill assigned a target to each member and increased their damage dealt and dodge ability in regard to their assigned target. My party members would suffer damage and dodge reductions against other opponents, but I was going to deal with the ambush so they wouldn't be affected.

I turned back to the ambush flying down at us from the ceiling.

"Stop!" I yelled out. The lesser vampires suddenly lost their wits and hit the ground hard.

Talker skill: *Stun Howl*. This skill stopped opponents. Higher-ranked bosses could resist it, but it worked fine against the ambush. I threw back my long black coat at once and unholstered my silver flame, aiming it at the ambush troops.

The silver flame was a gun that shot magic bullets: a .38-caliber, eight-chamber revolver crafted of mithril, a material with high magic power conductivity. The grip was carved from beast and redwolf fangs retrieved from an abyssal depth of 9. The life ring inside was also engraved with a spell that increased the power of the magic bullets. Because Talkers lack magic attack skills, the silver flame was my only weapon in combat against beasts.

Of course, magic bullets were expensive, so I couldn't just shoot at will. All I currently had chambered were a pair of ice bullets. I fired the first round at the ambush.

The ice bullet hit the ground and froze everything around it. It wouldn't kill instantly, but it froze the limbs of two ambushers. The third, who had quickly recovered from *Stun Howl*, dodged and ran at me, zigzagging, spoiling my aim. I had no aim assist skills to help draw a bead on such a fast-moving target, and I'd have to wait ten minutes to use *Stun Howl* a second time.

Fifteen of the eighteen seconds had passed. The beasts' claws would reach me in four.

It was all going according to plan.

I turned my silver flame toward the boss and bellowed from my abdomen, "Now! Lloyd and Walter, use your limit break on the boss!"

I squeezed the trigger. Of course, there was no way I could hit a target behind me. However, since I had been busy with the ambush, my sudden attack on him made the boss flinch, just for a split second.

That split second would be fatal.

The ice bullet barely missed the boss, hitting the wall instead and freezing the surrounding area. During the moment the boss was watching the bullet whizz past, the vanguard leapt.

"Aura Blade!" "Deadly Drive!"

They each had their own skill, and both had the ability to momentarily increase their attack power fivefold. The boss tried to parry the attacks with his claws, but it was futile.

Talker skill: *Assault Command.* The power of all ally attack skills increased tenfold for ten seconds. I had embedded that in my order.

Assault Command was the strongest of all my skills, but it came with a strong blowback, too. Attack skills are depleted immediately after the ten seconds are up, leaving targeted allies weak and vulnerable for several minutes. *Assault Command* had to be used at exactly the right time. And my timing was perfect.

Their fierce blades sent the boss's severed head flying through the air. The claw of the ambusher stopped short right in front of my eye and fell to the ground.

I stopped the stopwatch and checked the second hand.

"Precisely eighteen seconds. Confirm the enemy is deceased."

As the one issuing orders to the party, it was crucial I plan my tactics down to the second. If my judgment was off, even by a millisecond, the entire party could die. That was why I always timed critical moments such as these to make sure my calculations were correct.

I grinned, just a little, at my achievement in commanding a perfect battle.

"Battle complete. Great job, everyone."

†

"To our victory!" We clinked our jugs of ale together over the table.

We had just taken a coach back from a successful Abyss purification without any casualties. Before calling it a night, we always stopped by our favorite tavern, The Orc's Club, to celebrate.

The table was laden with many tasty dishes besides the frosty ales. Most of them were meat: thick steaks, pork ribs and sausage, roast chicken, and giblet stew. Everything was greasy, but we cleaned all the plates, refueling our most important assets—our bodies.

Seekers are all gluttons. Tall, brawny Walter could pack it away, as you might expect, but even dainty Tanya, the only woman in our party, ate more than the average man.

The more we ate, the more we drank. Although the conversation had started out serious as we reflected on the battle, before I knew it, we were drunk and laughing. It was always like that. Since this job had been so lucrative, we were also ordering and reordering ever faster.

"We did really well today! We got away with five million fil! Five million! That's our biggest haul ever!" Walter reminded us for the fifth time that night. He had a habit of loudly repeating things when he was drunk.

But I knew how he felt. I'd inherited my grandfather's resistance to alcohol, so it took a lot to get me drunk. But if I did, I would behave just like Walter.

Five million fil... A great bag of coins occupied a place of honor as our table's centerpiece. It was full—fifty coins for each of the lesser vampires we'd dispatched. The graceful Tanya was entranced by the bright and shiny coins, and the normally macho leader, Lloyd, also looked elated.

I was happy, but it wasn't enough.

We should have made more. We earned *only* five million fil. That fact made my stomach knot up.

"Look how far we've come..." Tanya muttered, sounding emotional.

Lloyd flipped up his bright-red hair and nodded in agreement. "It's only our first year, and we're already doing so well. We can afford to aim higher. We should all be close to B-Rank by now."

He was full of confidence, and I agreed. Everyone here was guaranteed to move up a rank.

A number of conditions had to be met to rank up, and we were very close to fulfilling the ones for B-Rank. There were three classes I could choose from upon ranking up, and naturally, I planned to pick one that would strengthen my current role. My team members all felt the same way.

It had been a year since we started out as Seekers. As Lloyd said, everything was going smoothly. But successful rookies like us attracted a fair amount of jealousy.

The imperial capital was home to a number of taverns that catered only to Seekers. They not only served food and drink but also served as centers for intelligence gathering and recruitment. Perhaps as a result, though these rules were unwritten at best, each tavern had a minimum rank and results for admission. C-Rank Seekers couldn't patronize taverns reserved for Bs, and were even kicked out of certain C taverns if they lacked the requisite number of kills. It was common to hear stories of ignorant newbies being "baptized."

The Orc's Club was appropriate for our rank and results, but even those with the same rank and results were further subdivided based on education and age. As we'd only been Seekers for a year, we were all between sixteen and eighteen years old. There were other tables around the bar, occupied by parties similar to the Blue Beyond, but dark clouds hung over the tables where older parties gathered. Those were the Seekers who were stuck, unable to move up in rank.

While they'd been active for a long time and earned the results necessary to get them into this tavern, such Seekers were often more arrogant than their abilities warranted, and they envied these promising young guns. In fact, one of them was glaring at us right now. When I glared back, he awkwardly averted his eyes and returned to nursing his drink.

I wasn't in the mood to make something of it, but if I did nothing, he'd peg me for a weakling and might try something later. Sometimes, you had to push back.

"Hey, who are you mean-mugging?" Walter asked me.

"Nobody."

Walter, red-faced from the alcohol, peered at me over the rim of his mug. The incident wasn't even worth sharing. I let it go and started chewing on a sausage, but he kept pressing me. "What, what is it? If you have a problem, talk to me."

"Shut up. It's not worth it."

"Are you still mad about our haul?"

"No. Forget about it, let's just drink."

"You care too much about money," he said. "There's a lot more to being a Seeker. I'm sure your beloved grandfather would say the same thing."

"Huh?" I was going to just ignore him, but it pissed me off that he was trying to use my grandfather against me. What did he know about my grandpa? I'd told them that I was the grandson of Overdeath, but I didn't remember saying anything about how he'd trained me, or even that he *had* trained me. Walter had a lot of nerve.

If anything, my grandfather had actually taught me the opposite. I was constantly told that as a Seeker, I needed to be concerned with money. Money, money, money. Everything a Seeker did required money. Buying all the equipment we needed in the field, procuring new gear, or repairing old gear—none of it was cheap.

But despite the financial practicalities of our profession, most Seekers put on airs about money. There was a culture among Seekers that dubbed mercenary concerns "unrefined," and this, in turn, often caused trouble. Had I negotiated our fee for this job instead of Lloyd, I would have demanded another 500,000 fil. The materials one could harvest from the corpses of lesser vampires had been in high demand lately.

But when I suggested negotiating, the attitude of the other three was "If we can get five million, then there's no reason to make a fuss over another five hundred thousand." Since I wasn't the party leader, I had no choice but to go along with the majority.

But 500,000 fil wasn't chump change. There was a lot we could do with that kind of money. To dismiss it as not worth negotiating for proved that the rest of my party didn't really understand money. They were oblivious to the market value of the materials we harvested from the beasts, and they had no concept of raising our compensation through negotiations.

It was infuriating. But I understood there was no point in letting my irritation spur me to rash behavior, so I kept those thoughts to myself.

"I'm not mad. That's over and done with." I swallowed my anger along with my drink and sighed. It was annoying to hear them talk down to me, but they were drunk. It would be a waste of effort to argue.

"Yeah, you're the one who keeps bringing it up, Walter. Noel might have had a strong opinion about our fee, but in the end, he went along with what we said. Right?" Tanya said. She was seeking to deescalate the situation, but I couldn't bring myself to nod along.

It wasn't like I'd acquiesced because they'd convinced me they were right. I'd given up because it was pointless to keep arguing. But they were just so misinformed...

All I could muster up was a weak smile, but for some reason, that got on Walter's nerves. He slammed his mug on the table and started yelling. "Stop sniggering like a fool! I'm pissed off!"

"What?"

"Your greed affects everyone in Blue Beyond! You better think long and hard about that!"

"What are you talking about?" I asked. "You're the ones babbling on about five million, five million, five million. It's okay if you do it, but not if anyone else does?"

"What's wrong with being happy about a just reward?! I'm not greedy like you!"

For such a big man, he sure could act like a child. But as the saying went, only other drunks could reason with a drunk. I decided to be polite and gentlemanly in my response.

"Yes, you're right, you're right. It's all my fault. You are always right, Mr. Walter. I agree with you completely. You are simply wonderful."

"What's with your attitude?! I'm two years older than you!" Walter snorted, glaring at me with wide eyes.

"What does age have to do with it? Are you saying you'll obey anyone just because they're older than you? Don't make me laugh. *Skill* is all that matters to a Seeker. It would be pretty naïve to try to hide behind your age, eh, Walter?" I said.

"Y-you..."

A vein bulged in Walter's forehead. For a second, I thought it might burst and start spurting blood. He stood up, kicking his chair away, glaring at me furiously the entire time.

"Watch yourself, Noel! All you can do is hide behind us and give orders. You have a lot of nerve for someone who's always running his mouth from safety, out of the line of fire!"

"You're precisely right; I have an easy life thanks to you, Mr. Walter. I really am grateful. You are a veritable god of war! Especially compared to my useless self, who can only bark orders! You are a Seeker among Seekers. I am in awe of you, truly."

I stuck my fingers in my mouth and whistled, escalating Walter's anger and frustration so rapidly that I thought he might shatter his own teeth from clenching his jaw.

"Noel...are you ready to back up what you're saying?"

"Huh, what? I'm just praising you. Don't get so worked up. Shouldn't a Seeker keep a cooler head? Or do you want me to coddle you? Shall I sing you a lullaby? You've gotten so big—a big *baby*, that is, eh, little Walter? Ah, such an adorable little fella, you are."

"I-I'll kill you!" Walter, finally reaching his limit, moved to grab me. I twisted my lips at the exact scene I was anticipating.

I decided to take him on. Just because he was a Warrior, the vanguard of our party, didn't mean he could win a punching contest while drunk. When I stood up, ready to throw my most powerful punch, Walter lunged at me. Lloyd, who had been watching quietly, stepped between us.

"Knock it off. You're pathetic!" He was angry with me. And I'd thought I had a free pass to beat Walter's face in...but my plans for the evening had been canceled by the party leader's intervention.

I held both hands up in truce and sat down. Walter clicked his tongue and buried the hatchet as well.

"You really are both idiots..." Lloyd said, rubbing the flustered Tanya's shoulders to soothe her. They were lovers. I had my doubts about intraparty romance, but I lacked the authority to object.

Incidentally, Walter also had feelings for Tanya. But Tanya had chosen the clean-cut, slender Lloyd, not the rough, masculine Walter. It was an extremely awkward love triangle.

"Let's get going. I'll divide the reward." Lloyd laughed easily, deescalating the situation.

His handsome smile was worlds apart from Walter's discontented scowl. No wonder Tanya had chosen him.

The five million fil were distributed as follows.

First, two million was set aside as capital for the party. This would be used to fund future activities. It also served as insurance in case something happened.

Next, two million was used for party expenses. This was needed to replenish our supplies, to repair and improve equipment, or buy new equipment. Lloyd and Walter's weapons had been blunted in the battle with the lesser vampires, so they needed sharpening. I also needed more bullets for my silver flame. It would probably all total two million fil even if we went to the armament shop that gave us good deals.

Finally, it was time for our individual compensation.

"This is all that's left?" Walter's shoulders slumped. Hard to believe how elated he'd been moments ago.

We each got 250,000 fil. Considering a normal job came with an hourly wage of one thousand fil, it was nothing to sniff at... but it was disappointing, compared to five million. Tanya was also somberly looking at the two gold coins and one larger silver coin in her hands.

I wasn't about to say I told them so. I might feel validated, but it would just make all of them feel worse.

"Come on, now, don't look so glum," Lloyd said with an uneasy laugh. "Our individual shares are a bit low, but our party's capital is growing steadily. Plus, if we get another big job, we can make just as much."

He was right...partly.

"Lloyd, this was a rare, high-paying job. They don't come along every day. More importantly, we didn't get this straight from the government. One of the clans passed it on to us. Normally, they'd keep this kind of job for themselves."

"That's true... That's true..."

Requests for Abyss purification were all handled by the government and normally only given to clans. There was a way to get Abyss requests without being part of a clan, though. Clans would often subcontract out Abyss missions rather than simply refuse them, since the assessment system granted higher ratings to clans that accepted more requests per year. The request to take out the lesser vampires had been outsourced to us by a clan.

Abyss-related work paid well and was excellent training. Seekers like us, who chose not to join an existing clan, would go around to the other clans and take on their excess missions and turn a decent profit. The plan was to earn enough money and rank up sufficiently to start our own clan one day.

Of course, the clans didn't hand over the entire fee to their subcontractors. We had to pay an expensive commission. The harvest rights to the beasts we killed also belonged to the clan, so if we didn't negotiate carefully, they'd just take advantage of us. On the other hand, if we drove too hard a bargain, the clan might never hire us again.

But given our successful track record and ability to fight at a level above our ranks, the time was right. So I asked, "Lloyd, how much party capital do we have?"

"Huh? Umm... With what we got today, we're up to 12.8 million fil," he said.

As the leader, Lloyd was responsible for managing the party capital. And 12.8 million was in line with what I remembered.

"That's enough for us to start our own clan."

"Huh?!" Lloyd was surprised. The other two cried out as well.

"Noel...you know as well as us that we have to pay the government twenty million fil in order to create a clan."

This twenty million fil wasn't just graft. It was insurance, in case a clan failed to complete a mission by the deadline that the government sent.

Abysses grow when left alone. Therefore, they needed to be purified as quickly as possible; any delay made an Abyss larger and more dangerous...and missions more expensive. The failure of one clan meant that the next contractor hired to try to purify an Abyss could demand a higher fee. That was why we had to pay twenty million fil up front. The fee was compulsory, due every six months.

"I know. But we've grown stronger over the past year. We've also built a reputation. We can't just live off of subcontracts forever."

"I mean, I know how you feel but..."

"I'll pay the remaining 7.2 million," I said.

"Huh?!"

They were even more surprised this time and it showed in their reactions. They'd never expected me to offer to pay the 7.2 million-fil difference myself. Honestly, it wasn't a small sum for me. I did have an inheritance from my grandfather, but there wasn't much left of it.

I had used a significant amount to help the vineyard staff get back on their feet after that terrible night, and to support myself until I became a Seeker. I was very particular about equipment thanks to my grandfather's teaching, and the best stuff was always priced at a premium. Quality equipment cost an arm and a leg, but it also let you keep your arms and legs attached to your body.

I didn't just have a silver flame—I also wore a long, black coat of the highest quality. This coat, made from the myocardial fibers of a black dragon, a beast with an abyssal depth of 8, was highly durable and also boosted my resistance. There were many other expensive items I'd purchased in order to become a Seeker, such as the instruction manual for the attainment of skills.

"Of course, you can pay me back once the clan is on track," I said. "It's not like I'm giving you a handout. I just want to save money for the future, and we'll earn more if we establish our own clan rather than just taking leftovers from others."

If I could put these three in my debt, it would be easier to convince them that I should be the leader too. It felt a little unfair, but I was ambitious.

"Where would our base be? We need a building in the imperial capital to be our base in order to form a clan. Land here isn't cheap. We could rent month-to-month, but that would cost too much," Lloyd said.

"Don't worry, I know a place we can rent for cheap."

"Seriously? But..."

Tanya jumped in, as if pained by the sight of Lloyd hemming and hawing. "Noel, I know you're serious, but don't be hasty. Even if we rush into forming a clan right now, I really don't think it'd be sustainable."

"Why?"

"Why? Well, we're still rookies. We're only C-Rank, and still young. I'm seventeen, Lloyd and Walter are eighteen, and you're only sixteen. Even though we're technically adults, in the eyes of the world, we're still children. It doesn't matter how strong we are—it won't go well."

"Why?"

"Well, because..."

I held up my hand to stop her. Tanya wasn't wrong, but she wasn't right either. Her reaction was normal, but trying to equivocate did no one any good.

"So when, then? How many years must we wait before you think we can start a real clan? What are the necessary conditions for success? If we never start a clan, then we'll always be newbies."

"Well..."

"I've been studying Seeker clan structures forever. I have all the knowledge we need. But book learning can only take us so far—we need real experience, the kind we can only get by actually founding a clan. We'll never move forward if we don't take the next step."

"Uh, uh..." Tanya tried to protest, but she couldn't find the words. She looked to Lloyd for help. They were a tight-knit couple.

"Noel does have a valid point. Some things can only be learned through doing. But the government controls the highest-paying Abyss-related work," said Lloyd. "If they dismiss us for our youth, then establishing a clan will be futile. Can we really afford to pay the compulsory insurance fee every six months? If we rush into this before we're ready, it'll bankrupt us."

"That's not right, Lloyd. We'll be able to get work precisely *because* we're young," I said.

"What do you mean?"

"We're young and we're good-looking. Both those things are important."

"I don't know what you're trying to say, but..." Lloyd tilted his head to the side. The other two had the same expression on their faces. They really didn't know, huh?

I looked closely at them again.

Lloyd, our leader, was a Swordsman. He was slender but lithe, with fiery red hair and delicate features that distinguished him from other Seekers, who were mostly a rough crowd. Every action he took was elegant and refined.

Tanya, our Healer, was beautiful, with a kind face and well-maintained hair that shone gold. She was friendly and mild-mannered and, thanks to her prowess as a healer, had a number of fans who idolized her as the Holy Mother.

Then there was our Warrior, Walter: tall, hulking, muscular.

He wasn't the type to care much about his appearance, keeping his black hair cut short, but he had chiseled features and there was an appealing wildness about him.

I was the final member, the Talker. I'd inherited my mom's looks, so I wasn't hard on the eyes. In fact, I was often mistaken for a girl, but I'd long since given up on caring about such things.

"The government is encouraging citizens to become Seekers right now," I continued. I had their attention. "Now, what kind of Seekers might inspire young people to want to be like them someday? Strong ones? Of course. Ones who conduct themselves well? That would certainly help. But most of all, they'd have to have charisma."

"I see..." Lloyd realized the point I was trying to make. He stroked his chin and chuckled.

"That's right—charisma, youth, and looks. The greatest Seekers are celebrities, after all. If we're strong, young, and attractive, the government could use us as their poster clan."

"In other words, they'll favor us because we're young and hot?" Walter asked, finally starting to sober up.

I nodded. My famous grandfather, Overdeath, had been both strong and handsome too. He'd always dressed well, and he had been pretty popular with the ladies in his day.

"Of course, we'd need the skills to back it up," I said. "But the most successful clans also all happen to have good-looking members."

"I won't deny that's one aspect of being a Seeker," said Tanya. "I only wanted to become one because of a certain Healer I admired.

But... I don't know how to put this, but I don't like the idea of selling myself like that." She stopped talking. She finally understood what I'd been getting at, but she didn't look happy about it.

"Do you two feel the same way?"

"I'm on board," Walter answered. He crossed his arms over his chest and laughed audaciously. "I'm getting tired of this low-paying work. Let's have our own clan. If we rake in more cash, we can have all the good ale and good women we want. Yep. No downsides at all."

"Walter! This is serious. Stop messing around!" Tanya raised an eyebrow in anger, but Walter wasn't joking.

"I am serious, Tanya. What's wrong with wanting status, honor, and money? You want the same things, if not to the same extent."

"Th-that..."

"Or what? You want to be my girl instead? In that case—"

"Walter!" Lloyd slammed his hand on the table, his face twisted in fury. Walter was hitting on his girlfriend right in front of him. That would piss anyone off, no matter how noble they were.

"I'm just joking. Don't get mad, leader," Walter said, offering a loose smile. Lloyd just sighed.

Intraparty romance really was a problem, and this was exactly the kind of trouble it caused. Tanya had clammed up, looking embarrassed. Walter wanted her even more than status, honor, or money. He didn't often show it, but he did seem to be just a romantic at heart.

"I'm serious about starting a clan, though," Walter said. Neither Lloyd nor Tanya argued.

"So that's two in favor. Lloyd, tell us your opinion as a leader," I said.

"That's tough... You really want to start a clan right away, no matter what?"

"I'm sorry," I said, "but this is one thing I won't back down on. If you decide to put it off to some undetermined date, then I want my portion of the capital back. I'll leave the party."

That caught them all off guard. "Noel...don't you think that's a little extreme?"

"I won't deny that it is. But if we're not going to move forward, I would rather go my own way than sit here and be berated by you guys. I told you when we formed the party that I had a dream. My dream is to become an even greater Seeker than the great Overdeath."

"A dream..."

Lloyd thought for a long moment before finally opening his mouth to speak. "Okay, then. Let's form a clan!"

"Lloyd, really?!" Tanya turned angrily toward Lloyd. She seemed really opposed to the idea.

"We're going to have to do it eventually anyway."

"B-but..."

Lloyd smiled gently at Tanya's persistence. It was strange... I couldn't put my finger on it, but something about this exchange nagged at me.

"Noel."

"Hmm?"

"This is my decision as leader. Are you happy now?"

"Yeah. I'm glad you understand. When should we discuss the details?"

"Let's talk after we've rested and sobered up. How about in the afternoon, the day after tomorrow?"

"Very well, then. The afternoon, the day after tomorrow. I'll come to your place," I said.

With that, our celebration—which had already lasted a bit longer than usual—came to an end.

As it turned out, this would be the last time Blue Beyond would celebrate.

✝

I wake early. It doesn't matter how tired I am from the day before, or if I have a job that day—I always wake at 5 a.m. and immediately start training. On the day I was supposed to meet with Lloyd in the afternoon, my morning routine was exactly the same as ever. I began by running the perimeter of the imperial capital—about 50 kilometers, carrying a pack as heavy as three large men the whole way. That took about three hours. After that, I ate breakfast at home, then performed a quick bodyweight routine of fingertip push-ups, sit-ups, and reverse sit-ups, all as a warm-up for two hours of resistance training with barbells.

One thing my grandfather taught me was that even members of the support classes needed physical training. In a pinch, your own body may be the only weapon you have.

Talker skills can be activated by simply speaking the words, so they don't deplete MP. It's still exhausting to use them continuously, just as giving a rousing, hours-long battlefield speech might be. Not to mention that hunting down Abysses and fighting beasts was far more strenuous than your usual morning promenade.

My skills had effects on my party members, but not on me. I couldn't use my skills to enhance my own physical prowess. If I were rendered unable to use my skills or think clearly because of exhaustion at a critical moment, I'd jeopardize the party.

I always carried potions with me during Seeker jobs, but it wasn't enough. You couldn't always find time to down one in the heat of battle, and if the bottles broke, I'd be sunk. Rigorous training was the only answer.

My morning training finally finished, I washed away my sweat in a hot shower and then gulped down a bottle of potion from the icebox.

"Yuck..." It tasted horrible as usual. Imagine a fine puree of apples and raw fish. It wasn't so bad that I couldn't handle it, though. A post-workout potion made my muscles heal themselves instantly, so I never needed to take rest days.

While I was doing my cool-down stretches, I heard loud footsteps coming down the hall. Walter burst into my room without knocking.

"Noel, it's terrible!" he cried, panting. He was a mess, his eyes were bloodshot, his face dripping in sweat. It looked like he was coming to tell me the world was ending.

I cleared my throat and crossed my arms in front of my shirtless chest to hide it from him. "Hey, pervert! How about knocking before you just barge in!"

"What are you playing at?! Who would want to see you naked?!"

He was angry with me. I was just trying to lighten the mood... Regardless, it looked like *Peer Support* was working perfectly. He started to calm, inhaled deeply, and was already looking a bit better.

"Anyway, it's important. Read this," he said, handing me a single letter. It was wet with sweat, probably because he had been holding it so tightly. I had to take care not to rip it as I spread it out to read. I instantly knew the handwriting. It was from our leader, Lloyd. He had signed it, and the signature was unmistakably genuine. There was no way someone else had written this.

The four-page letter was long and most of it unnecessary. However, the message was extremely simple.

"Hmm. I see. In summary, Lloyd made a bad investment and he's in a lot of debt. And he embezzled the 12.8 million fil to pay it off. But since I was in such a hurry to establish a clan, he and Tanya fled the capital, so we couldn't grab them before the truth came out. Ha ha. What an imbecile."

The letter explained the entire situation in detail. It was padded aplenty with excuses and apologies that only served him, but that was the gist of it.

That explained the strange feeling I'd had when we were discussing it at the tavern. It was so ridiculous I couldn't help but laugh.

Seeing me in paroxysms only made Walter angrier. "What's so funny?! They betrayed us!"

"That's why I'm laughing. I never thought that straight-arrow Lloyd would embezzle the party funds and then disappear in the night. Ha ha ha! C'mon, Walter, laugh!"

"How can you laugh, idiot?" Walter was so furious that spittle flew from his lips. He crossed his arms and leaned against the wall. "Dammit...what are we going to do? What *can* we do?"

"By the way, where and when did you get this letter?"

"Huh? Just now. I heard about a good job at a tavern last night. I wanted to grab it before someone else could, so I went to Lloyd's boardinghouse first thing in the morning and the old man said he left this letter..."

"When did the man say Lloyd left his room?"

"He said about eight last night."

The city gates closed at 8 p.m. and opened again at 5 a.m. He must have left right before the gates closed so he could get away in the cover of night. A true midnight escape.

"It's 9:30 now, so it's been about half a day. I doubt they hired a coach or borrowed a horse, for fear of leaving a trail we could follow. So even moving at night, they can't have gotten far on foot. With some fast horses, I'm sure we could catch up by evening."

"Maybe so, but we don't know where they went," Walter said.

"We can ask the city immigration officials. As long as we know which gate they left from, we can determine where they're headed. They wouldn't dare wander off the road in the middle of the night.

I know the limits of their stamina. They'd need some rest by now, so they're likely in a nearby village."

Walter snapped his fingers. "That's it! Let's go to the immigration officials!"

"Hold on a minute. What do you intend to ask them?"

"Huh? Are you dumb? You just told me how to find them. I'll find Lloyd and knock him out! It's just gonna eat at me if I don't!"

This guy had no idea. It was true that I had given him a way to find Lloyd, but my point was only that we had options and therefore didn't need to be hasty. After all, we had more issues to deal with than just finding our wayward comrades.

"Do you plan to resolve this with a fistfight? Or if Lloyd weeps and tells you he's sorry, will you forgive him and take him back?" I asked. "What are you, some kind of muscle-bound fairy frolicking through flowery fields? Shall we hold hands and sing a song as we dance? Use your brain and stop living in a fairy tale, dummy."

"Wh-what did you say?!"

"Listen, they're idiots too, but they're desperate. Hunting them down won't solve anything. We won't just wind up fighting... We could kill each other."

If the situation hadn't been dire, Lloyd and Tanya wouldn't have fled. The 12.8 million fil Lloyd embezzled was already gone. They likely didn't even have their share of the bounty from hunting the lesser vampires anymore. We'd been paid our share for the job, but Lloyd had been in charge of the party funds.

They'd absconded with 16.8 million fil, 8.4 million of which belonged to Walter and me. It was a lot of money to steal from your own teammates. Skilled Seekers like Lloyd and Tanya would have had no problem paying it back. But they had chosen to run instead.

This was betrayal, plain and simple. They'd severed all ties with us. Now that they had forsaken the path of restitution, it was clear they had made up their minds. If we ever encountered them again, it would be as enemies, not allies.

"Walter, are you sure you can take out Lloyd?"

Walter and Lloyd were both C-Ranked fighters, but Lloyd was better at close-quarters combat. It wasn't even a near thing—he was far stronger than Walter.

"I'm sure I can," said Walter, "with your support."

It was tempting. I quickly calculated the odds and concluded we had about a 60 percent chance of victory. Even if we won, it would be close, and we'd probably be hurt badly. Lloyd wasn't alone. He had Tanya, a Healer, at his side.

"Can you take out Tanya, too? Dealing with the Healer first is a basic strategy."

Walter looked away and said nothing, finally understanding what I meant. He was in love with Tanya. He'd never be able to raise a hand against her. Given his weakness for her, he'd never prevail against Lloyd, even with my buffs.

Even if he could bring himself to fight her, they were a stronger duo than we were. In a two-on-two battle, we were looking at 20 percent odds of victory. The combination of a high-performance Swordsman and a Healer who could cure wounds even during pitched battle was simple but effective. The combination of a Warrior and Talker of the same rank wasn't nearly a match.

"Even if we beat them, somehow, we'll never get the money back. Chasing them now would be a waste. They know that, too. That's why they ran—they figured it was unlikely that we would pursue them."

"Dammit! So what're we supposed to do, just cry ourselves to sleep?!"

"Cry ourselves to sleep? How stupid are you?"

That was never going to happen. Those two had determined their best option was to abscond in the night. They knew Walter would never harm Tanya. I didn't care about Walter's pure heart, but I absolutely would not tolerate them thinking of *me* as weak.

They had underestimated me.

"My motto is: pay them back a thousand times over. I'll teach them a lesson," I declared, just as I heard a knock on the door.

"Noel! I'm doing laundryyy, so give me your laundryyy!"

The singsong voice with a lisp belonged to Marie, the daughter of the owner of the Stardrop Inn. When I opened the door, a short girl wearing a cute, frilly maid uniform was standing in the hall, a basket balanced on one hip.

"Wow! Noel, you're just as skinny—and manly—as ever!"

I looked at Marie's red cheeks, suddenly remembering I had no shirt on. This little brat was too young to be commenting on a man's body. According to her father, Marie's room was covered with posters of handsome models she liked—including some pictures of male models snuggling up with each other. It's amazing what parents will allow their children to do.

"Laundry huh? Wait just a second—"

"Ha ha ha. Were you busy by chance?!"

"What?"

Marie looked back and forth between Walter and me, her eyes sparkling. "A handsome prince without a shirt and a studly, brawny, big-brother type... I wonder why you would shut yourselves alone in a room..."

"Miss Marie, what are you talking about? Didn't you come for the laundry?"

"Ahhh! All that is holy!" Marie squealed and fled. "Inssspiraaaation!"

I didn't know or even want to imagine what inspiration had struck her, but clearly she was off in her own fantasy world. I hoped from the bottom of my heart that she would stay in that world forever and never come back.

"Wh-what was that all about?" Walter asked, but that was a question no one could answer. All I could do was tell him to look for himself.

"As you saw, some weird kid."

"Anyway, go get ready and come back. I'll get ready too," I ordered Walter. He'd been in such a rush to get here that he was still in casual clothes. He wouldn't be able to fight like that.

"Okay. But what are we going to do?"

"I have an idea. For now, just go get your weapons and arms," I said. Walter looked dissatisfied but left the room anyway.

I needed to prepare to fight too. I quickly donned a shirt and then the holster for my silver flame. I hadn't replenished my bullets yet, but I could still use it to bluff. I also got my knife, some throwing weapons, and my medical pouch, and strapped the lot around my waist and thighs. Finally, I put on my coat and was ready for battle.

Once I was ready, I headed downstairs. At the Stardrop Inn, the guest rooms were on the second floor, and the restaurant on the first. There were plenty of patrons enjoying breakfast this morning.

"Chief, give me five thick steak sandwiches, and put it on my room tab, as always," I told Gaston, the owner, who looked surprised.

"It's a bit early for lunch," he said. "That's quite a princely snack."

"I have a long way to go, so I need to fill up before I leave."

"How about a lunch box?"

"No, it's not that big of a deal."

"I'll whip that right up for you, then," he said. "Do you happen to know where my daughter ran off to?"

"She looked like she was having one of her fits."

"Again?!" Gaston sighed, rapping his hand on his bald head. "What is she doing so early in the day, when we're so busy?"

"You know being a single parent is no reason to let her walk all over you, right?"

"Shut up! She's my only daughter, and she's adorable. What am I supposed to do?"

Gaston and Marie ran the Stardrop Inn pretty much on their own, his wife having succumbed to illness about two years prior. They had some employees, but only for the lunch and dinner rushes.

I sat at the counter, waiting until my steak sandwiches came out, arranged on a large plate with a side of fried potatoes. I bit into one, the umami taste of juicy meat filling my mouth. The steak was medium-rare, the toasted bread slathered with a special mustard. It was delicious and had clearly been made with care.

And it wasn't *just* delicious either. Everything Gaston cooked was imbued with performance-enhancing effects. The change wasn't dramatic, but I felt my energy levels rising with every bite.

The Stardrop was a good inn. The owner was a hard worker and a great cook, providing excellent service, which was why I had chosen his establishment. It was a little pricier than others, but since Seekers' most important assets were our bodies, it was important to live a hygienic and healthy life. If my body broke down, it was all over.

By the time I had eaten three of the steak sandwiches, Walter was back and in full gear: wearing thick armor and carrying a battle-axe that could separate a horse's head from its body in a single stroke. The gear was still dinged up from our most recent battle, but it should do for now.

"You made me rush while you sit here and enjoy a meal..."

"I never said to hurry. And I thought we would need to eat first to get ready. You better eat too." I pushed the plate over to the puzzled Walter, who picked up a steak sandwich and took a big bite out of it.

"It's good."

"Right?!"

Gaston gave us a charming smile from the other side of the counter. Walter must have been hungry, because he polished off the remaining sandwiches and all the fries.

"There, I ate! Now what? Are we going to immigration?"

It was almost 11 a.m. The timing was perfect.

"No. First, we're going to The Orc's Club."

We made our way down a bustling street toward The Orc's Club, passing elves, dwarves, gnomes, halflings, and even demi-human hybrid beasts. The imperial capital was a thriving, cosmopolitan town. While species tended to self-segregate elsewhere, we all lived side by side here. The throngs of people and the heavily loaded horse carts constantly coming and going made for a colorful spectacle.

"Why're we headed to the tavern? I don't get it..." Walter grumbled. It would be easy to explain why, but I chose not to. We didn't have time for the argument that would surely ensue. However, I did decide to give him a bit more explanation rather than just telling him to shut up and obey me.

"Walter." I turned and looked at him. "You're dumb, but you're not useless. You're an excellent Warrior."

"What are you talking about?"

"You have your role and I have mine. In other words, leave the thinking to me. I've commanded this party for a year now. Have I ever steered you wrong? Trust me a little."

"Er...I know that!" Walter clicked his tongue and sped up, basically forced into accepting what I said. Now I was following behind him.

Eventually, we caught sight of the familiar sign of The Orc's Club across the street.

Seekers-only taverns were open during the day to serve Seekers arriving via coach or just returning from missions. Business hours were usually 10 a.m. to 1 p.m., and then from 7 p.m. to midnight. This tavern was already full of Seekers, though it wasn't even noon, some of them freshly returned from a mission and enjoying an after-work pint.

"Now what?" Walter asked quietly. I ignored him and raised my voice.

"I would like to make a request of everyone here! Lloyd and Tanya, members of our party, Blue Beyond, have embezzled our party's assets and fled the capital! Whoever finds them and brings them to us alive will be rewarded with two million fils!"

A hush fell over the tavern when I started speaking, quickly replaced by commotion. Those who didn't get it started talking among themselves, while others started jeering because they did understand. The number of voices mocking us grew, but I didn't care. Word would get out eventually. We'd be ridiculed sooner or later, and I was happy to just get it over with.

Walter, on the other hand, looked panicked. "Noel! Why did you announce that to everyone?!"

I'd expected that reaction; he was a proud man and this was too much for him. That vein was bulging in his forehead again.

"I'm doing exactly what I said. I issued a request. Now someone will capture Lloyd and Tanya for us. We couldn't possibly have done it ourselves."

"But you don't have to tell the entire town!"

"Then how would we know who's willing to take the job?"

"What do you mean? Explain it to me!" Walter demanded.

"I'll explain later. For now, just shut up." I looked back at the other Seekers and called out again. "How about it? Will anyone accept my request?"

In answer, one Swordsman raised his hand. He was a young man with brown hair and sharp features. Under his fur cape, he wore leather armor with golden rivets. Two swords were sheathed across his back, marking him as a dual wielder. I knew him as Wolf, the leader of Lightning Bite.

The C-Ranks of Seekers was swollen with beginners, so it was usually pointless to try to remember everyone's names, even if we did frequent the same taverns. But Lightning Bite, led by Wolf, was widely known as a rookie group that was fast on the rise, just like Blue Beyond.

"You'll really pay me two million fil just for bringing Lloyd and Tanya to you alive?"

"I promise I will pay you on the spot."

"Then I accept. Do you have any idea where they went?"

"Not a clue. But I know they left before the capital gates closed last night."

"They're probably on foot, then," Wolf said. "Got it. I'll leave now." He stood up and the rest of his party followed. He probably had the same idea I had—to ask the gatekeepers about last night.

"Is there anyone else? I'll pay whoever captures them first!"

Two more people raised their hands.

"I accept."

"We will too."

Two more parties left the tavern. Then three more rushed out, each trying to get ahead of the others. This cleared out about half the tavern. No one else volunteered.

All the parties that accepted my challenge were young and ambitious like ours. But none of them fit the profile I was looking for.

I was starting to think I had made a mistake when a single Scout approached me.

"Hey, I have a question about your request," he said in a low voice. The Scout was a skinny, bearded man who looked to be in his mid-thirties—an unremarkable man who showed no sign of enthusiasm or excitement. Maybe he was the one.

"Something you can't talk about here?"

"Heh, yeah. Can we talk in the back? You won't be sorry."

I motioned for the irritated Walter to follow, and we went with the bearded man. I was on my guard in case of a surprise attack, but there was no need to worry.

Once we were at the back of the tavern, the bearded man's expression turned smug. "I know where Lloyd and Tanya are," he said. "I saw a couple of travelers who looked like them on my way back from a job. What you said confirmed it. I'm sure it was them."

"Seriously? Where? Tell us!" Walter cried out, eyes wide.

This man was the one. Seekers came and went through the capital gates at all times, either on their way to a job or on their way back from one. I'd predicted that one of these Seekers, on their way back from a mission, would have seen Lloyd and Tanya fleeing at night. As long as we knew where they were, the rest would be easy.

Lloyd and Tanya's fates were sealed. They couldn't escape now.

"Don't get so worked up. I'm not going to talk for free," the bearded man said, dexterously sliding away from Walter. "It's two million if I bring them back alive, right?"

"That's right. If what you say is true, you should head out with your party immediately. The reward stands as promised," I told him. But the bearded man shrugged his shoulders.

"C'mon now, don't brush me off like that. I'd already be after them if I could. But there's a reason I can't..."

"Let me see. Is it because your party can't take on Lloyd and Tanya? Knowing where they are is pointless if you can't catch them. That's why you want us to go with you, right?"

The bearded man looked flustered for a moment but quickly recovered his nonchalant smile. "That's right. Those guys are strong."

"What's the makeup of your party?" I asked.

"We have one Swordsman, one Wizard, one Healer, and me, the Scout. We don't belong to a clan, so it's just the four of us."

I scrutinized the bearded man again, trying to gauge his skill. He looked older, and on the weaker side for The Orc's Club customers. A party of four at his level wouldn't stand a chance against Lloyd and Tanya. But if Walter and I were to join them, we'd have more than adequate odds of success.

"Am I right to assume the other three are the same level as you?" I asked.

"Oh, yeah. So, how about it? Will you work with us? Of course, you can reduce the reward in exchange for your help. For one and a half million fil—"

"One million. If you need our help, then the two million-fil reward is cut in half."

"O-one million?! No way. Not for only half!" The bearded man was flustered, but I had no intention of giving in.

"One million."

"O-one and a half!"

"One million."

"One million, four hundred thousand!"

"One million."

"Don't make this difficult! You need our help!"

I scoffed at the bearded man, whose face was now bright red. "I do need your help," I said. "But there are other ways. All the other parties who accepted the request are excellent. If we wait here patiently, perhaps someone will capture them."

"B-but they took your money, right? In that case, you need to catch them fast! The other teams might be good, but without the information I have, it will take them forever!"

"Probably. But so what? I have no intention of negotiating. It's that simple. If you don't like it, forget about working together. That's fine by me. What do you want to do? If the deal's off, we're going to go. That all right with you?"

The bearded man looked frustrated and gnashed his teeth, finally shaking his head.

"Fine... One million."

My bargaining had been a success. I knew from the start that an older Seeker with no money, one down on his luck like this guy, would have to give in eventually. In negotiations like these, the one with the money always had an advantage over the one being paid.

"And...where are they?" I asked.

"We passed them on Varley Road, just outside the south gate," the bearded man said. "Considering where we passed them and how much time has elapsed since then, they're probably in Carnot Village or Eulen Village by now."

"Understood. Get your party and wait for us at the south gate. Walter, you go with them. There's something I need to do."

"What do you need to do?" Walter tilted his head.

I forced a grin. "I'll tell you later."

†

Walter, the bearded man, and the man's party were waiting for me at the city gate as we agreed. They also had fast horses rented from the livery stable. We were ready.

"Noel...can you fight Lloyd?" Walter asked me with deep concern when I joined up with them, having finished what I needed to do.

It seemed he still had doubts, even after coming this far. I mean, I did understand how he felt. Though we'd only been a party for a year, Blue Beyond had been through a lot together. But traitors were traitors. It was a fight to either get our money back or cry ourselves to sleep. Not to mention nursing the bitterness of

betrayal in our hearts forever. We had to take care of this ourselves. We had to resolve this, then start over.

"I can fight them," I said. "No mercy."

"Even if you have to...kill them?"

"Of course. If it's us or them, I won't hold anything back."

I meant what I said. I was ready to kill whoever I had to, if
necessary. Being a Seeker meant taking lives. I had already killed
many beasts and more than a few humans with bounties on their
heads. I couldn't very well justify not killing someone just because
they used to be a friend.

"Don't you have a heart?" Walter asked. It was so ridiculous,
I laughed at him.

"Walter, I've frequently contemplated what to do if an ally betrayed me. People stray easily. I wasn't even surprised that Lloyd
and Tanya betrayed us. I just thought, 'Ah, the time has come.'"

"But they were our friends! You mean you never trusted them?"

"Trust, sure, but not blind trust. You can't be sure of everything.
To ally with someone, you need to be able to gauge how far you
can trust them."

And they *had* betrayed us. It was that simple.

It looked like Walter had more to say, but I was done talking.
I looked away from him and mounted one of the borrowed
horses. "If you can't fight them, then you can wait here. I'll get
your money back for you."

Without Walter, our chances at winning dropped significantly,
but there were other approaches we could take. A Warrior that
couldn't fight would just get in the way.

"Don't be an idiot... I'm not that weak," Walter said, mounting his own horse. He goaded it through the gate first. The bearded man and his party followed at a short distance.

"He's soft. Too soft," I muttered to myself without thinking. "If he's not committed, it will just make things harder."

After about three hours of following Lloyd and Tanya's trail, we arrived in Carnot, one of the villages the bearded man had mentioned. It was a quiet farming village about a half-day's walk from the imperial capital. As soon as we saw our two targets leaving a restaurant, we initiated our capture plan.

Not that it was a special strategy. It was clear, even from this distance, that my erstwhile allies had their guard down.

"On a date to the farm, eh? You guys have rich taste," I called out to them. Hearing my voice, they both spun around.

"N-Noel!"

Lloyd's face was twisted in surprise and he put his hand on his sword, as I expected.

But it was already too late.

"Don't move!"

Talker skill: *Stun Howl.*

It worked. The bearded Scout, who had been lurking in the shadows, leapt upon Tanya, pinning her to the ground. In the instant that Lloyd was distracted by Tanya's scream, everyone else, including Walter, sprang from hiding and surrounded them.

A moment later, the effects of *Stun Howl* dissipated. Lloyd and Tanya couldn't hide the look of despair on their face after being completely overtaken in only two seconds.

There were plenty of ways they could have fought back if they'd faced only the bearded man's party. Lloyd could have thrown the knife hidden in his sleeve at the bearded man's forehead, freeing Tanya to blind their opponents with her *Flash* skill. Lloyd could have then used that moment to take out the entire party. Such tactics required perfect timing and cooperation, but they were both skilled enough for that.

However, thanks to me and Walter being present, they were afforded no such opportunities. It looked like Lloyd had assessed the odds and understood that there was nothing he could do. He dropped his sword and surrendered.

The captured pair bowed their heads at my feet.

"Lloyd!" Walter cried out, grabbing Lloyd by the collar. "Why?! Why did you betray us?!"

"Sorry..."

"That's it? You're sorry?!"

I stopped Walter's hand before he could punch Lloyd.

"Lloyd, I understand what happened from your letter. But what about the reward from the lesser vampires two days ago? Where is the party's capital from that?"

"I'm sorry...I used that too."

"For an investment?"

"No...to pay back a debt."

So he had no problem betraying his friends and running away, but he felt morally obligated to repay his debts? It didn't make sense. There was only one explanation.

"The bad investment story was a lie. It was gambling, right? What's your vice? Cards? Dice? Roulette? Betting on fights? It doesn't matter. You lost a lot gambling and got in debt with some bad people, so you used the party's money. Right?"

Investments had an element of luck to them, but they stood a much better chance of paying off—hence the numbers of rich investors around. But with gambling, the house always wins in the long run. The bettor is just a fish, hooked and reeled in. Gambling was nothing more than a slightly more hygienic way of flushing your money down a latrine.

"Answer, Lloyd. Did you gamble away the money I left with you?"

"Sorry..."

"Shut up, you idiot!" Walter shouted, livid. He picked Lloyd up. "I spent years of my life to earn that money! Where do you get off using it to gamble?!"

"You don't understand the pressures of being a leader!"

This surprised me. Apparently, Lloyd had decided to snap back and hold his ground.

"It's not like I wanted to use the party's money!" he said. "But before I knew it, my debts had mounted so high, there was nothing else I could do... Blame me if you want. But are you so much better? You dump all the responsibilities of leadership upon me, and then demand your own rights when it serves you—ugh!"

I kicked Lloyd in the stomach as hard as I could. He flew out of Walter's hands and rolled onto the ground. While he was squirming around, I kicked him again.

"Ugh!"

"Are we better than you? Of course we are. You're the one who said you wanted to be the leader in the first place!"

My third kick struck him in the back, right over his kidney.

"Argh!"

I ignored Lloyd's shrieks, kicking him over and over.

"The pressures of leadership? You think that's an excuse? You have some nerve! The only reason you gambled yourself into debt was because you're an incompetent imbecile!"

"Argh! Ugh, bleeech..."

My eighth or ninth kick must have landed a good hit, because Lloyd started puking blood.

"S-sorry... P-please...stop..." He looked pathetic, his face covered in dirt, tears, snot, and puke as he begged for mercy. "Please...I can't take...any more...argh!"

Oops, kicked him in the face. His pleading after having the audacity to snap back at Walter was so infuriating, I couldn't stop my foot.

That said, this was no more than he deserved. I was a Talker and didn't have much physical strength. By contrast, Lloyd was a Swordsman with the maximum vanguard attribute. My kicks weren't even close to deadly to him. He would be fine.

"If you want to be forgiven, then take a thousand more kicks. I'll listen to your apology after that."

"Eee, eeek!"

I went to kick the quivering Lloyd again when Walter grabbed my shoulder.

"That's enough..."

"Why?"

"Because..."

"P-please, for me! Please forgive Lloyd!" Tanya chose this moment to speak up. She could defend him if she wanted, but did this girl understand her own position? No. No, I didn't think she did.

"Shall I kick you instead, then? I don't discriminate against women. I won't hold back just because you're a girl."

"Huh? W-wait, that's not what I meant!"

"Apparently, you don't understand your role in all of this. You're just as guilty as he is, Tanya. You were gambling with the party money too, right? You wouldn't have needed to run with him, if not."

"N-no! I... I just thought I couldn't let Lloyd go alone..."

Playing innocent. What a fool.

"I'll ask you one more time. You were gambling with him, right? Confess."

"I was. But it was Lloyd's fault. Had he loaned me more money, we would have won. This all happened because he wanted to place all the wagers himself."

After that sudden confession spilled from her lips, Tanya looked up at me, her face red with anger.

"Noel! You used a skill on me!"

"I did. What about it?"

Talker skill: *Confess*. A skill that forced its target to tell the truth. There were laws restricting the use of mind-control skills like this, given their potential to wreak havoc on society. Using them for personal gain could result in immediate imprisonment.

"Do you know what you just did? You can't get away with that!"

"Normally, no. But you're a criminal who embezzled party assets. According to imperial law, use of mind-control skills is allowed when coaxing a confession of a crime from a criminal. I've committed no crime—you have."

"B-but..."

The blood drained from Tanya's face. Apparently, she hadn't even realized she was a criminal.

"The punishment for embezzlement is ten years hard labor. Congratulations! I'm sure your skills will be put to great use breaking rocks! I'm proud to have risked my life for you so many times!" I said sarcastically, applauding slowly as I spoke.

Their faces went white. They knew what embezzlement was but probably hadn't realized until this moment that it was what they were guilty of. People only commit crimes when they're being foolish. And fools are blind to their own foolishness.

"It looks like you're done talking," snorted the bearded man, who had been watching in silence. "It was a good show. Thank you. That's enough. I'm ready for my reward now. You better not try and say you forgot about the one million fil you promised."

"I'll pay your money. You wait there."

"No, I'm done waiting. We're busy. Pay what you owe."

If they'd really been that busy with work, they wouldn't be so down on their luck. "I'm not telling you to wait until tomorrow. Just wait a little longer. The money will be here soon."

"What are you talking about? If you don't have the money, we'll take something else!"

The bearded man reached for my silver flame. Silver flames were worth a lot of money. Even used, they could sell for three million fil. I predicted the man's intentions and movements, and when he reached for my gun, I grabbed his wrist and twisted it up.

"Don't touch me. Your hands stink like squid."

"Y-you tricked me..."

"Don't make me sound like a bad guy. I told you I'll pay you." I glanced around to the rest of his party. "Oops—don't move. You don't want to lose your precious Scout, do you?"

I unsheathed a knife and held it to the Scout's throat, making sure they knew that if they made even a tiny move, their friend was dead.

"Did you think you could steal from me, right to my face, just because I'm not a frontline fighter?" I said. "That's too bad. I may not have the same raw combat power as you, but I have both Walter and Lloyd beat when it comes to guts."

"Erg..." The bearded man succumbed to my wrist lock and stopped struggling. Annoying as it was, I was going to have to keep him like this for a bit. Walter, who had no idea what was going on, nervously gripped his battle-axe and glared at the man's party.

Eventually, we heard the whinny of a horse.

"There it is," I said, releasing my grip on the bearded man and kicking him to the ground.

The horse was pulling an extravagant purple carriage at a great speed. It pulled to a halt before us and a tall man in elaborate, aristocratic clothing, which were the same ugly purple as the carriage, stepped out. His hair was silver and parted straight down the middle. He had sickeningly symmetrical features, highlighted with makeup. Under all that, he looked to be in his mid-thirties.

The man put a purple lace handkerchief over his mouth and twisted his face.

"Ew! The countryside is just covered in dust! Must this whole town smell of manure?" he said as he gestured dramatically. He was the epitome of a foppish dandy, and yet everyone around was frozen in fear at the sight of him.

Then someone said in a shaky voice:

"Finocchio Barzini...the slave trader?"

Light always cast shadow, and the prosperous imperial capital was no different. In fact, it was lousy with deep, dark secrets. Namely, organized crime.

The biggest mob family in the imperial capital were the Lucianos. With branches in multiple countries, they did all the usual shady business you'd expect: prostitution, drugs, gambling, extortion, and murder. They also had tremendous influence on the legitimate side of society. They even had connections to the imperial family, and they virtually ran the capital as a result.

Finocchio Barzini, boss of the subfamily whose name he bore, was one of the leading lights of the Lucianos. His main sources of

income were the slave trade and brothels. The Barzini family held the monopoly on the capital's slave market, and so every denizen of the capital knew who he was.

He was sophisticated but had vulgar taste. He was cheerful but cruel. He was generous but cunning. He despised violence, but he was a purebred sadist. His foppish lifestyle was part of the dichotomy that characterized everything he did; his world was split down the middle, and people called him "the mad clown."

"Oh, there you are, little Noel! Did I keep you?" Finocchio came sauntering toward me with pigeon-toed strides, fluttering his hands. Behind him were two brawny guards.

"You're late. I thought you'd get here faster."

"Ugh! Don't be nasty! I rushed here for you! I came all the way here, at top speed, just for my little Noel!" Finocchio puffed up his cheeks in discontent and twisted his torso, half-stretching, half-posing. He probably thought it was cute, but he just looked like an eel out of water to me.

I'd met Finocchio about six months ago, while working a part-time job without Blue Beyond. We'd been using each other ever since. Everyone else, unaware of our relationship, just looked confused.

"Now then, let's talk turkey," he said. "You've already obtained permission from both of them?"

"Yeah, it's settled. I'll be selling Lloyd and Tanya as slaves," I answered, causing everyone to gasp in surprise.

"Noel, this is what you said you had to do...?" Walter asked in disbelief, and I nodded.

"I suspected Lloyd and Tanya would be broke, so I made a deal with Finocchio to earn back the money we lost. We knew where they were headed, so we agreed the exchange would take place wherever we met up."

I'd had Walter go ahead with the party while I arranged this. I hadn't imagined Finocchio would come personally to seal the deal, but I guess he was so excited at the chance to buy half of Blue Beyond that he'd decided not to trust the job to his underlings.

"This isn't funny!" Lloyd cried out tearfully. "We're Seekers! Heroes!"

"I will never submit to slavery!" Tanya joined in, but her voice was shaking with fear.

"You don't want to be slaves?" I asked.

They lashed out in response.

"Of course not!"

"You shouldn't even have to ask!"

"Well, then, all we can do is hand you over to the military police," I said. "As I said before, the penalty for embezzlement is ten years of hard labor. Do you know the survival rate for prisoners put to endless work in the mines on starvation rations? It's about two percent."

Lloyd and Tanya looked horrified.

"I think you'd do better being sold off as slaves and hoping for a kind master. You're both young and attractive. I don't know how a master might make use of you, but they'd probably take good care of you, in their own way."

They were at a loss for words, but their silence spoke consent.

They had a much better chance at life in a collar than down in the mines. They never really had a choice.

"Now then. Finocchio, try to find them good masters."

"Of course, my little Noel. I shall begin my appraisal!"

Finocchio examined every inch of the two criminals, who were frozen like frogs under the eye of a snake, with his grasping hands as well as his eyes. He finished with Tanya's physical exam quickly, but spent a lot of time on Lloyd's, which involved more penetration.

The average price for a slave in the imperial capital was around five million fil. Taking Lloyd and Tanya's talents into account, I expected they'd fetch at least thirty million as a pair.

Of course, that would be the price at which *Finocchio* sold them. As was customary, I would only get a third of that—ten million fil. Still enough to cover the 8.4 million fil they'd embezzled, pay the bearded man his reward, and have a profit left over.

However, considering that the Blue Beyond was now down a Swordsman and a Healer, it was still an overall loss. I was hoping that Finocchio might pay a premium. My actions going forward all depended on that price...

"Mm! I already knew it, but you both have great bodies! Strong and healthy! You'll live a long time. Lloyd is a bit worse for wear, though."

"We had some trouble apprehending him. It was an unavoidable accident."

"Unavoidable accident? Doesn't look like he put up a fight... Well, how does this sound for a purchase price, anyway?"

Finocchio removed a traditional Eastern abacus from his interior breast pocket and performed a quick calculation with the beads. I frowned at the number he showed me.

"Six million fil?" Far lower than I'd estimated. I wouldn't be able to recover my losses.

"I'm sorry. But there's a reason for this. It's not been announced publicly yet, but the Holy Cross Church is about to issue a religious ordinance of honorable poverty—which is to say, they'll be demanding that the wealthy tithe far more substantially than we have been so far. Even aristocrats and the bourgeoisie can't defy the church, so we all must cut back on extravagances."

The Holy Cross Church worshiped the creation god, Emeth. While the capital was home to many religions, this one boasted the most followers and was historically the best-known cult of the empire. Falling out of grace with the church meant betraying your ancestors and shaming yourself, so no believers dared risk their wrath. In a way, it was an organization even more fearsome than the Luciano family.

"If I were to spend too much on slaves, who knows what the church might say? Both my clients and I have been tightening our purse strings to demonstrate our devotion. Of course, I must keep trading slaves if I wish to be able to afford tasty treats, but my purchase points are greatly reduced for now."

"That's the reason for the extremely low price?"

"That's right. It's just bad timing. Once the church's coffers are refilled, I hope to return to free market prices, but six million is all I could do for now, young friend."

I didn't think Finocchio was lying. He wouldn't tell a lie that could be so easily double-checked back at the capital. There was no way I could defy the Holy Cross Church either.

"I understand. We suffer through hard times together."

"Oh I knew you'd understand. I love you, little Noel! Mwah!"

"So I'll sell them for eleven million fil," I said.

"Thank you, thank you. If you can accept eleven million then— wha?! That's five million more than what I offered!"

I ignored Finocchio's wide-eyed surprise and continued matter- -of-factly, "In fact, I'm increasing the price to twelve million fil."

"Whaaat?! What are you saying?!"

"Thirteen million fil."

"Wh-wait, wait a second!"

"Fourteen million fil."

"Hey, Noel!"

"Now it's fifteen million fil."

"You stupid brat! Just how do you intend to keep up this farce?! Do you think I'm a fool? Huh?! If you want to be fed to the pigs so bad, I'd happily reduce you to slop right now!"

When Finocchio was angry, his clown mask came off, reveal- ing the wild beast that lay underneath. So this was his limit, huh?

I moved closer to Finocchio and whispered, "If you buy them from me for fifteen million fil, I'll tell everyone you bought them for double that. Thirty million."

"You...plan to fudge your own sale price?"

He was as perceptive as I would expect. Finocchio calmed down in an instant and smiled at me.

Normally, market prices are determined by the great tug-of-war between supply and demand. But sometimes, it is the price itself that determines the demand for something. In other words, the higher the price placed on something, the rarer it is perceived to be, stimulating the interest of wealthy buyers. Regardless of his religious obligations, if Finocchio claimed that he bought Lloyd and Tanya for thirty million fil, their value would definitely increase far beyond that. A procurement cost of thirty million fil meant a selling price of ninety million fil. Frankly, that was a fair price for the pair.

"Of course, when an ordinance for honorable poverty is issued, the wealthy try to cut back on unnecessary spending. But the more people deprive themselves, the more they are tempted, don't you think?" I asked. "True luxury items will attract buyers who'll do anything to win the bidding war. You should pay more for things—or people—you can definitely sell. Not less."

"I'm going to be honest... If I say I bought them for thirty million fil, then, as you say, their value will rise," Finocchio replied. "If you'll support my story, then I'm happy to oblige. But it won't be good for either of us if we're caught."

"That's just a risk assessment, right? What's the problem?" I said.

Finocchio put his hand to his forehead and looked up to the sky.

"Agh... I knew you were nuts, but this is something else. You're the only person in the capital who'd ever dare to try to squeeze money out of me. How about joining my family? You can start at the executive level," he said.

"No thank you. I was born to be a Seeker. So, what's your answer?"

"Yes, yes, I know, I know... I'll buy them for fifteen million fil! I'm sure you're already aware, but I'm never giving you a deal like this again! Oh, my, my!"

My negotiations had been a success, helped along by Finocchio's shrewd business instincts. The money would cover my losses until I could put together a new party.

"You actually out-negotiated the mad clown..." the bearded man muttered, dumbfounded. When Finocchio heard that, he pointed his finger at the bearded man. "You, nasty beard!"

"Uh-uh! Wh-what is it?"

"If you ever speak a word of what happened here to anyone, you, your family, your lovers, and your friends will all be dinner for my pigs! You got it?"

"I-I got it! I will never tell a soul!"

"And all of you too! Got it?"

"Y-yes! We got it!" everyone said.

"Fine then! Oh, little Noel. Here is the million on the spot I promised. I'll transfer the rest to your account tomorrow," Finocchio said, handing me a leather bag, which I then tossed to the bearded man.

"The reward I promised," I said.

"O-oh..."

I'd gotten back what was mine, and I'd paid what I owed. There was nothing left to do here. Time to head back to the capital and think about my next move.

"Walter, we're going."

"W-wait, Noel!" Just when I thought she had resigned herself to her fate, Tanya called out, still appealing for mercy. "A-are you really going to sell me off? Please...save me. Aren't we friends?"

"I don't need friends who gamble with my money."

"I'm sorry! Please give me another chance. I'll pay you back even more than I lost!" she pleaded.

"No. I can't trust you. Goodbye, farewell."

Once a traitor, always a traitor. There was no merit to keeping someone untrustworthy by your side.

When I brushed Tanya off, she switched her focus to Walter.

"Walter, please! Save me!"

"There's...nothing I can do." As soon as Walter looked awkwardly away, Tanya let out a bloodcurdling shriek I had never heard before.

"Oh, knock it off! You're supposed to be in love with me, aren't you? So save me, then! Are you useless when it comes to it 'cause of your virgin balls? Do you have goblin snot for brains? I hope you die! Just die, you useless muscle-bound piece of shit! A half-dead cur would be more useful than you!"

The torrent of abuse poured from her, as if a dam had burst, and Walter took it all in, staring at the ground. Lloyd simply looked stunned. His body was there, but his mind was gone.

This was a nightmare. "Finocchio, take them away. I'm tired of them."

"Oh, really? I'm having a great time. This is a wonderful show."

I glared at Finocchio and he shrugged his shoulders.

"Fine, fine, I understand. Come, my puppies, let's go."

At Finocchio's signal, the brawny guards loaded Lloyd and Tanya onto their shoulders and shoved them into the carriage. Tanya cursed me the whole time, calling me every name she could think of.

"Buh-bye, little Noel! Ha ha! Mwah!" Finocchio blew me a kiss goodbye and sauntered away with a sway of his hips. We watched Finocchio and his gang drive off toward the capital and I let out the sigh I had been holding in.

"Ahh... Walter, we're going back now."

"Yeah..."

And then I heard the bearded man let slip an insult I couldn't overlook.

"This weak-ass buffer thinks he can get away with anything just because he's connected..."

Such poor form. He should have learned something from Tanya.

"You're so right," I said. "I'm just a weak-ass buffer who can't even defend myself. Yet somehow, I managed to make all this money. Maybe you useful people should try a little harder, huh?"

When I antagonized them with a huge grin on my face, the bearded man and his team gnashed their teeth. Sarcasm was often the best way to deal with arrogant Seekers, especially failures like these.

"Now then, I wish you luck in your future endeavors," I said, turning to take my leave.

Unable to contain himself, the bearded man spat in frustration, "Just a damn beast who sold his friends off as slaves!"

And now he'd called me a beast.

Beasts were what Seekers hunted for a living. Calling me a beast was akin to calling me the most despicable creature in existence...but also the most notorious one. That suited me.

I decided, then and there, that I would become the most notorious Talker in all the world.

†

"Here. That's your share."

Noel placed a leather bag with seventy coins—seven million fil—in it before Walter. Apparently, the rest of the fee for selling Lloyd and Tanya had been transferred into his account that morning. Noel had called Walter to this non-Seeker tavern on the outskirts of town to hand over his share.

Walter stared at the bag. He'd gotten his money back, but it brought him no joy. No matter what they'd done to him, this money came from selling his friends. But he wasn't man enough to throw it back in Noel's face.

Instead, he silently put the leather bag in his satchel, then took a gulp of the local whiskey. He felt compelled to drink but also felt like he couldn't get drunk, no matter how much he imbibed. He'd been drinking at home even before Noel summoned him, but he remained articulate. He couldn't even taste the whiskey on his tongue.

"So...what are you going to do now?" Walter asked.

Noel replied matter-of-factly. "First, we need to fill the two empty slots on the team. Then we need to train with the new party until we're in sync. If there are no major issues, we can start working again."

"You think you can fill the empty slots?"

"Well, it probably won't be easy. The best Seekers are all already in parties, and even if we could lure them away, they wouldn't want to join a half-broken party. All we can do is wait patiently and do our best to recruit new members. It's too risky to take on any Abysses until we do, and there's not much other work we can do with just the two of us—"

"That's not what I meant!" Walter shouted, standing up and kicking his chair away. "No one can replace Lloyd and Tanya. The four of us were Blue Beyond! It doesn't matter how good the new members are—they can't replace them. Don't you get it, Noel?"

"Nope," Noel said firmly, his expression unchanging. "It's true Lloyd and Tanya were excellent, but no one is fundamentally irreplaceable. They were talented, but ultimately still just C-Rankers. There's an endless supply of those in the capital."

"That's not what I mean either."

"But that's everything there is. A Seeker's profession isn't child's play. Allowing emotion to dictate your decisions is the height of stupidity."

"Erg..." Walter had no response to that. He knew he wasn't capable of making cool-headed judgments. But was he really in the wrong here?

"Hmph. Idiotic," Noel snorted. A cruel smile spread over his face. "You're just hurt because Tanya showed you her true colors. Don't get too sentimental. That's who she was."

"You..."

"Oh, are you mad now? If you still like her after that verbal lashing she gave you, you must be the most faithful dog of all time. Maybe you should buy her? Then she'll always be yours, and you'll live happily ever after."

"Noel, you ass!" Walter grabbed Noel by his collar and raised his fist, but couldn't bring himself to swing. "Why... Why did you..."

Despite being torn from his chair, Noel had the same, thoughtful expression as always. It was almost as if he was keen for Walter to hit him. *If it will make you feel better, I'll take a punch.* He didn't say it aloud, but Walter couldn't help but feel that was what Noel was thinking.

Walter let go and slumped in his chair.

"We'll...never find new members. Who would be dumb enough to join a party with a guy who sold off his teammates to a slave trader?" he muttered despondently.

Noel shook his head. "You're right. Cowards may be turned off. But truly excellent Seekers will understand that the circumstances called for it. They'll probably even appreciate that we punished them properly rather than leaving a scandal in the party unresolved."

"But most people will despise us... The world is full of cowards."

"There's no point in worrying about the riffraff. Forget about making enemies; we need to find new allies. And in order to recruit, we need to be clear on our policies. Up-and-coming villains. It has a nice ring to it. They'll know we're not like the rest," Noel declared, his voice full of confidence. There might be some truth to his words. You could dress it up pretty, but Seekers were hooligans at heart. Their profession didn't attract the weak.

"You're tough..."

Looking back, he had been tough as long as Walter had known him. Noel was always cool and collected and never made a mistake. Walter couldn't even bring himself to envy him. He only felt admiration.

"You're not like me. I'm...weak." Saying it out loud made it easy to accept. The pride he'd tried so hard to defend seemed to melt like ice in the sun, bringing with it a surprising sense of relief. Maybe that was why Walter understood what he should do. "Should I quit being a Seeker?"

There it was. The crux of the matter. While he struggled to put his thoughts in words, Noel continued, "You lack conviction. But we fought quite a lot of battles that we would never have survived without you. No matter what you say, I understand your strength. You are stronger than anyone."

"Noel..."

"Walter, recruiting new members isn't such a rare thing. Let's start Blue Beyond again, you and me. I need you."

Hearing that warmed Walter's heart. He'd butted heads with Noel in the past and said things he didn't mean, but Walter knew as well as anyone that Noel was an amazing Seeker. Most buffers were weak. They could grant allies with powerful buffs but had almost no combat power in their own right. Buffers always needed their teammates to protect them, limiting the party's tactics.

Parties without buffer members were more flexible and more likely to emerge victorious. Or so most people believed, anyway.

But Noel was different.

Noel, a Talker, lacked raw physical strength. But Walter had never once considered Noel useless. Even if he weren't a skilled close-combat fighter, he could defend himself, and he was so good at handling attacks from the rear that Walter felt secure entrusting their backs to him.

Of course, Walter knew of Noel's special training under his grandfather, Overdeath. But it was more than that. Noel was *persistent*, putting himself through a harsh training regimen every single day. Walter never skipped his training, either, but he wasn't sure he could keep up with the same regimen while also completing Seeker missions.

The main reason Noel drew the eye of so many Seekers, including Walter, was his indomitable will. It was only natural that Walter felt proud to know that such an amazing Seeker thought him necessary.

He fought back tears, but his mind was made up.

"I'm sorry. I'm going to quit being a Seeker... I'm really sorry..."

Walter moved out of his room and withdrew all his money from the bank. He also traded in his armor and weapons. He'd resolved to quit seeking and go back to his hometown, but he hadn't decided when yet.

He wondered what would happen to Lloyd and Tanya. Could he really work an ordinary job when all he'd ever done was follow orders in battle? No matter how hard he thought, he couldn't come up with any answers. His head spun.

He was glumly waiting for a coach at the station when—

"Hey."

He turned around to see Noel.

"What, you came to see me off?"

"Yeah, exactly."

"Oh. Well, thanks." He hadn't expected that. He didn't think Noel was the type.

"Here, a farewell gift," Noel said, proffering a bottle of the famous imperial capital whiskey Walter loved.

"For me?"

"It's going to be hard to make it home, yeah?"

"Oh, yeah. Well..."

"Well, that's all I came for, so, bye. Take care of yourself, Walter." Noel literally walked away without looking back once. Walter watched him in a daze, then looked down at the whiskey in his hand.

"I can't tell if that guy really has a heart, or if he's just brusque."

Strangely enough, he felt no ill will. His dark thoughts began to clear, leaving him feeling like he might laugh.

"Did you know? You were actually the one Tanya liked..." But Tanya never got the chance to stand by Noel's side. Noel wanted strong allies he could work with, not a lover, and she'd known he would rebuff her if she confessed her feelings. It was while she was talking to Lloyd about it, seeking advice, that those two had fallen in love.

What if she'd confided in me instead? Walter wondered. Would she have chosen him? But even if she had, Walter would just have been a poor substitute for Noel.

"You were right, Noel. The capital is full of replacements. You were the only special one. You're different."

Lloyd had been the most talented member of their party, followed by Tanya, and then Walter. But even if the Blue Beyond had remained intact, only Noel would have ever become a top Seeker.

"We didn't deserve a commander as great as you." Walter opened the cap of the whiskey and took a swig. "Go for it, Noel. You can become the greatest Seeker... You were the best brother-in-arms a man could ask for."

The taste of the familiar whiskey set off tears that wet his cheeks.

†

"I'm starting again from square one."

Now that Walter was gone, the Blue Beyond was no more. The name still held some value, but that reputation was all I had.

I wasn't worried, though. I'd been the one who created Blue Beyond. I'd found the other three and formed the party, and I could do it again.

Obviously, I needed to learn from my mistakes—such as trusting Lloyd with the role of leader. Clearly, I couldn't let anyone else assume that role. Had I been in charge, he would never have had access to our money or been able to gamble it all away.

I needed to do better this time around. I would never make the same mistake again.

"Now then—"

I stepped into a back alley and stopped.

"Don't you think it's about time you came out?"

As if answering an invitation, the bearded man and the rest of his party stepped out of the shadows. They had been following me, and now they drew their weapons.

"You got your reward. What else could you want?" I asked.

The bearded man gave me a cheesy grin in response. "So Walter's left you too, huh? Now you're all alone."

No wonder they'd thought this the perfect chance to get revenge for being made into fools. But they *were* fools. They were such fools, it wasn't even funny anymore. Their sheer idiocy made me sick.

"I have a question," I said.

"Huh?"

"Why didn't you gather some more people? You know people outside of your party, right?"

"Four is plenty to take care of you. It doesn't even matter that you're connected to the Luciano family," the bearded man said. "We're gonna mess up that pretty little face of yours and toss you in the gutter."

Four was plenty, eh? At least they understood that none of them could take me on alone. Mocking me for my weakness while simultaneously refusing to fight me any way but four-on-one demonstrated a wonderfully ironic sense of pride.

Unfortunately, they were dead wrong.

"At your level? You should go off and find another forty people to help."

"The Talker, always gotta be talking. You'll regret that attitude." The bearded man's mouth twisted, his words dripping with arrogance.

They were the ones with the attitude. They probably expected me to rely only on *Stun Howl*. The party wizard would likely use a skill to counter me. It was obvious that they were convinced they could win as long as they avoided *Stun Howl*.

They were all fools. *They* would regret their attitude; I'd beat it into them to make sure.

"Heh heh. Don't pretend to be so tough," I told them. "You know you can't beat me, don't you? How about I give you a handicap? I'll fight you with my eyes closed."

"You'll what?!"

"Hey, what's wrong? C'mon, pipsqueaks. Come get me."

I closed my eyes as promised. When I motioned for them to come get me, the entire party screamed in unison and rushed me.

"What are you playing at?! I'll kill you!"

The moment they let my provocation erode their judgment, I pulled out a flash bomb and tossed it in front of me.

"Wha?! Arg!"

The intense flash burned the eyes of everyone except me. I then opened my eyes and punched every one of them directly in the heart with every bit of strength I possessed.

"Ugh?! Er."

Just one strike—but it was enough. The blow to their chests caused a cardiac concussion, and they lost consciousness.

"Since we're in the capital, I'll let you live. Instead..." I took out my knife and took the time to collect each of their left ears. "These wounds will serve as a message. You can show everyone what happens if you mess with me."

I left the bearded man's party, all of them now more handsome than before, and exited the alley. On the way out, I noticed an unusual item.

A snake exuvia. A rare find at any time, let alone in the city. Maybe it was food for a pet, or it had escaped and was now living in the sewers.

Snakes shed their old skins in order to grow new, stronger scales. Blue Beyond was the same. We'd cast off our old scales, and now we could grow better ones.

"As of this moment, Blue Beyond is reborn."

2 Reawakening

T HE MOST EFFECTIVE WAY to recruit members is to post an advertisement on the bulletin board in the central square. You can also place an ad in local newspapers. Seekers on the hunt for a party get potential recruiters' info from there, check the terms and conditions of the job, then submit to an interview.

I chose The Orc's Club as the site for my interviews. It was 11 a.m. now, and the joint was filling up, but it wasn't too loud, and it would do well for interviews. Now I just needed to wait for someone to show up.

"No one is coming," Wolf of Lightning Bite babbled next to me, even though no one asked him.

"Shut up. You're getting in the way of my interviews."

"Interviews? I told you, no one's coming. Any Seekers who come in here already have a party or a clan."

"That's just the people you know, right?"

"Well, it's *possible* there's some hidden talent out there, but the odds are very low. And even if such people exist, they probably come with other baggage. That's pretty much a given for tough guys who can't find a team to tolerate them. You really think you can build a good party with guys like that?"

"It's not your concern. Now go away."

"Don't be like that. Aren't you lonely here all by yourself?" Wolf rubbed my shoulders a little too softly and gave me a friendly smile. "Join our party. You're more than welcome."

"Ahhh."

How many times had I sighed like that? Wolf wasn't just annoying me; he was trying to interfere with my interviews to recruit me for Lightning Bite. He'd been doing this since I stepped into the tavern, and no matter how emphatically I declined, he kept at it. I was really getting tired of him.

"That's enough, Wolf. Noel said no already," came a disgusted voice from the table next to us. It was an elf girl, a dignified beauty with two half-pigtails that formed her signature style. Lycia, one of Wolf's teammates. She was lightly garbed in a sleeveless blouse and skirt, her only armor a leather breastplate. Lycia was an archer and capable Seeker who was well known at The Orc's Club.

A number of others murmured their agreement.

"You said you'd take care of it so we let you, but instead of inviting him to join us, you've just been harassing him. Who would ever accept an 'invitation' like that?"

"Wolf's just not very creative. Bulldozing people is the only strategy he knows."

"Poor Noel. Wolf, ewww."

"That's why the girl from the flower shop turned you down."

The Lightning Bite members were digging in. They'd been watching all morning, and apparently, they'd finally decided to intervene.

"Shaddup, you guys! And stop telling everyone I was rejected! I'm just about to start the real negotiation!"

He wasn't done yet? C'mon...

"Wolf..."

"What? You're ready to join our party?"

"I've changed my mind," I said. "I would be happy to join your party under certain conditions."

"Oh, seriously?! Ya hear that, guys? Master negotiator right here!" Wolf stood up, pleased with himself, and Lycia promptly tripped him. "Ow! What was that for?!"

"You're in the way, Wolf. Lie down."

Lycia coldly nudged Wolf aside and took his seat. "What conditions? We're serious when we say we want you, so we're ready to listen. If we had a skilled commander on the team, we could take on anything."

"They're not difficult requirements. It's simple."

"What is it? Tell us, tell us." Lycia bent forward and leaned closer.

Why was she doing that? Was this an elf thing? Ugh. Too close. She was practically breathing on me, and I could count her eyelashes.

"It's just one condition, actually..." I said.

"Yeah, yeah?"

"I want to be the leader of Lightning Bite."

"Huh? Sure. Everyone's okay with that right?" Lycia asked and the other members nodded.

"I'm fine with that."

"Me too."

"Me too..."

"No problem."

Wolf stood up, flustered, at these quick responses. "That was quick! What about my opinion? I'm the leader! You can't just decide without me!"

"But Noel is smarter than you, Wolf. None of us care who the leader is. See? It's fine," Lycia said firmly.

Wolf nodded for a moment. "Well, when you put it like that... I guess. Wait a second. No, it's *not* fine! I'm the leader! I'm the founder of Lightning Bite!"

His teammates burst into laughter, continuing to poke fun at Wolf. They weren't actually slighting him. It was all a joke, evidence of the trust they shared. None of them truly wanted to replace their leader.

But I wasn't joking. Not being party leader was a dealbreaker for me. I'd already told Wolf I would never work under someone again, and he must have understood I meant it, for he left me alone and returned to drinking and joking around with his team.

"That's too bad. I wanted to go on some adventures with you, Noel," Lycia pouted, putting her chin on the table. She hadn't returned to her seat. "What will you do if you don't get anyone?"

"I'll cross that bridge when I come to it. I may just have to switch from recruiting to headhunting."

"Do you have anyone in mind?" she asked.

"Well, maybe."

My dream recruit was Hugo Coppélia, a Puppeteer. There was a certain problem that needed solving before I could approach him, but if I was successful, it would make my party immeasurably stronger. Hugo could help us outperform the former Blue Beyond. I wanted him in my party, no matter what.

"Really, who? Is it someone I know?"

"Trade secret."

"Hey! Why? C'mon, tell me!"

She wasn't as bad as Wolf, but this girl was annoying too. While I was trying to decide how to get rid of her, I suddenly heard a voice, barely more than a whisper.

"Are you Noel Stollen?"

The voice was so sudden that Lycia and I jumped a little in surprise. We hadn't sensed anyone approaching at all. I might lack the skills, but Lycia was an archer with sharp senses. Maybe this short, cloaked person really had appeared out of thin air.

"I am Noel. And who are you?"

"I—"

The person lifted their hood, revealing a head of silver hair with a purple tint to it.

She was a young girl. Her bright silver hair was cut in an even bob, her skin was tanned, and she had delicate, doll-like features. Her eyes were different colors, the left being the color of a sapphire, while her right eye was amethyst. She wasn't as small as a halfling, but she looked like a child at first glance, though upon closer inspection, she had the charms of a grown woman—particularly her sharp cheekbones and nicely shaped nose.

"I'm Alma. I saw your sign in the square."

So, a potential recruit. But a woman... Considering what happened last time, I was hoping to avoid female Seekers. Maybe I should have declared that I was looking only for men, but the ratio of female to male Seekers was so low that I hadn't really expected any women to show up. I should have foreseen this.

Well, now that she was here, I couldn't just turn her away. It would look bad if I suddenly said "no girls allowed" at this point. As long as she met my requirements, I should remain open to accepting her, gender aside.

Besides, it might be best not to limit my recruitment to males. I wasn't quite sure yet, but this woman seemed very powerful, considering her ensemble and the way she'd suddenly appeared out of nowhere.

"Alma, thank you for coming. Please sit down." I gestured to the seat across from me.

"Okay," Alma said, sitting down in front of me.

"You're going to start the interview now?" Lycia whispered in my ear, her head cocked to the side. "This girl's just a child, right? She can't become a Seeker yet."

"No, uh—"

"Incorrect. I'm not a child. I am an adult."

Apparently, Alma overheard her. She shook her head, holding up two fingers on her right hand and one on her left.

"Twenty-one. Well into adulthood."

"You're five years older than me..." I'd figured her for an adult but hadn't thought she was that much older. This woman sure was full of surprises.

"I want to ask you a few questions. Is that all right?"

"It's fine."

"Okay, then. First—"

"Favorite food?" interjected Wolf.

"Strawberries."

"Wolf! Don't interrupt me!" I was caught off guard. Wolf, whom I'd thought was sitting at his own table, had come back here to tease me.

"You're the leader of a different party. Why would you be asking questions? And who cares about favorite foods?"

"Why so serious? This recruit seems interesting."

"This isn't a game!"

"Favorite book?"

"Elizabeth Grese, *100 Techniques for a Girl Who Wants to Be a Tough Guy.*"

While I tried desperately to get Wolf to leave us alone, Lycia started asking questions. Before I knew it, all of Lightning Bite was seated at my table.

"Hobbies?"

"Taking walks."

"Are you good with money?"

"Here and there."

"What are your measurements?"

"They're 90-53-82 centimeters."

Why were they asking such ridiculous questions? I couldn't even bring myself to try to stop them anymore. I decided to just join.

"What's your class type and rank?"

"Scout. Rank C."

A Scout. That was good. A Scout or Archer skilled at detection would come in handy when exploring Abysses. Ironic that a class Blue Beyond had never included would appear now.

"Are you interested in fashion?"

"Somewhat."

"What sort of experience do you have? Have you ever belonged to another party?"

"None. I just registered as a Seeker now. I've been living in the mountains, training."

She had no experience as a Seeker at all? I didn't want someone inexperienced, but I was more intrigued by this talk of training. Why would she continue training until she was twenty-one?

"What's your motto?"

"If it can be done tomorrow, then do it tomorrow."

"I have one last question. Why do you want to be a Seeker?"

"I have no interest in being a Seeker. My interest is—" Alma cut herself off, staring at me the entire time. "You, the grandson of Overdeath."

"Are you related to my grandfather?"

My grandfather was famous as a hero, but I wasn't sure why someone who had been holed up in a mountain and wasn't even a Seeker would know of him. Alma or one of her relatives must have had some kind of personal connection to him.

"Not me. My gramps said he fought your grandfather."

"Ohh..."

"My gramps didn't have a right arm. Overdeath had sliced it right off."

Under the table, I had my hand on my silver flame.

"You're not here to avenge him, are you?"

"No. I wouldn't do something so unproductive. I am just interested to see what kind of Seeker the grandson of a hero has become," she said.

"I-I see... Well, I apologize on behalf of my grandfather. I'm sorry. My grandfather has passed away, so I hope you will accept my apology as his."

"Gramps passed last month, so no one is holding a grudge. The past is the past. I don't need an apology," Alma said, looking truly unbothered.

So "Gramps" had been one of Overdeath's many vanquished foes. I had heard of numerous such people, enough that I had no idea who she was talking about. My grandfather had fought anyone and everyone in his youth.

"Incidentally, what was your grandfather's name?"

"Alcor Judikhali."

As soon as I heard the name, I got goosebumps. The members of Lightning Bite grew pale with terror.

Alcor Judikhali was a name synonymous with fear.

There existed a secret society within the underworld where the criminal syndicates held all the power. The Society of Assassins, as the name suggested, was made up of professional killers. They were merciless, slaughtering even newborn babies if requested, and were considered the worst kind of scum, fouler than even the most sadistic mobster. They were feared and avoided by all.

The founder of the Society was a legendary Assassin named Alcor Judikhali.

The most famous tale of his exploits was the time he was hired to annihilate all competing religious organizations by the Pope of the Holy Cross Church. He completed the mission single-handedly, killing over a thousand people on that one job alone. He was untouchable. People hesitated to even say his name in public. And here Alma was, claiming to be his granddaughter. If it was true, she would be a rare talent. I wanted her on the team.

I was also surprised to hear that Grandpa had tangled with the Society of Assassins. He'd never said anything about that. What had he been hiding? Not to mention cutting off the arm of the legendary Alcor—it sounded absurd.

I caught myself. Alma's revelation was so intriguing that it had distracted me. I closed my eyes for a moment to gather my thoughts.

"You're the grandchild of *that* Alcor? That's not funny," a huge man with a crew cut bellowed as he stood up from a table across from us.

His name was Logan, leader of the King of Dukes. He wore a leather jacket with no shirt underneath and had gauntlets on his thick arms. I'd thought him a Seeker who showed promise, but he had a bit of a behavior problem and got in fights all the time.

"You think you can come around here spouting nonsense? Maybe you can get away with that in the slums, but we don't put up with liars like that, you pig." Logan looked down at us, his lips twisting cruelly.

"Hey, it's nothing to do with you. Leave them be," Wolf cut in, stepping up to Logan and glaring at the other man, who was a full two heads taller and made Wolf look like a child by comparison. But despite being smaller, Wolf didn't back down. Instead, he seemed to be puffing himself up. Those two had never gotten along.

But today, Logan had his eye on Alma, not Wolf.

"And what does it have to do with you? You're the one who should be backing off."

"Ah, er, uh, well..." Wolf, having no comeback, grew flustered.

"Well, it's true it's got nothing to do with me. I don't tend to interrupt other parties' interviews. Unlike this dumbass Wolf here."

"Argh..."

"But, from what I hear, this pig isn't fit to patronize The Orc's Club. And she's a big fat liar, besides. You can't expect me to just stand by and allow that. Am I mistaken, Noel?"

I chuckled at Logan's claim. "I don't know if she's a liar, but you're right about her not being fit to patronize this tavern."

Alma almost certainly had no idea what we were talking about. I needed to explain.

"You may not know this, but Seeker taverns restrict entrance to certain ranks. It's customary for the regulars to beat up anyone who violates those restrictions."

"News to me."

"It's an unwritten rule. But it applies to everyone, and there are no exceptions for people coming in for interviews. In fact, the reason I chose this spot to hold my interviews is because I wanted Seekers who are the same level as me."

"But I was able to sit here."

"That's because neither Lightning Bite nor I warned you off. Normally, what Logan says would hold true," I explained.

Alma nodded with interest. "I see. I understand now."

"In that case, get your ass outta here. I'll let you go this time out of consideration for Noel. But if it happens again, you'll get no mercy, pig," Logan snorted, motioning toward the exit with his chin. Alma ignored him and raised her right hand.

"Noel, I have a question."

"What is it?"

"How is the ranking of a Seeker decided?"

"A number of ways. Your class rank, for one. The accumulated results of your missions, for another. In other words, it's a measure of your reputation as a Seeker."

"I see. Results. I understand now. In that case..." Alma flew from her chair and put up her fists, facing Logan. "I just need to pound this self-important gorilla into the ground, right?"

Ding. Right answer.

I knew letting Alma's lacking rank slide would just piss off the other Seekers. The only way to appease them was for Alma to prove her strength. And lucky for me, she had the perfect opponent: Logan, the strongest Seeker in The Orc's Club. He was the perfect guinea pig to test if she really was who she'd said.

"Who are you calling a gorilla?!" Provoked by Alma, Logan was beyond furious.

"Hey, Noel! I just wanna make sure! You don't mind if I kill this pig, right?! I can't hit hard without killing her!"

With that, they'd both consented to trade blows. In other words, this would be a fight to the death.

"Fine with me. She's not my friend. Do whatever you want."

Once I gave my approval, the rest of the customers in the tavern stood up to watch.

"Get her!"

"Show her what a real Seeker is!"

"Don't let that tiny girl beat you!"

"Who are you betting on? I got ten thousand fil on Logan!"

"Idiot, no one would take that bet!"

The onlookers thought she didn't stand a chance. Logan won out in size, the intrinsic difference in combat ability between a fighter and a Scout, and most of all, experience. His victory was guaranteed.

But Logan didn't look so confident anymore. In fact, his brow was sheened with sweat. Alma had thrown him for a loop just by daring to challenge him.

And she was calm, her face expressionless.

"Alma's gonna win," Lycia muttered next to me.

"Whoooa!"

Logan made the first move. There was a flash as he bellowed mightily and threw a sharp, straight right jab at Alma's face. A direct hit would have made her head part company with her body. However...

"You're too slow."

He hit the air where she'd been standing. After dodging the attack too quickly for the human eye to follow, she leapt in close to Logan and chopped his throat with the side of her palm.

"Argh!"

Taking that fierce blow to a vital point, Logan vomited blood. He fell to his knees and hunched over, looking like a criminal waiting to be beheaded.

"It's over."

Only it wasn't a guillotine that chopped off Logan's head. It was Alma's heel. The powerful blow took out his medulla oblongata and he lost consciousness.

The fight was over in under three seconds.

She was strong. To think a Scout could take out Logan so easily... Even from my perspective, after training in classical martial arts with my grandfather, Alma's fighting ability was beyond what I knew. And she wasn't even winded. She could have killed him immediately with a single chop had she wanted to. It was true, instant defeat.

While the onlookers went crazy over the results, I called out to Alma, "You're hired!"

We left The Orc's Club, Alma humming to herself as if nothing had happened.

"That was an amazing fight. You really are the grandchild of Alcor."

"You didn't believe me either?" Alma puffed up her cheeks, looking dissatisfied.

"I mean, if someone just shows up and tells you they're the grandchild of a legendary Assassin... No one would believe I was Overdeath's grandson at first either."

"But I believed you right away."

"Huh? Why is that?" I asked.

"Your eyes are different. You have eyes that say you'll do anything to win. Gramps told me to never fight with Overdeath. He said the man always went beyond what you could anticipate and was impossible to beat, no matter how well you fought. Your eyes reminded me of that."

All I could do was chuckle. I didn't mind being told I had eyes like my grandfather, but Alma made him sound like some sort of sadistic goon.

"Like I said before, I'd like you to join Blue Beyond," I said. "However, you said you had no interest in being a Seeker. Wouldn't that be a problem if you were to join a Seeker party?"

"No. I have nothing better to do, anyway."

"So you're bored? I know you're strong. But if you don't take Seeker work seriously, it will get you killed sooner or later. Beasts are merciless."

"You need skill to fight, not conviction. I may be unmotivated, but I'll produce results. You needn't to worry. Strength is its own form of justice. I'm pretty sure the same applies to Seekers."

She was assertive. I sensed some arrogance, but she wasn't incorrect in her thinking.

"Noel," Alma said, stopping. I looked back to see her holding her stomach. "I'm hungry. I haven't eaten anything since this morning."

"Then let's eat," I said, realizing I was hungry too. We walked down the restaurant district together looking for a good place, but all the highly reviewed restaurants were crowded.

"Do you mind waiting in line?"

"I don't want to wait that long. I'll have that." Alma pointed to a fried sweet bun stand. There were a few people waiting, but the line was moving fast. Ten minutes later, we each had piping-hot fried buns in our hands, both huge and looking delicious. I chose meat filling and Alma had custard cream.

"Mm?! This is delicious!" Alma's eyes shone as she bit into her bun.

I took a bite of mine too. It really was delicious. The outside was flaky over the soft, sticky dough, and the meat filling was wonderfully juicy, mixed with sweet veggies that enhanced the flavor of the meat.

"Noel, let me have a bite."

"Huh? You're so strange. Here." I held my bun out to her and Alma took a little bite.

"Mm, this one is good too. I've never eaten anything so delicious."

Alma put her hand to her cheek and closed her eyes. I thought she was exaggerating but then remembered she had lived in the mountains all her life.

"Is this your first time venturing out from the mountains?"

"Yup."

"You're doing pretty well for it being your first time."

"Gramps taught me how to blend into my surroundings."

"I see. Hey, there's something I've been wanting to ask you. In the mountains, were you training to be an Assassin?"

"Yeah," she said. "I was training to advance from Scout to Assassin, and then beyond that. I haven't jumped to B-Rank yet, but I've cleared all the required training."

"Ah, I thought so."

She was clearly too strong to be C-Rank. It made sense that she had already fulfilled all the requirements to advance. A new appraisal was required to move up a rank, so she was probably just putting it off.

"But you didn't join the Society of Assassins. Didn't your grandfather train you for that purpose?"

"Yeah. That was my plan. But I was rejected. They said I wasn't fit for the Society."

"Really? You sure seem strong enough for it..."

"I was strong enough. But they said I was lacking in other attributes."

"What does that mean?"

Alma shook her head. "Sorry, I don't want to talk about this anymore."

"I see... Sorry to push you. Thanks for telling me so much."

Everyone had a secret or two they didn't want to share. If she didn't want to talk, I wasn't going to force her.

"Well, they said they were making changes and they didn't need the Assassins trained in the 'old style' anymore," she said, suddenly doing a complete about-face.

"Wait, you're going to tell me now?!"

What was going through this dumb girl's mind?

"The Society has always been an independent, secret organization," she continued, "but the current leader has said he intends to affiliate with the crown soon."

"What? So they'll work solely for the emperor?"

"Seems that way. They said they're shifting to focus more on espionage work than contract killing, though they're probably still going to keep doing some assassination. The whole organization is going to change."

"Alma... that's extremely important information. It's not something you talk about while munching on some sweet buns. I mean, you shouldn't be talking about it at all!"

"Ah, they did say it was an absolute secret. Damn."

"'Damn'? That's all you have to say?"

Was this a problem? Now that I knew this information, would they send a bunch of Assassins to silence me?

Was I going to die?

"Noel, don't worry."

"Worry?"

"If anything happens, your big sister will protect you. It's okay."

"I don't remember having a big sister."

She only brought up her age when it suited her...and now, thanks to her, I was in possession of some very dangerous information. I decided then and there that I'd cut her loose and run for my life if I had to.

✝

"How much do you know about buffers?"

We had left the capital and walked to a forest nearby. It was dense with coniferous trees and home to many wild animals, making it a perfect hunting ground. We were following the game trails when I asked my question, and she tilted her head in thought.

"Honestly, not much. Just that they're weak when it comes to individual combat but have potent support skills that can make a party much stronger."

"Well, that's the gist of it. However, we do far more than provide support."

"You have other jobs?"

"First of all, there are a variety of support skills at our disposal. For example, my class is Talker, and one of my skills is *Assault Command*. It can end the battle in an instant, but it comes with consequences. If used incorrectly, it could annihilate the entire party."

"That's horrific," Alma said.

"Yeah, it's extremely dangerous. That's why buffers must be able to evaluate the battlefield before providing support. Then we take command and control the situation so that our support effects can be best put to use. Such is the role of a true buffer," I explained.

Alma nodded, engaged.

"That's interesting. Very interesting. But it sounds difficult. There's only so much you can do to influence the battle by issuing orders. You have to be thinking ahead at all times."

"That's why so few buffers are skilled in combat. They can't defend themselves, which makes it hard for them to rank up. And to be in control of the entire battlefield and direct a party to victory, all while fighting...it's practically impossible."

"But you can do it, eh, Noel?"

"If I couldn't, I would be dead already. Here, this looks like a good spot."

We stopped at a clearing deep in the forest. In the center was a cobalt-blue lake. Judging by the animal droppings and footprints, the local fauna used this as a watering hole.

"I'm going to have you capture a monster."

"Monsters" were what we called animals mutated by the influence of an Abyss. Although not as dangerous as beasts, capturing them was one of a Seeker's duties.

"It's called a killer rabbit, and it's a rabbit with iron horns."

Rabbits were normally cute and furry, but these had horns sharp enough to kill a human. They also loved to fight, so they had a habit of jumping out and skewering their prey whenever a likely target passed by.

"Why am I going to catch a killer rabbit? To eat?"

"We're not going to eat it. This is an experiment."

"An experiment?"

"You're not just going to catch it. I'm going to provide you with support while you do it."

"I don't need support to catch a killer rabbit," Alma huffed, seeming insulted.

"With your skill, I'm sure the killer rabbit will pose no challenge. But what about if you have support?"

"The easy task will be all the easier," she said.

"Is that what you think? Yes, buffs improve your abilities. But whether you're able to take *advantage* of that improvement will depend on you, the one receiving the support."

"Ah. I see..." Alma understood what I was trying to say.

"As a Scout, do you have the *Accel* skill?"

"Yup. It doubles my speed. I can use it up to five times in a row."

So she could increase her speed fivefold. Amazing. A normal Rank C could only increase theirs threefold.

"Were you able to use that skill perfectly from the very start?"

"Not at all. The acceleration is sudden; I had to work to build up my body for a long time. Otherwise, I would shred my tendons and shatter my bones."

"And that's with your *own* skills. It's even harder to adjust to the skill improvements provided by buffs. We need to train you to adapt to my support skills."

That was the experiment: to see whether Alma could quickly learn to use my support skills. Our plans going forward would be determined by her performance.

Even my former allies, excellent Seekers all, took two weeks to get used to my support skills. I wondered how Alma would do. Her individual abilities were far more advanced than theirs, but that meant the boost from my buffs would be correspondingly extreme. She might need more time to get used to them. Of the former Blue Beyond members, it had taken Lloyd the longest to adapt to my support skills, and he'd been the most advanced of the three.

"How many killer rabbits can you find around here?" I asked, and Alma closed her eyes, straining her ears.

"Thirteen within two hundred meters."

"That's perfect for the experiment. I want you to use *Accel* to catch them. I'm also going to apply two support spells. Your mission is to catch at least one within ten seconds. I'll triple your speed. We'll see how quickly it takes you to adapt to working with buffs."

"Got it."

"Okay, let's start the experiment now."

Talker skill: *Battle Voice*. The support granted with my declaration activated Alma's body.

"How does that feel?"

"It's a strange sensation. I feel endless energy welling up within me."

"That's *Battle Voice*. Right now your HP, MP, and recovery speed are up by 25 percent."

"In other words, I won't tire easily?"

"That's right. The next skill is the real one: *Tactician*. As long as you follow my orders, the results and effects of all of your actions will be increased by 25 percent. We'll cover the details later—for now, just focus on that 25 percent increase."

I stepped away from Alma so she'd have more room to take off.

"Now, use *Accel* to the max. Based on simple math, your normal fivefold speed boost will increase to more than sixfold. When I say 'go,' we'll start. I'll be using *Tactician* skill on that instruction."

"Understood. But give me a second," Alma said, tossing her robe away. Underneath, she wore a white leather suit cut like a leotard. The design was revealing, exposing half her bosom, and accented with a corset belt that called even more attention to her cleavage. The holster on the belt held a long blade. There was also a pouch for small items, and a case with throwing darts. The effect of all that exposed skin was a bit attention-gathering, but she was dressed like an authentic Scout. She looked alert and prepared to take out enemies from the shadows.

"I can move easier now. Bring it on!"

I turned up my left sleeve and tapped the stopwatch function on my watch.

"Once you're ready, use *Accel*."

"Understood. *Accel—Quintuple!*"

"Order! Catch killer rabbits!" I yelled at the same moment that Alma reached her maximum speed.

A gust of wind swirled up and she vanished, thanks to the limit-breaking, ultra-fast movement brought on by my *Tactician* support. Even though I was watching carefully, she moved so fast that it gave the illusion she'd disappeared.

My stopwatch tracked time in tenths of a second. Two seconds. Three seconds. Four seconds, five seconds, six seconds, seven seconds, eight seconds—

"I'm back." I stopped the timer the moment I heard Alma's voice.

"Here are your killer rabbits." Alma, who returned in another gust of wind behind me, tossed the animals that filled her arms onto the ground. "Thirteen in all. I've knocked them unconscious."

"Thirteen...? You mean you caught all of them?"

"Yeah. Sorry, was there a rule that I was supposed to get only one?"

"No, I wanted at least one, so you're fine."

"Oh. Phew. What was my time?"

"8.6 seconds."

"So I'm within the time limit too. Great. I accidentally caught all of them. Is there more to the experiment?" Alma asked me, her head tilted to the side.

"No. We're done. Given these results, we need no further training."

She was incredible. I couldn't believe she'd adapted that easily to support skills on her first experience with them. I felt silly for even trying to test her. Is this what it meant to be heir to a legend? How enviable...

"Since you don't need any further training, Alma, that leaves us with some free time. Perhaps we can take on some work as a party instead."

"Ooh, my first job. I've never been in an Abyss before."

"Unfortunately, it won't be an Abyss job. Even though you're super strong, it's too dangerous to go into an Abyss without a tank. This is the job I had in mind."

I took a letter out of my pocket and showed it to Alma. I'd received it by owl post that morning.

"Hmm? Um... 'Dear Noel Stollen. A band of thieves has appeared in the outskirts of Mintz Village. I am requesting your assistance in defeating them. Sincerely, the Mayor of Mintz Village.'"

Alma looked up at me confused.

"A band of thieves?"

"That's correct. Our first job will be to subdue a band of thieves."

Seekers did more than hunt beasts and eliminate Abysses. They also went treasure hunting, explored places, brought down monsters, and went after bounties. The first two were rare; the last two more common. It didn't pay as much as Abyss-related work, but it was easy enough. Even Blue Beyond didn't start out with Abyss work, doing odd jobs to rack up experience and cash.

Requests like these were posted directly on the bulletin boards in the city square. Customers came from all walks of life, but most were from villages. The lords who were supposed to protect those living on their fiefs were often slow to risk their own necks. If their subjects waited to be rescued by their lords, they'd have a very long wait, or a very short one, depending on how hungry the beasts and monsters setting upon them were. Instead, they hired Seekers on their own to solve their problems.

I knew the mayor of Mintz Village through a previous job of that sort. Back then, he'd asked us to take care of some monsters. After completing that mission, Lloyd had promised him we'd help if he ever needed us again... Lloyd, who was now a slave. I was guessing the mayor remembered that promise and had decided to reach directly out to us this time.

I'd been planning to respond with a rejection, but since Alma was good to go, I was ready to fight at her side. The reward would be meager, but it was the perfect opportunity to test out our party's strength. We could extract our payment from the bad guys preying on the villagers.

✝

A stagecoach ran on the highway. It was a ten-hour trip, each way, to Mintz Village from the imperial capital. We would have to switch coaches on the way, so we stayed in the capital overnight and left the next morning, due to arrive in Mintz by afternoon the day after that.

"My bum is stiff... I don't like carriages..."

The stagecoach arrived at the town of Eudora, our transfer point, and Alma disembarked with a sigh, rubbing her bum. The sun was already setting and the stars were coming out. After seven hours in a shaky stagecoach, my butt hurt too. I was queasy and travel-sick and just wanted to take a bath and get in bed.

Weary from travel, we started searching for an inn. But as it was a transit hub, Eudora's inns were all booked. When we did happen to find a vacancy, only one room was open. A guy and a girl sharing the same room was unacceptable to me. I wanted this to be a shenanigans-free party.

"Alma, you take the room. I'll stay in the shed."

"Huh? Why don't we just sleep together?"

"It's inappropriate for me to share a room with you."

"You're worrying about nothing. Wait, are you blushing? That's adorable."

"No, I'm *not* blushing. But..."

Maybe she was right, and I was overthinking this. It was unfair to treat one's comrades differently because of their gender, even if the goal was a moral one. A proper Seeker should be able to sleep next to a member of their party without concern. The trouble with Lloyd and Tanya had colored my perceptions without my realizing it.

Alma was right—we should be able to share a room without concern.

We checked in, got the key to our room, then headed to the dining room. We were exhausted but also hungry. The food looked delicious, and we were ready to fuel up for tomorrow's endeavors.

As it turned out, though, the food was actually terrible. It had been a while since I had eaten anything so foul. It actually gave me a headache. Even Alma, who had lived her entire life in the mountains, looked nauseated afterward.

We ate the disgusting food without a word and went back to our room.

"That food was awful, but this looks good." Alma breathed a sigh of relief as she looked around. It was clean, and there were no stains on the walls or the floor. The bed looked nice and soft, the furnishings were fashionable, and some incense had been lit in the room.

"I was worried about what we'd find, but I think I can rest well here," I said.

"Yeah. You can take a shower first," said Alma.

I accepted her offer and headed to the bathroom. After undressing, I stepped into the shower room, which was spacious, with a large bath. A nice long soak would be great, but we had an early start the next morning, so I decided a shower would be enough. There was plenty of hot water, and just letting it rain down upon my head left me instantly relaxed, my exhaustion washing down the drain.

I cleaned off, got dressed, and went back to the room.

Alma was stretching when I walked in. She was clearly flexible—currently doing a full split, her stomach flat against the floor and her legs spread at 90-degree angles to her torso.

"Noel, are you done with the shower?"

"Yeah, it was good. You should go too."

"I will."

Alma sat up, then kicked her legs over her head to rise to a standing position from a front walkover. She looked my shirt-clad form up and down. "Your muscles are really apparent when you're not wearing your coat. You look good. Great. Like a wild beast. Not the kind we hunt—just a powerful one."

"O-oh, really? Well, thank you."

"Can I touch you?"

"Well, maybe just a little..."

As I assented, Alma started to caress my body. She didn't hold back, rubbing me and stroking me with her finger. It tickled, and I thought I might laugh.

"I said a little. I'm going to get angry soon."

"You're right. That's enough, then." Alma reluctantly took her hand away from my body. "That was a good experience. Thank you."

"You're welcome..."

"You really do have a great body. It's unfortunate."

"What is unfortunate?"

"You only get a body like that by working incredibly hard. Regular training won't do it. But no matter how much you train, you'll never have the body of a vanguard type," she said. "In the end, hard work can't trump talent. That's why it's unfortunate. If you were a Warrior, like Overdeath, you could have become the most powerful Seeker in the world."

Her frank words left me dumbfounded for a moment.

"Alma..."

"What?"

"Close your eyes."

"Hmm? Like this?"

Alma closed her eyes as I told her. I flicked her unguarded forehead with my finger.

"Ouch! Why?!"

"Because it's none of your business."

I clicked my tongue at her, laid down on the bed, then pointed to the bathroom.

"I'm going to sleep. You go take your bath."

"Hmph...fine..."

As Alma headed to the bath, I let out a sigh. "I know that better than anyone..."

I was well aware of the fact that I lacked the skills of a combat class. All I could do was do the best with what I had. I had to, if I was going to keep my promise to my grandfather and achieve my dream.

Even if it was hopeless, I had no intention of giving up.

I closed my eyes, starting to think about the next day, when I heard the sound of the bath filling with water. No mere shower for Alma.

"I hope she can wake up in the morning..."

The only stagecoaches to Mintz Village left at 8 a.m. and 3 p.m. If we missed the morning coach, we would have to wait for the later one.

Completely oblivious to my concerns, Alma seemed to be in a good mood, singing in the bath. It was a gentle, calming melody. As I lay there listening, I started to drift off to someplace far away.

"—You must become the greatest Seeker of them all. Do not bring shame to the Stollen name. That is my last wish."

I heard Grandpa's voice in my dream. I'd had that dream many times since the day he died. In my village that had been reduced to ash and ruin, with me holding Grandpa as he grew cold in my arms.

"I promise, Grandpa... I'll become the strongest Seeker ever."

Every time I had this dream, my heart became a whirlpool of cold grief and burning passion. Just as the meeting of cool and hot air gave rise to strong winds, this dream roused a powerful sense of ambition that swallowed all my other feelings.

That ambition was to become the strongest Seeker ever.

†

I heard the faint sound of birds chirping. It was morning. Maybe because of my recurring dream, my mind was clear and I was awake and alert.

Dreams end. Doors open. A new day begins.

"Mmm… Hmm?"

The first thing I noticed was that I was having trouble breathing. Then I felt a soft, flower-scented sensation on my face. When I realized that the warm and slightly moist object atop me was a human being, I immediately sat bolt upright.

"This dumb girl…"

Alma was sleeping soundly next to me. That was fine—we'd planned to sleep in the same bed. The problem was that she was completely *naked*…and that my face had been covered by her oversized breasts. She'd been using me as a body pillow!

"I thought I was overthinking things, but this is ridiculous…" I was dizzy, and it wasn't just leftover grogginess from sleep. In fact, my head hurt.

"Mmm…so many sweet buns…heh heh…" As I held my head in agony, Alma murmured happily in her sleep.

"I hope you drown in those sweet buns and die!" Finally hitting my limits of tolerance, I slapped Alma's chest away from me.

"I can't believe you'd hit a girl in the chest…"

"Shut up! This is all your fault."

"Is that what you're into, Noel? That's a little scary for me, little brother."

"Shut up! You're not my sister. And enough of this foolishness—we need to hurry."

Somehow, we made it in time to catch the early morning coach. After three hours riding that old, run-down stagecoach along bumpy roads, we were finally at Mintz Village.

"Blue Beyond, it's been so long. Thank you for coming all this way so quickly...wait?" The mayor, a man with thinning hair, looked at us in confusion. "Uh-um, where are the others?"

"The other three quit. But we have a new member. Please meet Alma, Mr. Mayor."

"Uh? I-is that so? Is everything okay?"

His concern was understandable. Two-person parties were a rarity, since they normally didn't last long. Also, Alma didn't look like a fighter.

"Mayor, rest assured," I said. "We will kill every last bandit before the end of the day."

The mayor looked startled to hear me promise that, but it was a good idea to demonstrate your conviction in times like these. It helped the customer feel more secure. And sure enough, the uneasiness faded from his face.

"U-understood. I'll leave it to you. Now, if you could join me at my house so we can discuss the details..."

Mintz Village was your run-of-the-mill village on the frontier. It lacked any heavy industry, its lord was as useless as one might expect, and its people lived hard lives. The mayor's house was a wooden building that didn't merit compliments, even out of politeness.

"Please. It isn't much, but have some tea," the mayor's wife said as we walked into the drawing room and sat at the table. His daughter, a freckle-faced girl with her hair in two braids, was there too. She was turning ten this year, if I remembered correctly—a country girl in every way, but blessed with good features. Once she got older and learned a bit about fashion, she could be the town beauty.

Her name was Chelsea, right? I remembered playing with her a year before. I'd been gazing at her while I thought all this, which apparently embarrassed her so much that she ran off to the back of the house.

"Sorry, she's at a...difficult age. She was actually really looking forward to seeing Blue Beyond again," the mayor said, hanging his head apologetically.

I chuckled. "Sorry about that. Our popular leader isn't here anymore. She must be disappointed."

"Actually, my daughter's always talking about...well, it's not important. Now then, let me tell you about the thieves."

According to the mayor, this was the fifth day the band of thieves had appeared on the outskirts of the village. They'd already decimated the neighboring village, murdering so many of its inhabitants that the entire village was now a wasteland. The band was about twenty strong. They didn't look to be from around here, so they were probably drifters. The mayor didn't know where their hideout was, but a number of witnesses had seen them disappear into the eastern forest.

"I understand. That's plenty of information."

If everything the mayor said was true, we should be able to get rid of them easily enough. The fact that they'd been able to lay the neighboring village to waste with only twenty men suggested some of them were capable fighters—capable enough to overcome any resistance the villagers could mount, anyway. But they were bandits, after all, preying on the weak. Their combat abilities simply weren't in the same league as those of a professional Seeker.

Not that I was going to take it easy on them. The way of the Seeker was total destruction, nothing less.

"Let's discuss compensation," I said. "To annihilate a group of twenty bandits, we'll need a deposit of 200,000 fil. When the job is done, you'll pay us another 350,000 fil, for a total of 550,000 fil."

"Wow, 550,000 fil...that's a lot..."

"I think 550,000 fil for killing twenty bandits is a pretty good deal," I told him. "It comes out to 25,000 fil a head. Or would you rather meet the same fate as the neighboring village?"

"N-no, that's not what I meant! I-I'll pay! I'll get the money!"

The mayor rushed out of the drawing room and came right back with a dirty leather bag.

"There are 200,000 fil inside. Please count it..."

I took the leather bag and counted the coins inside. There wasn't a single piece of gold. within, just aged and blackened silvers and coppers. He was even more strapped for cash than he looked.

"Yup, there's 200,000 fil here. I'll come back for the rest when the job is finished. Also, please gather the young men of the village."

"The young men? What for?"

"After we defeat the bandits, we'll distribute some practical items to them. The armor of twenty bandits wouldn't sell for much even if we could transport it back to the capital, but it'll be useful for the beginnings of a village militia. Every little bit helps, right?"

"U-understood! I'll call for them right away!"

Once the mayor thought there might be some soldiers to boss around in his future, his greasy face shone even more.

How the possessions of the defeated were handled would differ depending on the party and clan. Most followed the policy that ownership rights belonged to those who'd done the fighting. Clients were owed nothing. Imperial law also stated that the right of salvage belonged to the victors unless otherwise specified in the contract with the client.

I preferred to get as much as I could out of a job, but stripping equipment from corpses was a lot of work. In this instance, letting the village have it was the right thing to do.

"We'll be off now. Wait here and don't worry."

We left the mayor's home and headed to the eastern forest, where witnesses had last seen the bandits.

"That balding man kept staring at my boobs," Alma said with a scowl.

"Huh, really?"

"Really. With his wife and daughter right there. Gross."

Tanya had said something similar last time. I vaguely remembered her saying that he'd been leering, and it had creeped her out. I understood being drawn to a beautiful woman, but like Alma had said, he was in a position of authority and should be more professional.

"Noel!"

I turned around to see Chelsea running toward us, breathing heavily.

"Haa, haa... U-um, you're going to defeat them now, right?" she asked.

"Yeah. We'll take care of it quickly, so don't worry."

"W-well... G-good luck! I'm cheering for you!"

"Huh? Uh, thanks." I was confused at the sudden declaration of support but tickled by her childish innocence. "Do you still remember how to make a bamboo dragonfly like I showed you last year?"

"Yes! Of course! Mine fly higher than all the other children's! They zoom up high!"

"That's wonderful. I'm glad I could teach you," I said with a smile.

The girl blushed, taking the toy out of her skirt pocket. It was old and sun-darkened.

"This is the one you made for me. I've kept it with me ever since, 'cause, uh...it's precious to me! So I'll wait for you! My mother and I will make a delicious meal and wait for your return!" she sputtered, then ran back the way she'd come.

As I watched her flee, I could see Alma smiling knowingly out of the corner of my eye.

"What are you so happy about?" I asked.

"You're a smooth operator yourself, Noel. You've been leading that innocent girl on. You may look sweet, but you're oh-so-sour. I'm surprised, bro."

"Shut up, you big-boobed bimbo."

"Big-boobed bimbo?! Me?!"

"Stop messing around. We need to find this band of thieves."

"Noel, wait! I can't let that go, bro!"

I ignored Alma's indignant protests. We didn't have time to waste on this.

As we stepped into the deep, dark forest, it felt like coming home. That was always my state of mind when I was preparing to kill someone. Deep and dark, like this forest.

†

"What made that bald pervert think there were only twenty bandits...?"

Around the time the sun started to set, we discovered the thieves' hideout in a rocky area that formed a sort of natural fort. We were scouting the situation from the branch of a high tree, about three hundred meters from the hideout. Since the sun was at our backs, they wouldn't be able to see us.

Examining the hideout through a monocular, I could see it lacked the towers and palisades of a true fort, but it did have archers stationed at the stone walls. It was already a tricky place to lay siege to, thanks to the terrain, but there were also at least sixty bandits in there. Three times as many as the mayor had said.

"With this many people, they're definitely not just drifters..."

I put the monocular to my eye and examined the state of the hideout.

"There he is. That's the boss."

I'd found a large man with tribal tattoos on the right half of his face. His armor was clearly better than that of the others.

A woman who looked to be his underling was pouring him a drink. He looked a bit drunk already, but also sharp-eyed, clearly a tough fighter. I tried to match his face to the list of criminals I'd committed to memory.

"I know him. The leader of the band is Gordo the Razor Blade."

Gordo the Razor Blade. A B-Ranked Scout who'd upgraded to bandit and become a big-time crook, forming the Gordo Bandits and wreaking havoc in the regions west of the capital.

"I'd heard the other Seekers who faced him were annihilated, but I didn't realize Gordo was still alive. The man's a cockroach."

It made sense that Gordo the Razor Blade could gather sixty followers and shape them into something approaching a disciplined force. They were probably preparing for something much bigger than a little village plunder.

"What do you think, Alma? Can you beat a B-Rank bandit?"

"Easy." Alma put her forefinger to her thumb, giving me the a-okay signal. "I can take out a B-Ranker before breakfast."

Obviously, Rank B is higher than C. But that's just on average. A C-Rank with sufficient skill and experience could handle some B-Rank fighters without issue. When Alma said it was easy, she wasn't overselling herself. She was just stating simple facts.

"But I mean one-on-one. I can't murder my way through three score henchmen to get to his throat."

"I know. That's why I'm going to take care of them."

"You're going to fight alongside me, Noel? But if we get any closer, the bandits will spot us. I have a skill to hide my presence, but you don't, do you?"

"Just listen. Here's my strategy..."

First, Alma would use her Scout skill: *Stealth* and get as close as possible without being detected by Gordo's Scouting skills. Once in position, I would initiate Talker skill: *Stun Howl*. Three hundred meters was well within the range of my Talker voice. This would freeze the underlings in place.

Since Gordo was a B-Ranker, he could resist me, but I didn't care about that. He'd be distracted by the sudden paralysis of his whole little army, and in that instant, Alma would come from behind and take him out. Once *Stun Howl* wore off and the underlings regained their senses, she would user her *Disturbance* skill to send the camp into chaos.

Bandits without a boss are just rabble, prone to getting in each other's way. Alma's *Disturbance* would send them scurrying in every direction, unable to join forces—easy pickings. Amid the confusion, I'd approach until the camp was in range of my silver flame and cut off their escape route. As long as we didn't miss anyone, it would be mission accomplished in less than an hour.

"That's my plan. Do you have anything to add or any questions?"

"No. It's perfect. Let's do that."

"Okay. From now on we'll use *Link* to communicate telepathically."

Talker skill: *Link* was a telepathic communication skill that allowed allies to share thoughts. With this skill, we would be able to coordinate details even while far away from one another.

"Are you ready?" I telepathically addressed Alma, then heard her voice in my head.

"Ready when you are."

"Okay, then, initiate strategy now."

Talker skill: *Battle Voice*. After I applied my support skill, Alma used her Scout skill: *Stealth*. Her presence became faint, as if she were transparent. She jumped down and dashed through the forest. A few seconds later, I received a message from her.

"I'm in position. Distance is ten meters. Ready to attack on command."

"Roger. I'll use Stun Howl."

I took as big of a breath as I could to fill my lungs with air, and then let out a yell at top volume.

"Stop!"

I looked through my monocular to make sure *Stun Howl* was successful in freezing the band of thieves. Only Gordo had been able to resist, rising from his seat to see what had happened.

"Order! Kill Gordo!"

Talker skill: *Tactician*. Alma, already 25 percent more powerful in all skills due to my support, used her own *Accel* skill and reached Gordo at lightning speed.

Scout skill: *Silent Killing*.

Scout skill: *Quick Attack*.

Through my monocular, I could see Gordo cough up a clot of blood and then collapse. The combination of a skill that causes triple damage when successfully paired with a surprise attack and a skill that lets one attack with blinding speed had left him with a hole in his chest big enough to see through to the other side. It was overkill: exceeding a fatal wound to focus on certain death.

"Death confirmed! Next order! Cause Disturbance *in enemies until I arrive!"*

As soon as I gave the order using *Link*, I jumped down from my perch on the branch. It took me thirty-two precious seconds, even running at top speed, to cross the three hundred meters I needed to block off the most likely escape route.

"One defeated, two defeated. Three defeated. Four defeated. Five defeated."

Alma was delivering the death count directly to my brain. She was mowing them down with a quickness that surprised me. I cared nothing for their lives, but did she understand the reason I'd given the *Disturbance* order? It would be fine if she could pick off every single bandit, but killing them would cause more fear than confusion, and some might manage to escape. Then I would be responsible for the ones that got away. Leaving even a single survivor was unacceptable.

I finally arrived at the open rocky area on the edge of the bandits' hideout. What I saw was Alma, ruthlessly slaughtering the bandits one after another.

"Bwa ha ha ha! Ah ha ha ha!"

It was the witching hour, and the white god of death howled madly as she swung her dark-gray Assassin's dagger. She scattered the blood and guts of the pitiful meat bags, tearing five of them to pieces in a matter of seconds. She was so quick that she never even got any of the blood splatter on her beautiful white skin.

"Wh-what is this monster?! S-stay away! Stay away, aaahh!" one of the bandits screamed in fear. An instant later, his head was rolling on the ground. Half of the bandits who saw this simply broke into a panicked stampede, running straight toward me.

I'd thought this might happen. Alma was drunk on killing. Even knowing she was my teammate, she looked mad to me right now, almost inhuman.

Well, it was fine. I was there now.

"There is no escape! Time to die!"

Upon hearing my loud voice, everyone focused on me.

"Alma, come back to your senses! I'm going to use a flash bomb!"

"Huh?! O-okay! Sorry!"

I gave another order using *Link*, adding in *Peer Support* to calm her down. I made sure Alma's eyes were closed, then closed my own before pulling a flash bomb out of my coat and tossing it overhand into the knot of frenzied bandits.

"Agggh!"

I opened my eyes to the sight of stumbling, flailing, blinded thieves. Even the ones who had tried to run were stopped in their tracks, holding their burned eyes. Without hesitation, I drew my silver flame and shot a flame bullet into their midst.

"It burns, it burrrns! Agggh!"

One bullet, one mighty conflagration, a dozen flaming bandits. Those few who survived for a number of seconds before succumbing would only spread the fire farther, trapping their panicked, blinded comrades. As the bandits reenacted old paintings that depicted scenes of hell, I issued another order.

"Alma, I'll get the center. You get the strays!"

"Roger!"

Alma drew her darts, held them up high, and then released them all at once. It looked like she had thrown them randomly, but every single one struck a bandit dead.

Scout skill: *Perfect Throw*. This skill made the darts track automatically so they would definitely hit a target, keeping the blinded riffraff from somehow escaping. This rocky clearing had been turned into a kill box. The survivors had nowhere to go. We didn't need to rush.

I pulled my knife. It flashed in the late afternoon sun as I approached the bandits, taking my time.

There had been sixty-four thieves in the band. Alma killed thirty-eight; I killed twenty-six. Now they were nothing but silent corpses, sprawled across the rocks.

I felt no guilt. These were evil men who deserved to die—especially Gordo. This band of thieves was famed for their atrocities as far away as the capital. We'd all heard the story of one village he had ransacked. After taking what he wanted, he distributed razor blades to the village children and ordered them to hack away at their own parents, centimeter by centimeter, until they all died. Thus, the nickname Razor Blade.

While choking on the foul odor of blood and guts, I chopped Gordo the Razor Blade's head off and shoved it in a sack I'd recovered from the hideout. If I brought this head to the military police in the capital, I'd get a reward. If I remembered correctly, the bounty was two million fil. Carrying around a severed head was disgusting, but I could distract myself with thoughts of how I'd spend the money.

"I found it. You were right, they had a lot. It's exactly one million fil," Alma said, holding up a leather bag as she walked toward me. She had been searching the camp for money while I took care of Gordo's head. I'd figured he'd need a lot of cash to pay all his goons, and I'd been right.

"You hold on to that, Alma. That's your share of today's haul. You get a bonus for your first job. You don't mind if I manage the reward from the village and the bounty for Gordo's head, do you?"

"Okay. Heh heh, a million fil! Imagine how many sweet buns I can buy with this!"

I promised the village mayor that they could take everything the bandits had, but that was when I'd thought there were only twenty thieves. There had turned out to be triple that number, not to mention their leader being the famous B-Ranker, Gordo the Razor Blade. We were claiming the money Gordo had been hiding to make up the difference. It was ours by right.

The mayor must have known he was sending us to face a sizable force headed by a vicious criminal. He had to have heard tell of the terrible fate of the neighboring villages, and I was sure he understood these were no ordinary thieves.

But he'd held out on us. That bald pervert had omitted necessary information to convince us to do the job on the cheap.

"Ahh, this is why I hate taking jobs from the pathetic poor..." I said.

"But we made a lot in the end. Hunting thieves isn't so bad."

"Yeah, in the end. But just taking jobs like this isn't a stable living, and it's not fun. I really don't like killing humans."

"No? You looked like you were enjoying yourself," Alma said.

"Don't make me sound like a homicidal maniac. I was just trying to get psyched up for the battle. Why would I be okay with killing my own kind?"

I sighed. They said the more you sighed, the more happiness you let escape with each breath, but I didn't feel like keeping it in. If we just had one more party member—a tank—then we could start doing Abyss work again...

I looked up at the ultramarine sky to see a large ship sailing overhead.

"Wow, an airship!" Alma cried out, looking up at the same sky.

Airships were the greatest invention of magic-engineered civilization. Most belonged to royalty or aristocrats, though a few special commoners had their own too. The one currently above us was huge, its special antigravity engine powered by the remains of beasts. It was emblazoned with an image of a black mountain goat.

"That ship must belong to the Goat Dinner clan. Three-star regalia."

Alma tilted her head to the side. "Regalia? What's that?"

"Regalia are distinctive decorations and designs that can only be displayed by royal decree. The most honored clans are granted permission to use them."

Clans were already higher in the pecking order than individual parties. Beyond that, emperors rewarded clans for great acts of service or heroism. Regalia were more than mere trophies, though. They granted the clan great authority, equivalent to that of the most influential aristocrats. Owning an airship was normally forbidden to commoners, but the most successful clans could possess them.

"There are only seven regalia clans—the seven stars that shine the brightest in the capital. And they aren't all equal. There are four three-star-ranked clans, a pair of two-star-ranked clans, and a single one-star-ranked clan. For a clan to gain regalia rights, another clan must lose theirs. The ship we just saw is owned by Goat Dinner. It's headed for the capital, so they must be on the way back from an assignment."

"Wow, that's amazing. So that ship is full of strong Seekers?"

"Not just strong. They're at the top of the Seeker charts when it comes to intelligence, courage, experience, and financial resources. You can't compare them to the Seekers we see on the street."

The Goat Dinner clan ship had already grown small in the early evening sky. I reached out as if I could touch it. To the Seekers within, who had wings and could soar across the sky, I was nothing but a tiny bug crawling on the ground.

But someday—

No, that wasn't right. "Someday" was a meaningless goal.

"One year..."

"Huh, what?"

"In one year, we will have a clan, and that clan will have regalia."

It was a foolhardy aspiration, even for me. But a Seeker must be prepared to dream big dreams if they wish to reach the top.

"One year from today, this I swear."

†

"I'm so glad you made it back safely! Thank you so much for taking care of the bandit problem!"

When we returned to Mintz Village after taking out the band of thieves, the village mayor greeted us with arms wide open. What kind of environment did it take to produce someone so brazen? I couldn't tell if he was just shameless, or if he was simply a guileless country bumpkin.

I'd planned to complain about him lowballing us, but that just felt silly now. "Mayor, we have completed the task you requested. Their hideout was in a rocky clearing deep in the eastern forest. We wiped them all out. And this is the head of the band leader."

I showed the mayor my sack.

"U-understood... I will send the young men of the village to their hideout tomorrow morning. U-uh, so we can collect everything from the bodies?"

"Do as you please."

"Thank you so much! You have saved us!"

"No need to thank us. Just pay us what you owe us."

"Uh, uh, of course! Well then, please come to my house. My wife and daughter have been hard at work preparing a feast! Please, come in and rest as much as you need!"

I really wanted to get out of the village as soon as possible, but we'd already missed the last stagecoach of the day. I didn't care about the mayor, but I didn't want to leave without thanking his little girl.

We would stay in Mintz Village for the night and depart for the capital first thing in the morning.

"Noel, can I become a Seeker too?" Chelsea asked me as we ate at the mayor's table.

"I'm sorry, she just got her appraisal," the mayor said. "My girl has an aptitude for combat..."

I nodded. "Do you want to become a Seeker?"

"Yes! I want to become a great Seeker like you, Noel!" the girl answered, her eyes sparkling. The mayor and his wife were laughing nervously. It looked like they thought it was just a phase.

"Any adult can become a Seeker," I said. "All you have to do is register with the public office. After that, you can go to an academy in the capital for training. The course is two years for a vanguard fighter, and one year for rearguard. It takes more time to acquire the skills needed to fight on the front line."

"I was assessed as a Swordsman, so I'd have to go for two years..."

"Once you graduate from the academy, you can form your own party, or join a clan and start working. Working alone is dangerous, so I don't recommend it."

"The academy...is it expensive?" the mayor asked.

"Nope, it's completely free. Government funding. The government can always use new Seekers, after all, since an Abyss can emerge anywhere."

"Really?!" Chelsea sounded excited. Her face suggested she'd opened a door and glimpsed her dream through it for the first time.

"But they don't cover room and board. The capital is an expensive place to live in. Part-time work won't cut it, and you can't work full time and still attend the academy. You'd need to save up enough beforehand."

"O-oh, I see..." Her face fell as the reality of money set in. "Couldn't I go to an academy outside of the capital? I heard there was one nearby, in Eudora."

"Unfortunately, the only government-subsidized school is in the imperial capital. The regional schools have expensive entrance fees and charge high tuition. And the classes are far inferior to those in the capital."

"What about becoming a Seeker without going to school?"

"It's possible, but I wouldn't recommend it. Going up against beasts without training is sure death. Even monsters and human criminals would likely be too much for you."

Unless you apprenticed under an experienced Seeker, the academy was still the best place to learn the Seeker's arts, and your best shot at developing the skills to keep you alive.

"I won't sugarcoat this: Seekers must constantly put their lives on the line. They also have to take the lives of others. Both hunters and the hunted are desperate. Wishful thinking will only get you killed."

"But..." Hearing my words, Chelsea looked down, eyes filled with sadness. I felt bad for bursting her bubble, but I would never forgive myself if she died because I lied about her chances. All I'd done was tell her the truth, hard as it was.

"If you really want to become a Seeker, you can start by becoming an apprentice," I said.

"Appren...tice?"

"It's a job where you carry a party's gear, help them navigate, and generally support Seekers in their work. The work is managed by an organization called the Apprentice Association. You can register, get paid for your work, and even witness combat firsthand. It can be dangerous, but apprentices don't actually participate in combat, so their survival rate is very high. The Association will also teach you skills to help you survive. You can gain knowledge, experience, and even some minimal skills without attending the academy."

Chelsea's eyes went wide. "So there is a way?!" she cried out happily. "Thank you so much for telling me!"

"It's important to keep an open mind and learn all that you can," I said. "If you do that, doors will open."

"I understand! I'll do some research on my own too!"

"That's a good idea. Good luck."

"Um...if I were to become a strong Seeker, could I join Blue Beyond?" she asked, looking up at me with puppy eyes.

I chuckled. "Fine with me. If you really do become a strong Seeker and can live up to my expectations, then we can fight together as allies."

"Oh, really?! I'm so happy. Thank you so much! I will become a strong Seeker! I promise!"

It was a hasty promise, but who knew what the future held? If this child really did become an excellent Seeker, I'd be more than willing to add her to our team.

But the mayor and his wife wore somber expressions. They probably had their own agenda for their girl's future, but they dared not interrupt me after I'd saved their lives. I was betting Chelsea would receive a lecture once Alma and I took our leave... but that was a family issue. There was nothing I could do about it.

One way or another, we'd find out eventually if this starry-eyed girl would submit to reality...or not.

"Thank you very much for the delicious meal," I told the mayor's family.

We had finished eating. My plate was clean. To be frank, it hadn't been particularly tasty, lacking salt to add flavor or seasonings to offset the smells. But they'd shown us hospitality despite their poverty, so it was only polite to eat everything they offered, regardless of the taste, especially since the little girl had helped prepare it.

Alma must have felt the same way because she'd also cleared her plate. Now she was having trouble fighting back her weariness, and her head was drooping.

"I'm very glad you liked it."

"We are very grateful. We need to get some rest, but first, we'd like to be paid the remaining balance," I said. "I find it hard to relax until my business is all taken care of."

"Understood. I'll bring it right away. But first we have one more gift for you. Please try it."

The mayor motioned toward his wife, who brought a bottle of wine to the table.

"This is a famous vintage. We bought it one year when crops were good. It cost a hundred thousand fil at the time, and had only matured since then, raising its value."

"You want to give us such an expensive wine?"

"Yes. Blue Beyond has done so much for us. Selling the bandits' belongings should tide us over for a while, and it would be dishonorable to clutch pennies now."

The mayor uncorked the wine and poured a glass for Alma and one for me.

"Now then, don't be shy. Drink!" he coaxed us. I picked up my glass but didn't drink. Instead, I sniffed the wine and then put my glass back on the table.

"You're right," I said. "It's excellent wine. I can tell from the color and fragrance that it's top-flight stuff."

"Yes, of course! You won't often come across wine like that, even in the capital!"

"I believe you're right. In fact, even as a guest, this wine is far too precious for me to have the first taste. Mayor, as our gracious host, won't you please start us off?"

"Huh...? M-me?" he said, obviously flustered. A reaction that suggested the wine wasn't of the finest vintage after all.

"I agree. You should have the first drink, Mayor. Please," Alma said, placing her own glass in front of the mayor, who grew pale. I smiled at the man, who was now shaking so violently, it was almost funny.

"What's wrong? Won't you have a drink?"

"N-no I...I don't really have a taste for alcohol..."

"Well, that's strange. If you don't have a taste for alcohol, why would you buy a hundred-thousand-fil bottle of wine?" I asked.

"Y-you see, I...that..."

The humor of the situation was wearing off. It was time to finish this.

"Poison, right? You poisoned the wine, didn't you?"

When I said this, the mayor stood up, eyes bulging. "P-poison? Why would I do something like that?!"

"Why? So you could kill us and take our valuables and armor, no?"

"Unbelievable! What an outrageous accusation! Based on what evidence?! How insulting to accuse me of such a horrendous act!"

"The evidence?" I held up my index finger. "Exhibit A. No one who lies about the number of bandits to avoid paying a fair reward is going to then offer up a hundred-thousand-fil bottle of wine. You told us there were twenty bandits, but there were actually three times that many. You lied to me."

"I-I had no idea! I didn't know!"

"Exhibit B," I said, putting up my middle finger as well. "This wine is not expensive. It's cheap. You might have been fooled by a merchant, but that doesn't matter. What *does* matter is that I could tell from its scent that there's been a decline in its quality because it's been opened before, and recently. You opened it, spiked it, and then recorked it. You probably made sure to uncork it in front of us so we wouldn't suspect anything, but you didn't reckon with my fine palate."

"Th-that..."

"Hmm. You thought a little boy and little girl so much younger than you wouldn't know anything about wine, did you? You imbecile. Anyone with half a brain would realize that living in the capital would have given me a well-developed palate."

"Er...I-I'm sure my wife just accidently brought out my usual nightcap! That's it! Look, the label is even different!" he stammered. "Dear, I told you to be careful when you served the wine!"

"I-I'm so sorry!" she said.

Still with the charade. It was so irritating, it made me want to kill them.

"Exhibit C," I said, raising my ring finger. "You and your wife have been overflowing with bloodlust ever since the wine appeared. You have been giving off the 'I'll kill you' vibe quite clearly. There wasn't an ounce of shame or humility in your voice when you presented us with this supposedly famous and expensive wine. You were hoping we'd confuse the smell of poison for the bouquet of an unusual grape, but such an asinine gambit won't work on us."

"You're right, Noel. The poison in that wine has a peculiar taste," Alma said. "That's why they needed to explain the flavor somehow, so we wouldn't notice it was contaminated. Although only a true idiot would be fooled by their dinner theater performance. Even if we *had* been fooled by this charade, Scouts spend years developing a tolerance for poisons, so I would have been fine."

She laughed, snorting gently. The mayor and his wife's faces twisted in frustration.

"Sh-shut up! None of what you say is evidence! It's all speculation!"

"The evidence is right before you, Honorable Mayor. If you want to prove we're lying, just take a drink of the wine. Now."

"Shut up, shut up, shut up!" the mayor barked. "No one will believe you! Get out of here! Leave my village this very instant!"

So this baldie was going to go on the offensive, hm? I was happy to leave, but they still owed us money. Letting him off the hook for trying to swindle us was out of the question.

"I'll ask you one more time. You poisoned the wine, correct? Confess."

"Yes, I poisoned it. I wanted you dumb Seekers to die after taking out the band of thieves so that I could steal their valuables and armor! And yours, for that matter. Kids who're only good at fighting things are usually gullible. I thought it would be easy..."

Talker skill: *Confess*. Once the mayor realized he'd admitted his crimes, he rushed to cover his mouth with his hands.

"Father...is that true?" Chelsea asked, peering at her father—a monster whose true nature had just been revealed to her. She looked stunned, unable to fully comprehend the situation.

"Er...I-I'm so sorry!" The mayor dropped to his knees before us and began to grovel. "I-I know I can't be forgiven for what I've done! B-but I had a good reason..."

"A good reason?"

"I am deep in debt... When the famine struck, I went into debt to save everyone... I need money to pay that back... If I don't pay it back on time, then horrible things will happen... I-I never wanted to do anything like this! But I had to think of the future of the village. Someone had to step up!"

"You're lying," I declared.

The mayor shook his head furiously. "I-I'm not lying! It's true!"

"You probably are in debt, but it's not because of the famine. Maybe you thought you could fool me because I'm young, but there hasn't been a famine in these parts for thirty years. If you were still in debt from that long ago, this village would already be defunct."

"Wh-why do you..."

"Remember the last time you hired us to hunt monsters?" I asked. "They were a breed whose strength depended on the fertility of the soil from which they emerged. That's why, before we took the job, we researched the types of crops grown here and how bountiful the harvest had been in recent years. After that, we estimated the soil quality. That's when I learned about the famine—which happened more than a decade before I was born."

After being caught in another lie, the mayor stood there, at a loss for words.

"You're still trying to lie to us, at a time like this. What are you hoping to achieve, exactly?"

"N-no I...er..."

"I presume the reason you're in debt is that you were tricked by a heinous merchant. Maybe he promised to sell you a magic goose that lays golden eggs? Well, it doesn't matter. Either way, you got swindled and wound up massively in debt for it."

"H-how do you know..."

Wait, seriously? I'd just made up that example on the spot...

"You're slow, stupid, despicable, and cowardly. You're a zit on the face of humanity, filled with the pus of every negative trait we possess as a species. I don't know how you can even live with yourself."

"Err, grrr..."

"Enough. This is exhausting. Bring us our money now. It's pointless to make garbage like you pay for your mistakes."

"Y-you have no right to talk to me like that! Where do you get off demanding the rest of your reward?! You have Gordo's head! Just go claim the bounty for that!" the mayor snapped, forgetting himself. Then he grew flustered, suddenly realizing what he said. "N-no, that was...just tit for tat, I..."

"Oh, so that's not how you really feel?" I asked.

"O-of c-course not! It was just...a joke. Ha ha ha."

"A joke, huh? A very funny joke. Ha ha ha!"

"Th-thank you very much! Aha ha ha."

"Ha ha ha!" I'd been trying to decide how to make him pay. Now I had an answer. "I'll start with your right eye."

"Huh? M-my right eye?"

I stood from my seat, kicking the chair away, and grabbed the mayor by his collar. I slammed him down onto the table and then, just as I'd declared, stuck my thumb into his right eye.

"Ooowww!"

"That's it? It's not every day you get to be penetrated so deeply by a boy so much younger than you. You can squeal louder than that."

"Owww! My eye, my eye, aggghhh!"

The mayor continued to shriek, but he was unable to lift a finger—because my thumb was currently gouging his eye from its socket. Seeing her husband's eye put out, the mayor's wife fell from her chair in a swoon, and his daughter stood where she was, frozen. The mayor himself quickly lost the vitality to even scream. He was panting like a dying dog.

"Don't think you're getting off with just losing one eye," I whispered in his ear. "I'll take your left eye next. Then I'll cut off your nose and ears. Then I'll smash each and every one of your teeth and pull out your tongue. I'm going to make you look like the scum you are."

"Eeek, pl-please forgive meee! I-I'll pay your money r-right away! Three hundred thousand fil, right now!"

"Three hundred thousand? Don't make me laugh. You think that's going to cut it now? If you want to keep the rest of your face, you'll bring me every last coin you have in the house."

"B-but! I can't! Please, anything but that!"

"In that case, negotiations have concluded."

I cracked my knuckles and put my hand to the mayor's cheek, letting my thumb slide up to his left eye. I pushed past his eyelid easily. His eye was going to be mine now.

"This is the last thing you'll ever see. Make sure you etch it into your mind."

"N-no! Please, forgive me! I borrowed the money from the Gambino family! If I don't pay them back, they'll kill me!"

"Do you think I care?"

Did he think that dropping a mob family's name would faze

me? How stupid could he be? You don't become a Seeker if you're weak enough to fear organized crime.

I started to press down on my thumb to crush the mayor's left eye. That was when it happened.

"Wait a second!"

The voice belonged to little Chelsea. She stood in front of me, her big eyes full of tears, her teeth chattering in fear. Then she held up a leather bag. "This is all the money we have in the house! It's 820,000 fil! We don't have a single copper more! Please take this and forgive my father!"

Somehow, his daughter had known where his money was hidden. She made the decision to surrender it herself, before it was too late for her father. But the mayor was furious with Chelsea's decision.

"You fool! What have you done?! If you give him that money, I'll be killed!"

"But if we don't give him this money now, you won't just lose both your eyes; you'll never be able to hire Seekers again! What will you do if we're attacked by bandits or monsters?!"

"Th-that...but...er..."

I was moved by his daughter's words. I'd thought she was just trying to save her father at first, but she was also acting with the village's future in mind.

It was an unwritten role—a social expectation, if you will—that Seekers were expected to share information with each other. If a Seeker was sold short by a customer, or even betrayed, as the mayor had done with his poisoned wine trick, we had to tell our colleagues, so none of them might be victimized in the same way. The tavern masters served as the repositories of this information, maintaining lists of malicious clients and taking responsibility for warning their regular customers and other tavern masters.

In other words, once the mayor's treachery got out, no Seeker would ever accept a job from Mintz Village again. An Abyss could pop up right in the village square, and every clan, every party would sit idly by and let it be destroyed.

I released the mayor and took the leather bag, checking the contents. "It does look like 820,000 fil. Is this really all of it?"

"Y-yes! I wouldn't lie to you!"

"I see. I believe you. I'll accept this, and we'll forget about what happened today. That's fine with you, right? Mr. Mayor?"

The mayor nodded reluctantly, hand clamped over his right eye. "Y-yes...that's fine..."

"You'd best not try to trick another Seeker again. Even if they've got nothing to do with me, I'll take everything you got."

I fixed the mayor with my best death glare. The man's pants darkened as he pissed himself, unable to do anything but nod over and over in my direction.

"All right. Let's go, Alma."

"Got it."

Once we got out of the house, I heard a bloodcurdling scream. "I...I hate Seekers!"

✝

"Seekers are pettier than I expected," Alma said knowingly as we walked together down the moonlit path.

I chuckled. "Are you ready to quit already?"

"Not at all."

"Well, that's good."

Alma moved ahead of me and tilted her head to the side.

"Are you all right, Noel?"

"I'm fine."

"I see. Still, no matter the circumstances, it's always hard to see a girl who once admired you then come to despise you."

"If I wanted to avoid people despising me, I'd be living on a deserted island."

"When you're feeling down, you can always come to me. I'll hold you tight," she said seductively, spreading her arms wide.

I snorted. "Why don't you go hug a cactus, you big-boobed bimbo?"

"More name-calling! Knock it off!"

"Then stop treating me like a child."

"Hmm...that's difficult. It's your fault for having such an adorable face."

"*That's* your reasoning?"

It might be acceptable when it was just the two of us, but if she kept this up once we recruited more members, it would reflect poorly on me as leader. I was letting her play it off as a joke for now, since we'd just met, but if it continued, I'd put my foot down sooner or later.

Still, she was thinking of me. I should probably be genuinely grateful for that. "Well...thanks for your concern."

"Noel, are you turning sweet?"

"Drop dead."

"You're so cute. I just want to squeeze you tight."

"If you lay a single finger on me, I'll pull rank and withhold your pay for the next job."

"That's just cruel!"

We bantered back and forth like that, teasing each other, as we walked down the road. There were no stagecoaches at this hour, so all we could do was walk to Eudora. My daily training meant I had enough stamina to get there, but I soon became terribly bored of the long, dark road. But I didn't want to sleep outside and wait until morning either. I'd rather spend the night getting to Eudora and take the morning coach back to the capital.

"Alma, have you decided not to become an Assassin after all?"

She said she'd been turned down by the Society of Assassins, but that was an issue of profession, not class. Alma had already fulfilled the requirements to move to the next rank and could do so at any time, which meant she could become an assassin if she wished.

"I haven't decided. Would you prefer an Assassin to a Scout?"

"I'm not sure. Your combat power would increase, but we have to consider skill overlap with any future recruits. Personally, I'd prefer it if you held off for a while."

Assassins were more specialized for offense than other Scout subclasses, making them excellent to have in a party's vanguard.

But vanguard-class Seekers were also a dime a dozen, and if I didn't make a point of prioritizing our rearguard, we could end up with all vanguard-types. Under those circumstances, it would be better for party balance if Alma became a rearguard attacker instead. Scouts could also take Chaser or Bandit specialties, both of which were B-Ranked rearguard attackers.

Of course, the future remained unwritten. It was entirely possible we'd end up with too many *rearguard* team members, which was why I was happy to have her postpone the decision for now.

"I understand. I'll wait."

"Yes, please. Let's discuss it again when the time comes. I should be able to move up a rank soon too."

"I look forward to it," she said. "Incidentally, do you know how it's determined whether you can move up or not?"

"I do. Certain marks appear on your skin, right?"

"Right. Like these." Alma stuck her hands between her breasts and pulled the big mounds apart. Along her sternum was a pattern of dagger shapes. "Once you're ready to rank up, this pattern appears. It's usually on your chest or the back of your hand, but I kind of hope yours is on your bum, Noel. That would be so cute."

"C'mon..."

It would be so embarrassing if that happened. No matter what I accomplished, having my rank mark on my butt would be a millstone around my neck. Just thinking about it made my stomach hurt.

"Noel," Alma said, sounding serious.

"Hmm?"

"A lot happened today, but it was fun. I only ever trained with my gramps, so I never knew how nice it is to fight alongside another until today."

"Well, I'm glad to hear it was beneficial for you," I said. "It wasn't a bad haul either. Having money makes it easier to keep your options open. I know how you feel."

"No, I'm not talking about money..." Alma frowned for a moment and then smiled. "I'm finally beginning to understand what kind of person you are, Noel."

"Huh? That came out of nowhere. What do you mean?"

"I mean, you're so cute. So—" She slipped her hand into my pocket and looked up at me with a huge, blooming grin. "I'll fight by your side forever."

✝

Alma had visited the secret headquarters of the Assassins' Society three days before she met Noel.

The headquarters were located in the tombs of an empty church in one corner of the capital. Her grandfather, Alcor, had told her of the secret door that led to them, and she'd already made an appointment with a middleman.

"Welcome, Alma, grandchild of Alcor. Come with me." The man in white robes who greeted her showed Alma to the secret headquarters.

No one had questioned her lineage so far, perhaps because she used Alcor's seal for all correspondence. Well, she was sure some of them had their doubts, even if they'd treated her as his grandchild so far. Either way, she was going to have to pass a test to join the Society. They would want to verify her skills.

The headquarters was drab and empty of furniture. The light of tallow candles reflected off the peeling walls. Finally, they came to a large iron door.

"Alma Judikhali. I ask again. Is it your true desire to become a member of our Society?"

"That's the plan," she said.

"Good. Then you may pass through this door and face your trial. May the infernal god bless you. Now, proceed."

Prompted by the guide, Alma pushed the door open with an echoing clank. The heavy door normally required multiple men to move, but she pushed through with ease. On the other side was a space resembling a practice arena. A man stood alone in the center; long-haired, garbed in Eastern fashion, and armed with claws on both hands.

"So you're Alcor's granddaughter," he said. "I've heard of you, but you're definitely not what I expected."

Alma sighed at his condescension. "The Society lets in petty underlings like you? That's disappointing..."

"What did you say?!"

"You're the examiner, right? If that's the case, let's get it over with."

"A mere C-Rank dares to speak to me this way?! I'll show you a true Assassin!"

The man flew at Alma with the speed and grace of the wind. Most C-Ranked Seekers would already be mincemeat.

But the girl before him was no ordinary C-Rank. She was Alma Judikhali, the blood and heir of the legendary Assassin, Alcor.

"I-impossible..."

Blood splattered across the gray walls, sending the torches sputtering. The man with the claws had thrown himself upon the blades of a whirlwind.

"Like I said, a petty underling. Pointless."

It was Alma's turn to condescend. She slowly walked toward the fallen man, who was panicked beyond belief. "Impossible! Where did you get power like that?!"

"Are you stupid? The Society's techniques were all created by my gramps. None of them will work on me."

"You...really are Alcor's grandchild?"

"You should have known that the moment you saw me. A petty underling *and* incurably stupid to boot. But don't worry. You needn't ever be troubled about your incompetence again."

Alma smiled and raised her knife.

"W-wait! The test is over! I lose!"

"No, it's not. It'll be over when I kill you."

"Stop!"

Alma swung her knife down, ignoring the man's cries.

But then—

"That's enough. Sheathe your blade."

Alma's knife would not kill the man that day. Two fingers held it in place. The fingers of an intruder who'd just appeared without her sensing the slightest hint of his presence.

He was clearly extraordinarily strong. Alma took a step back to pull herself together, putting space between her and the newcomer, who was a brown-skinned man dressed in a white vestment with a mandarin collar. He looked middle-aged, his rock-hard muscles visible even under his robes. His physique and short hair made him look more like a warrior monk than a priest.

"Who are you?"

"I am the Society leader, Simon Gregory," the man said in a low voice that carried well.

"I see. If you are the head of the Society, then your strength makes sense." Alma sheathed her knife and tilted her head to the side. "But I don't understand. Why did you stop me?"

"Let me ask you this, instead: Why did you try to kill him?"

"Gramps told me that was the test. The stronger combatant survives, and the life of the loser is offered to the god of hell."

"That was in the past. Under me, those ancient and sinister traditions have been abandoned," the leader declared, leaving no room for argument. He gave the claw-handed man a look that told him to leave.

It had been decades since Alcor retired from the Society. Apparently, a lot had changed in that time. Alma didn't object.

"Got it. Did I pass, then?"

"You passed...in terms of technique."

"Is there more?"

"Let me ask you a simple question. All you need to do is answer." The leader's eyes were looking directly at Alma and seemed to search deep inside of her.

"Were you the one who killed Alcor?"

"Yes," Alma answered without hesitation. She'd written in her letter that he was sick, but if Simon Gregory already knew the truth, there was nothing to hide. Alcor hadn't been sick. Alma had killed him.

"Even an EX-Rank can no longer fight when his mind is gone," Alma said. "A senile man is an easy kill."

"Allow me to go ahead and ask you why as well."

"Do you need to ask?"

"No...I don't," Simon said. "It's a silly question, but you will indulge me."

She had harbored thoughts of killing Alcor ever since she could remember. The man had never once shown her the affection of a grandparent. The only thing he gave her was the knowledge required of an Assassin, putting her through daily eccentric training regimes until both her body and her very soul were worn thin. The only way she could avoid her own imminent death was to kill Alcor and gain her freedom.

"Alcor always sought power. He was more reaper than man. He existed only to kill," Simon said, putting his memories into words as his eyes looked to the past. "A terrifying individual. Though I am EX-Ranked today, and leader of the Society, I do not think I could have beaten Alcor in his prime. His strength was inhuman. He was death in the shape of a man."

"But he lost to Overdeath." Alma said.

"Yes, he lost. There is always someone stronger. Even the reaper himself could not defeat Overdeath. It's fitting, in a way, when you think about it. His defeat at Overdeath's hands was when Alcor started come apart."

A wave of compassion suddenly washed over Simon Gregory's expression.

"Alma, you are not the granddaughter of Alcor. You are actually his daughter, are you not?"

It seemed the leader had thoroughly investigated her background.

"That's right. I'm Alcor's daughter, not his granddaughter. I was one of the children born to a woman he raped in some village."

When Alcor lost to Overdeath, he lost his mind. To a powerful Seeker, one's only value lies in one's strength. After surrendering his arm to Noel's grandfather, Alcor was utterly bereft. Stripped of judgment and reason, he grew more fanatical by the day, obsessed with delusions. He'd lost the one battle he should never have lost. But if he could create a version of himself that had won, then he could erase the past—or so he believed.

"That man didn't want a successor," Alma said. "He wanted to be reborn. He truly believed that would wipe out all the blemishes left on his soul."

"So that's how his legend ended. Pitiful."

"No. It was his victims who were pitiful. The women who were raped and forced to birth children they didn't want. My brothers and sisters, who were sacrificed to feed Alcor's delusions."

So many innocent lives were snuffed out in pursuit of that man's madness. There was no crime in killing such a man, even if he is one's own father. Alma believed that with all her heart.

"That man believed I was his greatest success," she said. "But he still told me, many times, never to challenge Overdeath. Even in the throes of madness, he could never forget the fear he felt when he lost. I still hate him, but remembering that brings me some satisfaction. Overdeath is old by now. It's silly."

"Overdeath died a few years ago."

"Huh?"

"The town he lived in became an Abyss, and he ended up in a standoff with the Lord at its core," Simon said.

"I didn't know Overdeath was dead..." Alma was the only one left. It was a relief, in a way, though she now felt like she had no place to go.

"Alma, I'm going to be honest. You are not suitable for the Society."

Simon Gregory's words were like a punch to the face. Even though she'd been forced to spend her whole life training for this, Alma couldn't believe what she was hearing. "Why?! I showed you my strength!"

"You certainly displayed amazing power. I can see that you will be EX-Ranked someday," Simon said. "But that doesn't necessarily mean you are suitable for the Society."

"I don't get it! Explain!"

He stroked his beard, vexed by Alma's interrogation. "What I'm about to tell you is top secret... You must promise not to tell."

"Very well, I promise."

"The Society of Assassins is about to undergo a transformation. Instead of an independent, secret organization, we will be rebuilt to serve at the pleasure of the emperor. The new Society of Assassins will focus on intelligence gathering, and we will channel all resources into protecting the nation."

"So...no more assassinations?" Alma asked.

"Unfortunately, we cannot dispense with killing altogether. But now, we shall only kill as a means to an end, and not as an end unto itself. A subtle difference, I admit, but at the very least, there is a future in service to the empire."

"Future..." Alma didn't know what sort of future he meant. But she *did* understand that no matter how bright that future might be, there was no place in it for her.

"There is carnage sleeping in your heart," Simon said. "We cannot place the fate of the empire in the hands of someone so dangerous."

"Ha ha ha..." Alma let out a dry laugh.

This felt like a nightmare, though she was wide awake. This was reality. No—"reality" was the name of the nightmare she'd been trapped in since she was born.

"Twenty-one years... This is the result of the twenty-one years I was forced to spend in this wretched existence? Not a single moment of joy. No friends, no boyfriend. Forced to endure that man's delusions forever, and still, in the end, my strength is completely useless... So why am I even alive? The past twenty-one years...for what?"

Alma began to cry and found she couldn't stop. She was empty and frustrated, and those feelings turned into an endless flow of tears.

"Give it back! Give me my life back!" She knew there was no point in blaming him. But she couldn't help but cry out. There was not a single person in this world who cared about Alma, except for Alma herself.

"Your life is your own," Simon Gregory said, turning on his heel to take his leave.

"Wait! What do I do now? Tell me!"

"Live how you want to live. The Society is not the only place where your talents are useful. There are plenty who seek your power. For example, Seekers."

"Seekers?"

Yes, Seekers might have need of skills such as hers...but she knew almost nothing about them. All she knew was that they put their combat prowess to use hunting beasts and closing up Abysses.

"That reminds me, I heard something interesting," Simon said, his back still to a perplexed Alma. "The grandson of Overdeath is a Seeker here in the capital. Apparently, he had some trouble with the other members of his party and he is currently looking to recruit."

"What does that mean?" Alma tilted her head, unsure what he was implying. "There's nothing odd about Overdeath's grandson being a Seeker. He simply followed in his grandfather's footsteps."

"Ah, but he is not a Warrior. He is but a Talker."

"Talker?! The grandson of Overdeath?!" Alma said, surprised.

"That's right, he's a buffer," Simon said, his smile invisible to Alma. "Everyone knows that Talkers are the weakest of all Seekers."

"And he still became a Seeker? Was he forced into it by Overdeath?"

"No, it was his own desire. He registered after Overdeath was killed."

"I see... But why?"

"I don't know. But I know this much: Noel Stollen, Talker and grandson of Overdeath, is strong."

Alma didn't know much about support classes, save that they were comparatively unskilled in battle, and hence naturally considered the weakest of the lot. She couldn't believe a Talker was that strong.

"Is that true?"

"I do believe so. He is currently called the Rookie Giant-Killer. He's still only Rank C, a rookie, but he's going to go far in days to come."

"I can't believe it..." Alma said,

"I told you it was interesting." Simon Gregory turned to look at Alma, broadening his smile. "If you're interested, pay him a visit."

Three days later, Alma made up her mind to meet Noel Stollen, Talker. He turned out to be a bold, clumsy boy. A boy with an eternally burning flame of indomitable fighting spirit deep within...

3 A World of Humanity and Justice

I WENT THROUGH THE PACES of my daily morning workout, then showered away the sweat. I'd just made it back to my room when I heard a knock on the door.

"Noel, it's time."

It was Alma. Since I had no specific plans for the day, I told Alma I'd show her around the capital. She called it a date, but I had no such intentions, of course. I was only going to show her the sites every Seeker should know. I'd already told her that she could find the tourist and entertainment spots herself.

I opened the door to find Alma standing there and gave her a little wave with my left hand.

"Good morning," she said,

"Good morning. Well, come in."

Alma stepped into the room and looked around with interest. "This is nice. I wish I could have stayed here too."

Our original plan had been for Alma to join me at the Stardrop

Inn. But there turned out to be no free rooms, forcing her to find different lodging.

"How is your place? Have you settled in?"

"Pretty much. It's not as nice as this, but it's all right."

"As long as it's comfortable. That said, you're early. It's barely 9 a.m. Nothing is open yet."

It was Alma, impatient as always, who'd suggested she come by my room. We could have picked another meeting place, but she'd wanted to see the inn.

"I'm glad to see you so early, little bro. You're so bullheaded, Noel."

"Shut up. How many times do I have to say this? You're not my sister. If you were going to show up this early, then you might as well have come by in time to train with me."

"Impossible. I can't wake up at 5 a.m."

"You're so lazy... If you don't keep up your exercise regimen, you'll get fat," I told her.

"I'm fine. Beautiful maidens have special combustion engines, so we don't get fat."

"What are you talking about? Maiden combustion engines?"

Alma gave me a sidelong glance and flopped onto my bed. "Ahh...I'm so bored. Noel, tell me a funny story."

"Buzz off. I'm not a clown, here to perform for you. If you're bored, read this." I handed Alma a book from my desk.

"What's this? Your autobiography?"

"Close. It's not an autobiography, it's my battle record. I've been recording the details of every battle I've been in, starting when I formed Blue Beyond and ending at the bandits we defeated last week."

"That's amazing. What page am I on?" Alma turned onto her stomach and crossed her feet as she started to read. "Ergh! Noel, this record is inaccurate! You left out our love scene!"

"No event of the sort ever occurred. Shut up and read. And if you add anything strange, I'll smack you again."

"Tsk..."

Why was she clicking her tongue at me? She wasn't seriously going to write in a love scene, was she? She was so incredibly stupid. The fact that she was five years older than me and still acted like this was so frustrating, I didn't even know what to say.

While Alma read my battle record, I sat in my chair and picked up a book about organizational theory. Naturally, I hadn't given up on my clan dreams. I was studying what I thought I might need to advance, with my eye on establishing a new clan as soon as we added one more worthy member. I would have to front most of the money required, but that would be fine. Unlike before, I was the leader now, and I had no reason to be tightfisted with my personal funds.

In fact, thanks to the price Lloyd and Tanya had fetched, I was flush with it. I had enough to register the new clan, whenever I was ready.

Of course, there was no point in starting a clan if we couldn't go Abyss-diving, which meant we still needed a third member. I was still recruiting in the central square and also considering putting ads in the classifieds section of the imperial capital newspaper.

If a skilled Seeker surfaced thanks to one such ad, then great. If not, then I'd just have to resort to headhunting.

But I needed more time before I could recruit Hugo, the Puppeteer Seeker I had my heart set on. So I was casting my net in the meantime, though finding good recruits was proving an uphill battle.

"I'm bored now," Alma announced ten minutes later, closing the book.

"That was too quick."

"Not true. Too much reading turns you into a bookworm."

"So you admit your brain is no bigger than a worm's."

"You must be hearing things. Anyway, I now have nothing to do again. Noel, I have a favor to ask."

"I will hear your request. But choose your words carefully."

"Let me touch your body."

"I told you to choose your words carefully!"

Was this dumb girl really brazen enough to openly declare her intent to commit sexual harassment? Even the perverted dudes who hung around the taverns were more eloquent than this.

"Then here I go."

"Wait! I didn't consent to this!"

Clearly, she'd had no intention of respecting my opinion in the first place. Alma stood from the bed and reached her hands out to grope me. But I had no intention of letting her cop a feel so easily. Right before she reached me, I grabbed her hand and used all my strength to thrust her aside.

"Stop it! You're not gonna touch me!"

"Impossible. Give up and let me touch that great body, li'l bro."

"I told you, you are not my sister—argh, ohhh, y-you're strong!"

She was powerful. Her slender, elegant arms held more strength than I could bring to bear even when giving it my all. And judging by her composed expression, she wasn't even using half of what she had.

"Tee hee hee. Impossible. No little brother can overtake his big sister."

"Knock it off, dummy!" I clenched my teeth and tried to push Alma away, but it was useless. Trying to move her small body was like trying to shift a mountain.

"It's so cute...watching you fight desperately. May I kiss you?"

"What?! You know I would say no!"

"I'm gonna kiss you. Mwah-mwah-mwah." She puckered up.

"Stop, stop it! I said stop, you moron!"

She moved her face close to mine. If I didn't act fast, this woman was going to steal my first kiss.

But just as I thought I was doomed, the door flung open.

"Noel! What's all this commotion?!"

It was Marie, the daughter of the Stardrop Inn's owner. Her eyes grew wide when she saw us wrestling with each other, and she dropped the laundry basket she was holding.

"B-but... Noel, trying to kish a girl..."

"No, she's forcing herself on me! Stop gawking and help me get this idiot off me! I'll pay you!"

But Marie was trembling so violently that she couldn't understand what I was saying.

"Why...why wouldn't you kish a man?! You can't kish a woman! Handshome men kish handshome men! Waaah, Noel, you traitor!"

Marie started bawling, riled up by her own incomprehensible nonsense, and ran off.

"Wh-who was that strange creature?"

After such an abrupt incident, even Alma was left dumb-founded, her mouth agape. I seized that moment to release her hands and punch her in the throat.

"Ow!"

The blow knocked her unconscious. Free from her evil clutches, I was able to catch my breath. But my heart was heavy.

"Why aren't there any decent women in my life..."

It wasn't long before Alma came to. Apparently, she'd lost her memory of recent events and thought she had just fallen asleep, suspecting nothing whatsoever. Somehow, I'd maintained my chastity.

"Where are you going to take me first?"

The commotion had eaten up plenty of time, so Alma and I left my room. The capital was as lively as ever. A sea of people of different races and backgrounds, on foot and in carriages, flowed down the street like a river.

"First we'll stop by the armament shop I always go to. Then—"

I listed the places that a Seeker needed to know. The armament shop, the equipment/supplies shop, the Appraiser Association, and the bookstore that sold skill guides. Alma had already been to the Seeker Association herself, so we didn't need to stop by there.

"So, you understand what today's plans are? Now don't get separated from me."

"Got it."

At the Appraiser Association, Alma researched her options for ranking up. She had four choices. The vanguard options were Assassin and Torturer; the rearguard options were Chaser and Bandit. After viewing all the information, she narrowed it down to Assassin and Chaser, reasoning that neither Torturer nor Bandit fit her personality.

Emotionally, she seemed partial to Assassin, the job she had trained for. However, she didn't seem to have a strong preference, saying instead that she would stick to the plan of deciding between Assassin and Chaser depending on what the party needed most.

Once we were done at the Appraiser Association, it was past noon.

"I'm so hungry. Noel, let's go eat."

"I am too. Let's take a lunch break."

We could go to the specialty bookshop after we ate. While we were looking for a restaurant, I saw a familiar face.

"Alma, I'm sorry but can you decide on a place and order for us both? I have to do something."

"What? Right now?"

"When I'm done, I'll send you a message with *Link*, so you can tell me where you ended up. I'll be back."

"Oh, wait! Noel!"

I heard her calling after me, but I ignored it and kept running.

†

The capital was cheerful and prosperous, but society was hardly egalitarian. I arrived at the slums of the capital: the final stop for those who had fallen into poverty. This dark, smelly apartment block behind the downtown area was overflowing with garbage and populated by dead-eyed unfortunates. It was the very bottom of the barrel in terms of both sanitation and safety, and it wasn't just the impoverished who lingered here. Criminals liked to use the area to gather and establish hideouts, with the result that no upstanding citizen would ever come here on purpose.

"Noel, over here."

I turned to see a man who could only be described as an insouciant-looking young thug step from the shadows, wearing a smirk. This was the familiar face I'd followed to the slums.

"Loki," I said. A false name, of course, but no one knew his real one. "You came to this dump on purpose. We could have made the deal somewhere else. What if my clothes wind up permeated with the stench? What will you do for me then?"

Loki shrugged. "Sorry about that, but you know I'm walking a fine line here. Didn't want to do business somewhere I might be recognized, and I thought you might feel the same way."

"Anywhere would be better than this. Unlike you, I live on the up and up. I can't have groundless rumors springing up about me because someone saw me slumming it."

"Those are some big words for a guy who sold his friends into slavery."

"Shut up. You're obligated to take my comfort levels into consideration. Am I wrong?"

"Okay, okay. Don't look so angry, Boss," Loki said.

I wasn't sure if he really did get it or not, but he wasn't stupid. He would probably be more careful next time. A real professional never acted on emotion.

"Here, today's yield. Take it," Loki said, handing me a thick envelope. I checked the contents to find dozens of sheets of paper covered in text. It was the information I requested.

"Good work, as always," I said. "You really are the best informant in the capital. I guess you're not called the Kaleidoscope for nothing. Nothing gets past you."

Loki was an information broker, and also the top hustler in the imperial capital. His skill with gathering intel was a direct result of his class. Loki was an Imitator, a combat class that could copy other people's physical guise. This ability allowed him to infiltrate any location he chose without detection. He never let conceit overwhelm his caution, changing his appearance for each customer to ensure no one knew what he really looked like. Today's devil-may-care thug was just one of his personas. He could freely alter his age and gender.

There was a type of monster called a shape-shifter with similar abilities. Word on the streets had it that Loki was a half-breed: part human, part shape-shifter. Beings with rare abilities often came from special lineages, so I was inclined to believe the rumors.

"I'll take that as a compliment," Loki said. "But I prefer cash to compliments. Feel free to puff it up a bit. You made a mint off Gordo's head, yeah?"

So, he knew I'd taken out Gordo. He really was terrifyingly quick on the uptake. It was how he'd earned the reputation he had, despite having plenty of competition in the form of the capital's existing, well-established information network.

"I'll pay you. I'll pay you the normal, fair reward." As I opened my purse to pay his reward, Loki snatched the coins from it.

"Hey, thanks!"

"I'll contact you by owl for the next job."

"Aye, sir. You are a man of taste, Boss." His brazen eyes looked at me with curiosity. Loki continued, seemingly enjoying himself. "I heard you want to add that homicidal Puppeteer, Hugo Coppélia, to your team. You really are nuts."

"That's none of your business. Shut your mouth if you want to keep your tongue," I said, glaring at him. Loki threw up his hands.

"Whoa, I'm scared, I'm scared. The grandson of Overdeath is scary!"

"Whatever. I'm leaving now," I said, starting to turn away.

"Oh, wait a sec," Loki called out. "Don't venture too deep into the slums at night. There's a bad drug doing the rounds of late. Should be fine in the daytime though, probably."

"A bad drug?"

"It's a new stimulant. They say the high is incredible, but one of the side effects is uncontrollable rage."

"Seriously? What kind of moron is selling a drug like that? The Lucianos won't let them get away with it for long."

Loki's expression changed.

"It's being sold by a Luciano subfamily, actually," he said. "The Gambinos."

†

There were some rare cases of Seekers holding dual classes. Normally, classes divided between combat-type and production-type attributes didn't mix. There were clear differences between skills related to combat, skills related to production, and skills that anyone could acquire. The only exception was dual classes—people who had a combination of both combat and production attributes.

One such dual class was that of Puppeteer. In addition to the combat skill that allowed him to command and strengthen puppet-like automata, a Puppeteer could also use production skills to *create* puppets as well as weapons for those puppets.

Hugo Coppélia was an incredibly powerful Puppeteer. Nicknamed "the Bloody Taxidermist," he was the most blood-thirsty killer to terrorize the imperial capital in years. He was currently imprisoned in the capital, on death row. The Appraiser Association was assessing Hugo's class skills for academic research, so he wouldn't be executed anytime soon, but once their research was complete, there would be no more reason to keep him alive. He had maybe three months left.

However, thanks to the information Loki was gathering for me, I was almost done putting together a plan to set Hugo free. Once successful, I planned to manipulate public opinion to clear his name. I could recruit him for Blue Beyond after he was fully exonerated.

Naturally, I would never do this if Hugo really was guilty of murder. No matter how skilled he was, it didn't make sense to set an uncontrollable monster free. But I'd done some investigating of my own. Hugo had been imprisoned on false charges. Someone had framed him. The poor Puppeteer had been sentenced to death for a crime he didn't commit.

It was actually quite easy to prove that the charges were false. The problem was withdrawing a sentence that had already been issued by the authoritarian Department of Justice. That was difficult and required a lot of preparation. If I made a single mistake, I could bring the state's wrath down on my own head, so I had to proceed carefully.

I only had three more months. How far I could get depended solely on my wits.

"Alma, I'm done. Where are you?" I sent Alma a message as I headed out of the slums, then heard her angry reply echo in my head.

"You took forever! I'm at The Stuffed Cat! Hurry up!"

"Stop yelling. I'll buy you lunch, so forgive me."

"Really? Huzzah!"

The moment I said I would treat her to lunch, she cheered up. Her priorities were so predictable.

I had been to The Stuffed Cat before. It would take about five minutes to get there on foot once I left the slums. However, I decided to take a different route, ignoring Loki's warning and cutting deeper through the slums on my way to the restaurant.

It was easy to see the impact of the new berserker drug. There were addicts covered in blood from fights or self-inflicted wounds scattered along the streets. The walls and dirt roads were just as blood-spattered, and I spotted more than a few loose teeth and torn fingernails on the ground. It was just as Loki had said—pure carnage, caused by the drug's side effects of uncontrollable rage.

The addicts who sprawled comatose across the ground were all well-dressed folks too. The deals were being made in the slums, but the users came from all over the capital. It was only a matter of time before the drug became available outside the slums. Loki had said the Gambinos were promoting the drug, but I couldn't understand why the Lucianos would let a subfamily get so out of control.

As I kept walking, pondering this, I drew near to the exit from slums. The sounds of downtown grew louder. But then, something caught my eye.

"That—"

Another dirty drifter. But something about him was different. Upon a closer look, his features were ones you didn't often see in the capital.

"An Asian..."

Besides the criminals, most of the people who lived here were immigrants who'd been rendered mentally or physically unable to work. Asians were rare, though. There was trade with Asia, but very few of these traders lived in the capital full time.

He looked to be about the same age as me. His disheveled black hair was infested with lice, and his black eyes were lifeless.

He was also gripping a dirty stick where he sat, suggesting his leg was hurt.

I pitied him. I couldn't imagine being stuck in a foreign country, just waiting for death. And he was so young. He probably had dreams and ambitions, once upon a time.

Clink. I'd impulsively dropped a silver coin in front of the Asian man while walking by him. It was just a miserable ten thousand fil. Not enough to change his life, but he could at least get a hot meal.

"Hold up, girl."

The Asian man's jarring accent startled me. When I turned back, he was standing up and staggering toward me.

"You dropped this money, yeh? Here."

He held the silver coin out to me. I was at a loss for words.

"You all right? That's your coin, yeh? Big silver coin like that's worth a whole lot. Mind you don't drop it again."

"But..."

"Also, this ain't a safe place for a cute gal like you to be walkin' around. I dunno why you're here, but hurry up and get out."

He'd just called me a cute girl. I didn't have a mirror, so I couldn't see my own face, but felt certain my expression was beyond description.

"Wh-what's with that foul face? You got a bellyache or somethin'?"

"First of all... I'll be brief. I'm not a girl. I'm a man."

"Huh? A man? O-oh, I'm so sorry..."

"Secondly, I don't need that money. I don't want a coin that someone as filthy as you has touched. Keep it."

A WORLD OF HUMANITY AND JUSTICE 183

"Wh-what did you say?!"

"Do as you please with it," I said, turning on my heel. I felt the Asian man following me.

"W-wait, you!"

The second I felt his hand on my shoulder, I spun around and kicked him away.

"Argh!" Staggered by the kick, the man held his stomach and gasped for breath.

"Don't touch me. Know your place."

"Ahh...ahhh... you've done it now." The man's face twisted in anger and he gripped his stick tight. Did he intend to fight me? "I don't like fightin', but I'm no chump who won't stick up for himself neither. Sorry 'bout this—I'm gonna have to teach you a lesson."

He took up a fighting stance, and I realized he was in better shape than I'd anticipated. I'd thought he had a bad leg, but it didn't seem that way now. What was more, he didn't look nervous at all. Clearly, he had some combat training.

Was he a ruined mercenary? All I knew was that he wasn't a mere drifter. He had a weapon, but a mere stick couldn't hurt me much.

This was interesting. Really interesting, actually. I decided to let him have a go at me.

"You can still say yer sorry."

"I'm not apologizing, dumbass."

"Oh? In that case—"

The man crouched down deep.

"Go to hell!"

In the blink of an eye, the man, who'd been several paces away, was right in my face. He was fast! He skillfully swung his stick. and I would have wound up with some broken bones if I hadn't dodged.

"Wha?!"

He probably thought that one hit would end me. But right when his attack should have made contact, I bent far backward. The stick just barely missed the tip of my nose. I used the momentum to do a back handspring and kicked hard from that position.

"Erg?!"

I aimed for his chin with a kick hard enough to knock him out, but the man rolled his head back. I just barely grazed him.

I scuttled back to put distance between us. He didn't pursue me, instead keeping his distance and staying alert.

"Those are some mighty fine acrobatics. You a neenja, boy?"

"Neenja?"

Ohh, Ninja! If memory served, there was an island nation far to the east where Ninja was a Scout subclass. This man must have been from that island.

"I'm not a Ninja. I'm a Talker."

"A Talker? You? Meh, dun matter to me. I can see you're strong. Lemme go ahead and use a skill, then."

The air around the man suddenly changed. He faced me with a murderous determination worthy of a powerful beast. The transformation was drastic—he hadn't been anywhere near this serious a few minutes ago.

"Ha ha ha. You're the best. Excuse me for my rudeness. You've piqued my interest, so I'll get serious too." I pulled the knife from its sheath on my thigh and held it in an overhand grip.

"Don't hold back if you want to live."

"Ha. That's what I was gonna say!"

This man was strong. He was comparable to Alma, and the blood of a legend flowed through her veins. I didn't know what to expect. But then—

"Koga! What're you doin?!" I heard what sounded like a young child scream.

An older halfling man appeared on the scene, so round and chubby that he seemed practically to roll across the ground. Even adult halflings looked like human children at first glance, thanks to their stumpy legs, though their pointed ears gave the game away.

Halflings were a generally mild-mannered race. They stood only a meter tall, with large, exaggerated facial features, and lived in quaint forest villages. You had to watch out for city-dwelling halflings, though. Only the most ill-tempered halflings abandoned their countryside lives, and when found in urban areas, they were usually up to no good.

"How many times did I tell you to wait for me?!" said the halfling. "Now I find you brandishing your stick? What if the military police had been patrolling the block?!"

He was making the scene even worse. Despite his wrinkles and an attempt at a mustache, he still looked and sounded like a child throwing a tantrum.

However, the Asian man he'd called Koga shrank back under his tongue-lashing. Koga actually looked afraid of the man, as if he weren't a halfling at all, but a giant who might devour him whole.

"Miguel...this...um..."

"I don't need your excuses! I hope you're prepared for the consequences of disobedience!"

"N-no! Please, forgive me!"

"No! Look at my ring, Restrain!"

The halfling held up his right fist to Koga. The silver ring on his middle finger flashed and black lightning erupted from it.

Koga's scream sounded like someone was tearing his throat out. The lightning wrapped around his body, bringing him to his knees. I could smell his burning hair and flesh as he writhed in agony on the filthy ground. The halfling used the power of the ring to torture Koga, like a snake slowly squeezing the life from its prey, before finally relenting, leaving the man on all fours on the ground, barely breathing.

Witnessing the terrifying scene, I knew that it was caused by a vulgar item.

"The Oath of Subordination..."

Most items forged from the flesh and bone of beasts are wondrous devices that improve our lives. However, the evil among us can harvest beast flesh as well as the good, and some magic items are designed simply for the sake of power and cruelty. The worst of these is the Oath of Subordination.

The Oath of Subordination is composed of two items: parchment and a ring. Whoever writes their name in blood upon the parchment can never defy the owner of the ring. More specifically, when the owner of the ring chants "Restrain," the signatory's MP goes haywire, forcibly generating an electric shock within their body.

Needless to say, using such a dangerous and vulgar item on another person is prohibited by law. There is one exception, though. That is—

"You worthless slave! You bring this on yourself by disobeying me!"

The halfling spat at Koga, who was still on the ground, smoldering.

Slave owners were granted the right to use the Oath of Subordination. Which meant Koga was somehow this old halfling's slave.

"Ugh...and just who are you?"

Out of breath from excitement, the halfling finally turned to me.

"Seems like you were scuffling with my Koga. What's a pretty girl like you doing in a place like this? I wanna hear all about it. Don't worry, I won't hurtcha—I'm a gentleman. Might ask you to pour me some wine, though, heh heh heh."

Maybe he couldn't see my knife since I was holding it in an overhand grip, but the halfling began to stroll casually toward me, still laughing that creepy laugh. I kicked him in the face with all my might.

"Grrgh?!"

He flew across the street and hit a wall, blood gushing from his nose and spewing everywhere. His jaw and back were clearly in agony from the blow, but once he recovered, he looked at me with abhor.

"Y-you bitch! What do you think you're doing?! I'll melt your lady bits shut and you'll never piss again!"

The mouth on this "gentleman"! Pretty sprightly for an old coot. I could have put my foot through his head like it was an overripe pumpkin, but there was something I wanted to ask this lowlife.

"Watch your mouth. Or I'll be forced to take offense..." I drew my silver flame and aimed it at the halfling. "And put a hole in you."

"A silver flame?!" Staring into the barrel of my gun, the color drained from the halfling's face. "Wh-why would a girl like you have a silver flame?"

"Shut up. I'm the one asking the questions here, and you're the one answering them. If you want to live, anyway. Got it?"

"I-I got it!" The halfling nodded desperately.

"I've never heard that accent before. Where did you come from?"

"W-way down south; a town called Soldiland!"

A city on the southern border of the empire. Their accents were known for being a bit harsh.

"You're not a trader, so what are you doing in the capital?"

"W-well, I..."

"Answer me."

I moved the barrel of the silver flame to his forehead and the halfling yelped. It would be faster to use *Confess* but I didn't want to. I wasn't ready to stop until this lowlife felt true fear.

"I-I'll tell you! I-I've been exiled from my city!"

"Why?"

"I was running the d'Alembert family's underground fighting ring, but I pocketed the bribe money meant for the cops myself, and got caught, so..."

The d'Alembert family was a small-time organized crime ring down south. They weren't by any means weak, but the Lucianos were far larger and better connected to imperial power.

"In other words, you brought it on yourself. So you came to the capital to seek refuge in Luciano territory, since d'Alemberts aren't allowed here."

"Y-yeah...that's right..."

"Then this man is your gladiator?"

"Yeah... Most fighters these days take up with Seeker parties or clans, so I bought this slave somewhere else and brought him with me when I fled..."

"I see. You plan to put him to work in the underground fighting pits and keep the winnings for yourself," I said. "He's your last lifeline."

I had only visited the illicit fighting pits once, but I had seen enough to know that Koga would dominate the field. The fight purses would be significant.

"If things went well, you were going to find a way to get involved in promoting underground fights yourself, right?"

"Uh, well, yeah," he said. "Oh...do you happen to be involved in the fights, miss? Perhaps we've gotten off on the wrong foot—let's be friends." Still trembling in fear, the halfling man rubbed his hands together and offered me a fake smile. He sure was brazen for someone with a gun to his head.

"No thanks. I have nothing to do with the fighting pits. I'm just a Seeker. And I should have corrected you earlier—I'm a man."

"Huh, a Seeker?! And a man?!" His eyes grew wide with surprise. He seemed more shocked to find that I was a man than that I was a Seeker, but I didn't care.

What should I do now? I knew no one would reprimand me if I killed this old halfling. The d'Alemberts had disowned him, and though they might not be thrilled if I killed him, they wouldn't dub me their enemy for it. Besides, if the halfling died, I could claim ownership of Koga uncontested. He'd be a powerful asset in battle.

It was a course of action with no downsides whatsoever. It would bring me nothing but good fortune. And yet...I couldn't do it.

"I'll give you ten seconds to disappear. If you don't, you're dead. One, two, three—"

I started counting without waiting for a response. The flustered halfling ran over to Koga and kicked him in the head.

"Get up! We gotta get outta here!"

Koga stood up, still clearly in pain, and shakily followed his master, who was running at full speed. I saw fear and sadness in the slave's eyes when he glanced back at me.

What an idiot. With his speed, he could easily kill his master before the halfling could finish saying the word "Restrain." Either he'd been put through some frightful disciplinary measures, or he was just too afraid to strike out on his own.

But no matter how Koga had wound up so weak-willed, he was strong. I'd pay a high price to add him to my team, based solely on the few seconds I'd seen him in action.

But I needed a fierce wolf for my party, not a cringing dog. I had no use for someone so emotionally fragile.

"What a disappointment..." I muttered to myself, the words disappearing into the darkness of the slums.

†

"Hey! Noel, over here!"

Arriving at The Stuffed Cat, I was met by a smiling face I wasn't expecting.

"Lycia, what are you—"

Lycia, Lightning Bite's archer, was sitting with Alma. There were already a number of dishes laid out on the table and half were empty. I took a seat, a bit suspicious.

"Noel, you took forever. If Lycia hadn't showed up, I would have been eating alone," Alma said, scowling. Apparently, this was just a chance meeting.

"I said I'm sorry."

"Noel, thanks for lunch!" Lycia cut in, a shameless smile on her face.

"Stop shaking me down. I don't owe you lunch."

"What? C'mon, don't be stingy!"

"You're not even in our party. Get Wolf to buy you lunch," I said.

"Wolf never has money," Lycia said. "I'm usually the one who has to pay."

So Wolf couldn't handle his money either, despite being a leader. It was pretty embarrassing to depend on the rank and file to pay their own way. He didn't seem to be squandering party capital and losing trust the way Lloyd did, but he was still careless.

"You made a mint off killing Gordo, right? Alma told me. If you're so flush, then you can afford to buy me lunch!"

Hearing that I looked at Alma, who whistled and looked off in the distance at nothing in particular.

"You really can't keep your mouth shut..."

I should have muzzled her. This wench talked more than a fishwife. Realizing I'd never be able to really confide in her, I decided to keep quiet about Hugo until the time came.

"I don't suppose Alma also told you that I was buying her lunch?"

"As a matter of fact, she did," Lycia said, poking Alma in the cheek. "We ran into each other on the main road and got to talking, so we decided to eat together. Then Alma told me that you'd be joining us later, and it would be your treat. Right?"

"Heh. I see."

With the facts out there, Alma averted her eyes. I *had* said I would buy her lunch—but only her. She'd probably let it slip in the process of showing off. Seriously. The girl needed to mind her reputation with more care. She was in danger of making a habit of lying.

I decided to give in and make Alma look good.

"I'll be happy to buy you lunch, Lycia."

"Huh, really?!"

"Yep. Eat and drink as much as you want. I'll just take it out of Alma's paycheck. Every last fil."

"Wow! Thank you, Alma!" Lycia said.

"Huh?!" Alma looked perplexed, but it was too late.

"Excuse me! Your most expensive liquor, please!" Lycia called out to a passing waiter. "The whole bottle, not a glass! And a full course of the highest-grade marbled beef, please!"

"A bottle and a full course of the highest-grade marbled beef for me too."

"Wait! This is a joke, right?!"

Alma looked ready to cry when Lycia and I started ordering with abandon. I felt sorry for her, but she had brought it upon herself. Besides, it was nice to have someone else treat me to lunch once in a while.

We had fun eating and drinking on Alma's fil, and time flew by before we knew it. I wanted to stay longer, but we still needed to stop by the specialty bookstore to look at skill guides. Lycia said she had plans too. I also needed to do something about Alma, whose carelessness was reaching new heights.

"That really was a fun lunch! Let's go eat together again!"

"I'm never paying again. I hope you know that!"

I restrained the urge to snap at Alma, but Lycia only laughed so hard, she had to wipe tears from the corners of her eyes. "Don't worry, I'm not that cheeky. I'll pay next time," she said.

"That's generous. Does that mean you have your next job lined up?" I asked her.

"Well, if we succeed, then it won't be long before we can start a clan."

"Sounds like you're doing well. I need some of that luck."

"How is it going? Have you found any new members yet?" Lycia asked.

"Not at all."

I shrugged. No reason to tell a lie I'd be caught in right away.

"Hmmm. Not at all? Well, that's too bad." Lycia leaned forward, close to my cheek. "C'mon, join Lightning Bite. Alma can join too. That would be the best! C'mon!"

"I told you—"

I was about to decline again, but Alma cut in. "I have no intention of working for anyone but Noel, and Noel feels the same way, right? So, no. Give it up, Lycia."

"Well...like she said."

Lycia frowned, then groaned at our resolution. "No? I bet we would make a great party. But I guess it can't be helped... In that case, let's just be friends. That's okay, right?"

Alma smiled. "That would be fine. We can be best friends."

"Oh, best friends! Hurrah! How about you, Noel?"

"What do you mean 'How about me'?"

I had nothing against Lycia, but I wasn't interested. Sharing a meal once or twice was fine, but becoming friends with a girl from another party would just invite trouble.

"You've had plenty of chances to befriend me in the past," I said. "Why now, all of a sudden?"

"Because you had Tanya then..."

"Tanya? Tanya being here was a problem?"

"Of course. Problems galore." Lycia tilted her head to the side, face turning sour. "Tanya was all smiles and friendliness most of the time, but when it came to you, Noel, she was scary. When another girl approached you, she'd get this huge wrinkle in the middle of her forehead."

She demonstrated the expression she meant. It was scary, all right. It was the face of someone hellbent on avenging her parents, or something of the sort.

"I understand now," I said. "But that was because of Lloyd, not me. She and Lloyd were dating."

"No, it was because of you! Lloyd was always surrounded by fangirls, even after he got together with Tanya, but that never made her angry, right?"

"Now that you mention it..."

Lloyd had had a lot of fans. Even when we just walked down the street together, he was constantly being stopped for autographs and handshakes. But even when Tanya was present, she just smiled as though fans were a welcome nuisance.

"That's right..."

"Yeah, see!"

"Well, Tanya did always think of me as a little brother," I said. "She was probably worried that I'd fall for some weirdo."

I'd treated her like a real older sister once, though I backed off to give them space once she started dating Lloyd. But she'd betrayed me in the end, so clearly any familial feelings she might have had for me were just her way of filling the lonely void of a Seeker's life.

"That wasn't the expression of a girl worried about her little brother..."

I chuckled at Lycia's persistence. "Are you trying to say that Tanya had feelings for me? Don't be stupid. She's the one who chose Lloyd. Besides, she betrayed me. It's a bit of a reach to claim someone like that had feelings for me."

Even if what Lycia said was true, it had nothing to do with me.

"I'm no mind reader, so I can't say for sure, but that was proba-bly...hmm, how do I put this?" Lycia hummed to herself.

"Noel, you don't understand how a girl's heart works," Alma interjected. "A girl's heart is a wild stallion. She may give up, even begin to like someone else, but her heart never truly relin-quishes the guy she really loves. And that makes her do stupid things."

"Right, that! That's what I was trying to say!" Lycia said.

"Huh? It was?" Alma's words made no sense. "How would you know anything about such matters after living in the mountains your entire life?"

"This is just common knowledge."

"That's right..."

"Noel, you need to learn more about girls' hearts," Alma said. "I have a novel you should read."

"A novel? Now, wait just a minute..."

That explained it, at least. No wonder what she was saying sounded weird—she'd just pulled it from a book. This dumb, big-mouthed, sexual harasser of a girl... Her only redeeming quality was her skill in combat.

"Huh, what novel? I want to read it too." Lycia and Alma started chatting excitedly about the book.

"Excuse me—"

They were free to have girl talk all they wanted, but it was getting awkward for me. I needed to add some men to the team, and quick.

Lycia checked her watch. "Oh, it's getting late. I gotta go. Alma, thanks for lunch."

"Next time, it's your turn," Alma retorted, crumpling the long restaurant receipt in her hand.

Lycia narrowed her eyes, "I know. Noel, you come too."

"If I'm free."

"That's what someone who never plans on coming would say! Ugh!" Lycia said, puffing up her cheeks like a chipmunk. If I had free time, I wanted to be training, not lunching with the ladies.

"There's something I want to ask before we leave, Lycia. I heard there's a dangerous drug going around. Do you know anything about it?"

"A dangerous drug? Ahh...I think I heard some rumors about a new stimulant. The one that makes people go berserk? What about it?"

"I heard the rumors too, so I was wondering if anyone knew more about it."

So, both the drug the Gambinos were distributing and news of its existence had spread beyond the slums. It had no direct bearing on my activities, but I decided to keep an eye on the situation nonetheless.

"Oh, I had a question too. Are you gonna be my friend?"

"Fine... Let's be friends," I said playfully.

Lycia lit up with a big smile. "Yes! Let's!"

"Noel, do you dislike Lycia?"

I supposed it was only natural that Alma would ask. I'd clearly been holding Lycia at arm's length.

"I don't dislike her. It's just that she belongs to a different party. If I become more friendly with her than necessary, some people will take it the wrong way, and that'll cause trouble for Lightning Bite."

"That's a little dramatic. You'll never find a lover if you keep going like that."

"My job is my lover. And I'd never cheat on my lover."

It wasn't that I had *no* interest in love, but my first and most important goal was to gain renown as a Seeker. I didn't have time to fall head over heels, or into bed, with anyone.

†

After The Stuffed Cat, Alma and I went to the specialty bookshop in Skill Guide Alley, a selection of similar shops lined up in a narrow alley with an arched glass ceiling. Other than the skill guides, the shops carried wide selections of novels and antiquarian titles. There was even a book cafe where customers could take books from the shelves to peruse while they ate. The alley was open to all, and so ordinary shoppers, even families with children, mixed with the Seeker clientele.

"It's not what I expected. This is so warm and cheerful," Alma said, her eyes sparkling.

"I was surprised the first time I came here, too. And they have every skill guide you could ever want. You can get any book you've ever heard of here, save for extremely rare editions."

"What skills do you want to learn, Noel?"

"Either support skills to improve defense or special skills to impede enemy actions. What about you, Alma?"

"I want more throwing skills. I'll need them if I become a Chaser, and they'll be useful even if I become an Assassin."

It was a good choice. Indeed, throwing skills would be useful no matter what job she ranked up to. I would have offered advice had she been unsure, but it sounded like we were on the same page regarding skill selection.

"In that case, we'll part ways here."

"Huh, you're not coming with me?"

"Unfortunately, the books we need are in different shops. Once you find what you want, buy it yourself. You can use these stamps to pay." I pulled a bundle of stamps from my pocket and gave one to Alma.

"Your budget is one million fil. I'll leave *Link* open, so let me know when you're done shopping, or if you need extra money."

"Which shop has skill guides for Scouts?"

"Scout books are in this shop. I'll be going into that shop over there," I said, pointing to each. Alma nodded.

"Got it. See you soon, then."

"Don't forget to ask for a cashier's receipt."

I made sure Alma entered the correct bookstore, then headed toward my own.

"Hey, if it isn't Noel. Long time no see," the old man behind the counter greeted me when I entered the store.

This was the store owner, who also happened to be a gnome, a race known for their long, curled, goat-like horns. Since this elderly gnome also had white hair and a long beard, he resembled a goat more than most.

"Are you looking for another new skill?" he said between puffs of his pipe.

This was only my second time in the store. The first time, I purchased skill guides for *Assault Command* and *Stun Howl*. They had been expensive, though, so the store owner remembered me.

"I need a good guide for defensive skills, and one for special ones. Do you have anything?"

"Hmph, I have both. I'll get you a list."

"Thanks. I appreciate it."

"It's my job. No need to thank me. Oh, that reminds me—it's not what you asked for, but I did just get a skill guide that I thought you might like," he said, pulling a blue book cinched shut with a belt from down by his feet. Once a skill guide was read, the words vanished from the pages, so they were all sold bound shut.

"What's the topic?"

"*Exorcism.*"

"What?!"

Exorcism was one of the very few attack skills Talkers possessed. It could only be used on the undead, but it was extremely powerful and could utterly destroy opponents of the same rank as the Talker. More highly ranked opponents could resist, of course, but even they could still be hurt by the command.

With this skill, most undead wouldn't stand a chance against me. I had to have that book.

"It's extremely rare. I've never seen it in stock..." I said.

"Right. I haven't seen one in decades."

"I'm almost afraid to ask...how much is it?"

"Thirty million fil."

"Thirty million?!" I knew it would be expensive—skill guides are always pricey, and skill guides for rare skills cost an arm and a leg—but I'd never have imagined it would be *this* expensive. My strongest skill was currently *Assault Command*, and the guide for it had cost me eighteen million fil.

"I don't suppose...there's a payment plan?"

"No. There are already a number of collectors asking for it," the gnome said. "I would rather sell it to someone like you, who would make good use of it, than to a collector who'd just let it collect dust. Unfortunately, I can't extend you any credit right now. You're still lacking a new party, yes?"

"News travels fast..."

Being memorable wasn't always a good thing. Everything I did was public knowledge, including the poor situation I was currently in. The owner was right. I couldn't accept Abyss work without a full party, which meant I lacked good credit, despite my past achievements. No one was credulous enough to approve me for an installment plan for thirty million fil.

"Thirty million... I really can't pay that all at once right now." It was frustrating, but I had to admit defeat. My shoulders slumped, and the shop owner smiled.

"One month. I'll hold onto it for you for one month."

"Huh? Hold onto it?"

"You try and come up with the money."

"I understand. I am eternally grateful." Considering my current situation, it would be hard to make eighteen million fil in a month. But this was a chance I couldn't let pass by.

"Noel, I believe in you," the old gnome said, giving me a serious look. I smiled and nodded.

"Leave it to me. A month is more than enough time."

Maybe it wouldn't be, but I had to try. I had plenty of plans to break out of my current situation. With a deadline, I'd be even more motivated.

I abandoned the skill guides I'd planned on buying, deciding to save that money for *Exorcism*. That new skill would be much more valuable in the long run than the incremental improvements I'd been planning.

But that was me. I still had to buy Alma her skill guides, but I hadn't heard from her. I thought she might be having a hard time using the stamps, so I went to check in on her at the other shop.

"Oh, Noel?" Alma noticed me as I walked in, tilting her head to the side. She was at the register, paying for her purchases.

"Yeah, I finished at my store. What skill guide did you buy?"

"*Armor Piercing*. It's a throwing skill that cuts the target's defense in half. It cost eight hundred thousand fil."

"I see. That's a good skill." There were any number of situations where it could be useful. It would remarkably expand the tactics available to us.

"Also, this—" Alma held up a big box that had been sitting on the counter.

"What is that?"

"Tee hee hee." She opened the box. Inside was a stuffed bear.

"What...is that?"

"A stuffed bear."

"Well, yes. Why was it even in stock?"

"We carry them because I like them," the shop owner, a human woman, answered for Alma. "It's cute, right? Please take good care of it."

"I have no idea what you're even talking about." I understood that they sold bear toys at the store. I didn't care about that. What I *didn't* understand was why Alma had decided to buy it. "And you're going to buy that?"

"That's my plan. The skill guide is eight hundred thousand fil, and this little guy is exactly two hundred thousand, the rest of my budget."

"You're trying to expense this?! That's not what I meant by a one-million-fil budget! Put it back right now!"

"What?! Please, please! Buy it for me!" Alma said.

"No! I'm not buying a bear for a spoiled brat!"

"Oooh...I wanted to cuddle with it when I slept..."

"You're twenty-one years old! What are you *talking* about?!"

Alma eyeballed me dramatically and let out a sigh, apparently too frustrated to keep arguing with me. "Fine. I give up."

"As you should."

"I'll just cuddle with *you* instead. I'll come sleep in your room from now on, so make sure to leave the window unlocked. Though I can get in even if you do lock it..."

"*Fine.* I'll buy it for you," I said.

Two hundred thousand fil was a cheap price for my own personal safety.

✝

Koga Tsukishima was born in the easternmost island nation, the oldest son of a successful kimono fabric merchant. A life of idle pleasure...or so you might think.

It's common for fathers to clash with sons, but Koga's father looked upon him as if he were a heap of excrement swarming with flies. There was a reason he held such extraordinary animosity for the boy, why he considered him a blight on the family—and it had to do with the secret of Koga's birth.

The young fabric merchant and his wife had been deeply in love and admired by their community. They went to the shrine in the mountains every single day to pray for a beautiful, healthy child to become their heir.

No one ever dreamed that this pious routine would prove to be their doom.

One day, the couple was on their way home from the shrine, as always, when they were waylaid by bandits. They were stripped naked, and Koga's mother was raped. While they escaped with their lives, Koga's mother's mental state deteriorated afterward. Ironically, her womb was also blessed with the new life they had longed for—Koga—mere days after the rape.

Koga's father didn't know what to do. He didn't even know if the child his wife was carrying was his or not. They could abort the pregnancy with drugs if they wanted, but what if the child *was* his?

As he remained paralyzed by his indecision, his wife's pregnancy advanced until it was too late to terminate. Then Koga was born. Days later, his mother took her own life by slitting her throat. Whether it was because she'd truly gone insane, or because she'd born a child she did not want—no one knew.

Koga looked a bit like his maternal grandmother. His eyes did resemble those of his father, but the man wasn't certain, and in time, his doubts multiplied. Once he let those doubts consume him, he became paranoid. He spent all his time looking for ways in which Koga might resemble the bandit that raped his wife, seeing the brute even in how Koga walked and spoke.

At some point, doubt turned into hostility, and then hatred. Koga was innocent, but his father blamed him for all the misfortune that had befallen him. He didn't physically abuse the boy, fearing community pushback, but he left his care to servants and treated him like a stranger, though they lived under the same roof.

Koga was raised in that home for six years. He came to understand that his family didn't want him. Starved for love, the child tried to win over those around him, always hoping for affection in return. He stifled his discontent and insecurities, pasting on a smile, and doing his best to treat others kindly.

"The boy's always grinning like a fool. How foul. It's like your wife burdened us with a loathsome parting gift. If she was going to die, she could have at least taken the child with her..."

But when he overheard his grandmother say those words to his father, he realized all his efforts had been in vain.

Then one day, Koga woke up to find himself bound and tied in a place he didn't know.

"Oh, you're awake, boy." An unfamiliar man looked down at him. "Stay still if you don't want to get hurt. It's not like you have anywhere to run anyway. No one's coming to save you."

He didn't understand what the man was saying. Frozen in fear, Koga was taken to the port, loaded onto a ship, and stowed alongside other bound prisoners of different ages and genders, every single one of them bathed in sorrow.

That was when he finally understood he'd been kidnapped. Although, if he were to believe what the man said, Koga had actually been handed off to a kidnapper, probably by his father, who was glad to be rid of him.

He was sad. He hated his family, but he was sad. But that feeling faded over the long sea journey, and by the time the ship made port, Koga was just happy to be alive.

"You're lucky," said the man who had kidnapped him. "Boys like you usually kick the bucket on the journey, but somehow, you survived. Make sure you keep it up for whoever buys you."

The Eastern slave ship had landed in a town on the southernmost border of the Velnant Empire, Soldiland, the territory of the d'Alembert family. Koga was purchased by a halfling, Miguel, who had relations with the d'Alembert family. Miguel put him to work in the fighting pits, and there he spent two decades honing his skills before even being assessed for a class.

†

"Umm, your name was...what was your name again?" asked a young, bored-looking blond man with his head propped on his hand. The question was aimed at Miguel, who stood next to Koga in this opulent room.

"Boss, it's Miguel of the d'Alembert family," said the large man standing behind the desk.

"Oh, Miguel! Yes, yes, yes, I remember now!" the blond boss said, pointing at Miguel. "Miguel, you've been bad. I hear you made off with family funds? That's unforgivable, you know. The don of the d'Alemberts is *quite* pissed off. He asked my father to hand you over as soon as you were found. Your wanted poster has already been seen by everyone related to the Luciano family."

The man pulled a single sheet of paper from a desk drawer. On it was a description of Miguel. "This is why we apprehended you."

Koga and Miguel had been captured on the road, thirty minutes earlier, by a squad of rough-featured men who dragged them to this luxurious mansion and deposited them before the boss's desk.

Miguel had been expecting something like this, but the crafty halfling had been confident that he could talk his way out of any-thing. Yet now he just stood there quivering, clammy and pale, unable to utter a word. This man who'd the courage to talk business with a gun pressed against his forehead was now completely consumed by fear.

He'd told himself the same thing every day since he'd made it to the capital.

"It's fine, I can get myself out of any situation with anyone. The only person I need to watch out for is Albert Gambino. As long as that rabid dog doesn't capture me, we'll be fine..."

Now Miguel wasn't just on the verge of wetting himself—he was so petrified by the man before him that he was about to shit his pants.

Because the man before him was, in fact, the one and only Albert Gambino.

He was the young boss of the Gambino family, a sub-organization of the Luciano family: a slender, gentle-looking man in his early twenties. He was dressed simply in a red shirt with gold embroidery, and his casual attitude gave no hint of strength. The large, quiet man standing next to him gave off more of the gangster vibe than Albert did.

But it was Albert who was the true madman. The true devil. The Luciano family had Finocchio, known on the streets as the mad clown. But while Finocchio faithfully performed his duties as a family boss—albeit imperfectly—Gambino was the kind of madman who dispersed tragedy aimlessly and at random. One moment, he might be enjoying tea with his guests, and the next, sinking his butter knife into the eye of whoever was seated next to him.

A dangerous drug had been making its way around the capital lately, sold by Gambino. An alchemist friend of the family was producing it. It was risky business, equivalent to spitting in the face of his parent family, the Lucianos. But Gambino's father, the deceased former boss, had sworn a brotherly truce with the head of the Luciano family, so they were turning a blind eye to Albert's entrepreneurship for now.

"Now, the Gambinos have succeeded in apprehending one bad little halfling, but honestly, handing you right over to them would be a bore," Albert said, twisting his mouth in pleasure. "I mean, why should I have to work for a puny little peasant gang like the d'Alemberts? Don't you agree, Miguel?"

Miguel swallowed the saliva that had accumulated in his mouth and mustered up the will to speak. "Y-you're precisely correct! You're a part of the illustrious Luciano family, and the famously brilliant Albert Gambino at that. You can't let the d'Alemberts order you about! Yes!"

Albert nodded, seemingly satisfied with Miguel's desperate flattery. "Mmm, it's just as you say. Why, Miguel, you're quite knowledgeable on matters of underworld ethics for a halfling. It's a shame you were wasted on the d'Alemberts."

"R-really?! In that case, I would be honored to—"

"So, how about this? We will return you and your slave...as stuffed toys."

"Uh...Stuffed. Toys?"

"That's right stuffed toys! We will skin you alive, stuff your skin with cotton, then process your insides into ham and sausages.

Then we can send the whole lot to the d'Alemberts. Oh, they will be so surprised! What fun! Don't you think it's a wonderful idea, Miguel?" he asked with excitement, looking for Miguel's agreement.

But Miguel shook his head furiously. "No, no, no. Why would you do that? Skinned alive? Why would you tell such a vicious joke?! C'mon now!"

"Oh, it's no joke. I'm absolutely serious," Albert declared blankly. "That's decided, then. Laios, please make the preparations."

"Understood. At once." The large man called Laios bowed gracefully.

"B-but..." Miguel was dumbfounded. His smooth talk was useless against the disinterested sociopath before him. His time had simply come.

Of course, this meant Koga's time had come too. But just as Koga let out a sigh of resignation, there was a knock on the door.

"Boss, we have a debtor who is overdue. It's the mayor of Mintz Village."

The mayor, a bald man with a patch over his right eye. entered the room.

Normally, a debtor would never see the likes of Albert, especially since the mayor had actually borrowed the money from a branch lender in Eudora. Problems with repayments were usually handled by local muscle. However, the mayor had pleaded to appeal directly to the boss and came all the way to the capital to do so.

"I see. So your story is that you had our money and were about to repay it, when you were robbed by the Seeker party known as Blue Beyond?" Albert repeated for confirmation.

The one-eyed man nodded desperately. "That's exactly right! I resisted with all my might, but my wife and daughter were taken hostage. They tortured me, gouged out my right eye! The only thing I could do to save us was hand over the money!"

It was none of Koga's business, but the story sounded suspicious to him. If the mayor were telling the truth, why complain to Albert Gambino rather than file a report with the military police in the capital? The man was hiding something.

"That's not all! That bastard—the leader of Blue Beyond, Noel Stollen—said this: 'If you have money to give to the weak-ass Gambino family, you'd be better off tossing it in the river, so I'll take it off your hands!' I heard him say that with my own ears! I'm sure of it!"

Koga felt as if he was about to burst. He didn't know the truth about what happened, but it was obvious the mayor was exaggerating. It was clear he had something against this Seeker named Noel, and he was looking to leverage his debt to the Gambino family to get revenge.

"The weak-ass Gambino family, huh? That's harsh. Why, we're just doing our best. It's heartbreaking to hear someone would say such things about us," Albert deadpanned, clearly seeing right through the mayor's lie.

But the foolish man carried on.

"Mr. Albert, there is no time to weep! You must administer justice to the corrupt Seekers! To prove the glory of the great Gambino family!"

"Yes, yes. Let's administer justice to the Seeker Noel Stollen. And I'll wait for your payment. Are you happy now?"

"Yes, thank you! Thank you so much!" The happy mayor bowed over and over.

"Now that that's settled—it's time for you to take responsibility for what you've done."

"Uh, responsibility?" the mayor asked, confused. Albert scoffed.

"Yes, responsibility. Regardless of the reason, you went back on your word to us. So now you must take responsibility."

"B-but...responsibility..."

"Hmm...I've decided. I will have your right arm. The Seekers gouged out your right eye, correct? So I need to take your right arm."

The mayor's remaining eye opened wide, stunned at Albert's idea of what passed for logic.

"B-but! I'll die without my right arm!"

"Oh, come now. That's a poor attitude. You just need to believe in yourself and you'll be fine."

It was possible Albert really didn't think losing an arm would kill the mayor, but it was more likely that he just didn't really care if the man lived or died, as long as he got to enjoy watching him in agony first.

"Hey, you," Albert called out to Koga. "I heard you are a Longswordsman. They say men such as you specialize in clean slices. Is that true?"

Koga nodded. He was of the battle-type class of Longswords-man. He was only C-Ranked, but he had been the undefeated champion of the underground fights in Soldiland.

"Hmm...interesting. I wonder what makes a Longswordsman so different from the base class. Since we're here, and you're here, cut off the mayor's right arm. With that stick you're holding," Albert said, gesturing toward the walking stick.

"Me?"

"That's right. Hurry up, now."

It was an offer he couldn't refuse. Koga turned toward the mayor. "Mayor, hold out your right arm, please."

The mayor shook his head, crying, at Albert's order.

"Hurry up, or I'll have to kill you," Koga said in a low, threatening voice. The mayor gave up and held out his right arm.

"Yes, yes, just like that! Oh, wait a second. I need to get ready."

Albert pulled a small transparent crystal from his drawer and placed it on the table. He drew a hammer from the same drawer and smashed the crystal into powder, then he lowered his face and snorted it through one nostril.

"Ahhh...that's great! This is the stuff! I always gotta spark this before I enjoy violence. Wooo, it's incredible!" Albert's pupils dilated with excitement. Apparently, he'd just sampled some of the dangerous new stimulant. "Okay, go ahead. Cut off the mayor's right arm."

He said it as though it were nothing. As a gladiator, Koga had killed countless people in the underground fighting rings. But he'd never wanted to. He didn't *want* to kill anyone. Especially pitiful weaklings.

"Is something the matter?" Albert asked. "Do hurry up and cut it off."

As Albert urged Koga on, the mayor twitched and started laughing. "Heh heh, there's no way he could cut me with that stick..."

Albert slammed his palm against his desktop in irritation. "Did you not hear me say to slice him?! Hey, Asian boy! Do you know what happens if you ignore me?! Say something!" he screamed angrily.

Koga muttered in response, "I already did..."

"What?" Albert said, sounding befuddled.

In that moment, the mayor's right arm fell to the floor.

"Huh? Ah, aaaaah, my arm! Agggh!"

Koga had cut off the mayor's right arm the instant that Albert gave the order. He moved so quickly and cut so cleanly that no one in the room noticed. Even the mayor, whose arm had been sliced off, was unaware of it until his arm actually fell to the floor.

Blood started spewing from the cut and the mayor fell to the floor. Seeing that, Albert howled with laughter.

"Ha ha ha! Wonderful! You did it, Asian boy! I like you! Starting today, you will be my slave!"

No one dared defy the Mad Dog Albert when he said he wanted something. Koga was Miguel's only remaining property, but when told he would be freed if he surrendered his slave, he presented the Oath of Subordination immediately. And thus, Albert became Koga's master.

However, he had no immediate tasks for Koga. Life on the streets had greatly weakened the Longswordsman, who was given a servant's room and provided with food. A few days later, when Koga had completely recovered, he was measured for his own special armor. Laios acquired a suit of dark red tosei-gusoku armor and two swords of differing lengths from a merchant who did business in Koga's birthplace.

"It looks pretty good on you," he said from the door of Koga's room, after Koga had suited up. "You look like you're feeling better. Can you go?"

Koga nodded quietly. His new master, Albert, had decided to employ Koga as the family assassin. His first job would be that night.

"Who's the mark?"

No good ever came from knowing more about his intended victim, but he hoped, despite himself, that it would be a bad guy.

"The target is a Seeker."

"A Seeker? Do mobsters kill Seekers?"

The gang member didn't try to hide his disgust in response to Koga's question. "This target doesn't need to be killed. It's just the boss's sickness kicking in. You heard the mayor of Mintz Village's story, right? So you know who the target is."

"What? You mean..."

"Exactly."

Koga's target would be the leader of Blue Beyond, Noel Stollen.

†

Nights in the imperial capital were always bright, between streetlamps and the light pouring out of building windows. The alleys were dark, but never pitch-black, so there was still light enough to recognize Loki, who stood before me.

I had come to get the latest Hugo-related research reports. When our exchange was complete and I turned to walk away, Loki suddenly said, "Boss, you know the Gambinos are after you?"

"What? What do you mean?" Caught completely off guard, I tilted my head to the side in confusion. "Why would the Gambino family be after me?"

"I don't know the details, but it's because of the issue with the mayor of Mintz Village."

"Mintz Village?"

"That mayor went to Albert the boss and pleaded, feeding him a mixture of fact and fiction. So now Albert is after you."

"Idiot." The mayor had probably fed the Gambinos some story about me, since I'd taken the money that he needed to pay off his debts. "And did Gambino believe him? What's going on with that family, exactly? Including the stimulant issue?"

"Don't waste time trying to understand his motives," Loki said. "Albert is a true madman."

"A madman. What a nuisance."

"His predecessor was a good man."

"Is that so?" I said.

"He died before you came to the capital, so you don't know of him. He was a Robin Hood-like figure, admired for opposing the strong and aiding the weak."

"And his son is a madman? Bad parenting strikes again."

But Loki shook his head.

"No, the old boss didn't raise Albert. He was his bastard son, already grown to adulthood when the old boss called upon him to be his successor."

"So there were special circumstances surrounding his ascension. And?"

Loki seemed about to continue, but he suddenly stopped himself.

We heard the footsteps of a single person walking into this alley that no one would dare cut through in the middle of the night. I could also hear the sound of metal on metal—whoever was approaching us was armed. It would be a few moments before they reached us, but they weren't far away.

I looked at Loki, who had moved a few feet away from me. It was clear what was going on.

"Loki...you sold me out?"

The timing was too perfect. He'd arranged to keep me here and hand me over to the assassin. That was the only thing that made sense.

"Sorry, Boss. I can't say no to Albert."

"It's not very professional for an informant to entrap a customer. Do you understand what that means?"

"I know that. But I can't defend you with my life. And Albert pays well. I'm gonna use the money to flee to another country and get a fresh start."

"I see. That's a good plan. But you forgot one thing. There's no reason for me not to kill you."

I drew my silver flame and aimed it at Loki.

"Sorry about this. I didn't dislike you."

"Well that's a coincidence. I didn't dislike you either, boss. You're cute. Ah, well...I suppose it can't be helped. I'm not ready for the kaleidoscope to end, but at least I'll die at your hands."

I thought he might try something, but Loki wasn't trying to run. In fact, he just stood there and closed his eyes, his body language all but saying *Please kill me.*

"You don't value your life?" I asked.

"I do. But I violated the information broker's greatest taboo to save my own life. It's made me realize that without my pride, I'm nothing..." Loki said.

"I see." My finger rested on the trigger of my silver flame. I went to pull it—and stopped myself. "Go. I'll forget about this."

Loki opened his eyes. "You'll...forgive me?"

"I won't forgive you. I just won't kill you."

"Boss..."

"And you don't need to leave the capital. I'll crush the Gambino family. You can reclaim your pride here at home," I declared.

Loki froze, his eyes wide. Then he laughed out loud. He laughed hard, holding his belly and when he finally stopped laughing, there were tears in the corners of his eyes.

"Ah...I laughed so hard there, I thought I might burst. Boss, you serious? You're talking about the Gambinos, direct subordinates of the Luciano family?"

"And?"

"And, well..."

"I need some money anyway. If I take them down and claim the rewards, then I can solve that problem too. It will be like a little bonus."

"Boss...you're a madman too."

"Hurry up and get out of here. You'll get in the way of the fight."

The assassin was closing in. I pointed to the alley exit directly across from the footsteps. There was no escaping without a fight. Facing my assailant head-on gave me a better chance at winning than running away and leaving my back open.

"Anything I can do, boss?"

"Not here. I'll need you later. Come to my aid then—for free, of course. Then we'll be even."

"Heh. Fine. Good luck...bye."

Loki disappeared into the shadows, and I pulled a battle stimulant from my pouch. It was a drug that stimulated brain activity, improving concentration and strength. It would last for ten minutes. The backlash afterward would be severe, but it basically doubled my ability to calmly analyze the situation.

The drug took effect immediately. I grew calmer, my perception expanded, and the world felt bigger. I could see clearly in all corners of the alley.

It was quiet. I couldn't hear what you would call noise, but instead, I could discern each individual sound clearly.

The footsteps belonged to a man. He was nearly 180 centimeters tall, slender but muscular, and young, in his late teens. The rhythm of his step marked him as a vanguard fighter. He carried with him two swords, and he wore a full suit of armor.

That was enough information. This alley was narrow. Even if he were a Swordmaster, it would be hard for him to battle to his full potential here.

I could see the assassin's silhouette in the dim light now. Exactly as I had predicted, he was a young, slender man nearly 180 centimeters tall, clad in red armor and brandishing two swords.

His face, on the other hand, was not what I expected at all. He was Asian. His features were defined but not chiseled; I suppose you would consider him handsome. But his cold eyes were what drew attention.

I knew this face. But the last time I'd seen him, he was covered in mud and grime.

"Y-you are Noel Shtollen?" the man asked when he recognized me, surprise in his voice. So it was him.

"Yes, I am Noel Stollen. Nice to see you again, Koga."

Standing face-to-face, I could see that unlike the last time we met, he was healthy. He wasn't quite prepared for battle, but he was a completely different person.

"I didn't expect you to be a Gambino assassin. You've come up in the world, from fighting pit thug to high-level hitman. Congratulations."

I applauded. Koga furrowed his brow.

"None of yer business."

"What happened to the old halfling man? Did Albert kill him?"

"I dunno. He disappeared as soon as he handed me over."

"Hmm. I see. And now you're Albert's dog?"

"I don' care whatcha say."

"Ahh, what's the fun in that? Well, that's fine. So you are my assassin, right? Then draw your sword. Let's continue what we started."

I turned my silver flame toward Koga. But Koga stood absolutely still.

"Hey? Why don't you move?"

"This...is not a fair fight," he said.

"What are you talking about?"

"Truth is, I don' wanna fight you. I hate you, but I still owe you one big silver."

All I could do was laugh at his inappropriate words. "What do you mean 'owe me?' I just dropped a coin and you just picked it up."

"I ain't smart. Don't get all that roundabout talk," Koga said. "All I know is, it's strange you dropped that money right in front of me."

"And? Are you saying you'll let me go over a debt of a single silver coin? I didn't think a slave had that kind of freedom."

"Yer right. I don' have that freedom. When my master says kill, I gotta kill. No matter who. But I got my pride."

Koga took in a deep breath and bellowed, "My name is Koga Tsukishima! Longswordsman, Rank C! Specialist in the *Slash Attack* skill. Got it? Remember that!"

Had he just revealed his rank and abilities to make it a fair fight? Why was this mobster's slave being so obstinate about something so mundane as a back-alley murder?

Then again—

"Hmph. When someone introduces themselves, it's only polite to return the favor. My name is Noel Stollen, Talker. My skills are focused on buffing my allies to prevent the depletion of their MP. I am the heir of the great hero, Overdeath, and was trained by him."

"Noel Stollen, Talker. I'm never gonna forget that name."

"I see. Except you only have a few minutes left to remember it."

"S-say what?! I will win!"

"It's been fun, but I'm done chatting. Let's get started."

"All right! Commence!"

It was nice to have a fight like this once in a while.

Koga made the first move. He closed in on me with just one step and drew his sword. He handled it just as he had his stick back then, but his speed, strength, and grace were magnitudes greater now.

He let out a battle cry in perfect harmony with his advance and unsheathing of his sword. For a split second, I saw an image of myself being cut in two in my mind's eye. The draw of his sword was perfection. It wasn't just that his bones and muscles were in sync—it was like every single cell in his body was following orders. With these skills, he could easily cut through my black-dragon coat if he hit me.

But he missed, because I leapt straight up into the air and out of his reach, far higher than any man could jump, thanks to a wire gimmick installed in my wristwatch. I'd previously tied one end of the ultrathin wire to a window grating four stories up while waiting for Loki, and now it reeled me upward.

I was ten meters over Koga's head. Were I to take him out right there, *Stun Howl* would have been my best option. If I could freeze him where he stood, the fight would be over in an instant. Nobody is stronger than my knife across their throat.

But I didn't use *Stun Howl.* To put it frankly, I *couldn't* use it. If I believed Koga's words, he was the same rank as me, so the skill should work...unless his Longswordsman class came with resistance to mental attacks.

If I remembered correctly, Longswordsman was the far eastern vanguard equivalent of Swordsman. But I didn't know enough about the class to be sure, and if I used *Stun Howl* only to have it be ineffective, I'd be leaving myself open to attack. With Koga's strength, he could jump up here and slice me in half on the way back down. Suspended in the sky, unable to move, I was easy prey.

So I shot at him instead. I aimed my silver flame and fired a flame bullet at Koga. He easily dodged the bullet, which traveled at the speed of sound, but the true power of the magic bullet only revealed itself a moment later.

"Wh—fire?!"

Koga panicked as a pillar of fire rose up in the alley. I didn't know what kinds of resistances he might have as a Longswordsman, but melee-combat vanguard-types generally had no special resistance to fire. Once he was surrounded by flames, he'd be cooked. Even if he could flee the alley, his clothing and skin would have already combusted. After that, killing him would be as easy as slicing a roasted chicken.

Or so I thought.

Koga, a flickering shadow in the corner of the alley, swung his sword and shouted "Haste!" The sweep of his weapon whipped up a storm of wind that snuffed out the entire pillar of flame.

"No way!" I yelled without thinking.

There was no way the wind of a sword sweep could put out fire created by a magic bullet. So what had he done? The answer was simple. By swinging his sword, he created a vacuum around him, eliminating the oxygen the fire needed to keep burning. In other words, he'd killed the very air around him.

While I hung there, flabbergasted, Koga looked up at me, twisting his mouth.

"Ugh, dammit!"

This was a horrible position to be in. I kicked off the wall of the building to swing across the alley, then kicked back and forth up both walls 'til I reached the roof.

Koga flew up after and beyond me. For a moment, he was silhouetted by the full moon, then he pirouetted in midair and swung down the sword he held high over his head. I rolled to the side, dodging before he opened me like a tin can. I tried to stand up and aim my silver flame at him, but Koga had already closed the gap between. I dodged his incessant slashing attacks, losing wisps of hair from the close calls.

I couldn't raise my silver flame or even to take a deep breath for *Stun Howl*. I was managing to evade him, but If I made one wrong move, it would all be over for me. There was only one thing I could do.

I heard the sound of the sword and ducked again. Sparks flew from the cornice behind me. I drew my knife and diverted the path of Koga's sword. I stayed low, got up close to Koga, and aimed for his crotch with my fist. But Koga took a step back, avoiding my punch to his balls.

"Y-you! You can't aim there! What would I do if I lost my balls?! Stop fightin' like a coward!" Koga objected, pointing his finger at me.

I shrugged.

"Are you stupid? We're fighting for our lives here. Gouging out eyes, aiming for the groin, biting—everything is allowed. You think calling me a coward will stop me?"

"You got a big head, but it's clear who's stronger. Talkin's just gonna drag this out."

"It's clear who's stronger? Who decided that?" I held my knife in a backhand grip and crouched down. "C'mon. I'll fight you."

"A rearguard like you...wants to fight me head-on?"

I didn't answer, but just motioned for him to come with my free hand.

"Oh... Talker. Noel Stollen. Never answered you back then. You're a great man."

The flash of Koga's blade descended on me like lightning. I couldn't possibly fight back with my knife. But close-quarter combat techniques exist so the underdog can take out the strong.

I warded off all the sword blows with optimized, minimum movements without opening up my guard.

"Ha ha ha, you ain't bad! I thought so! How long can you keep this up?!"

But it was the other way around. I would gradually tire of dodging, but if I warded his blows off, I could break through his form. It wouldn't be easy to—his core was strong—but I could do it.

Each time I warded off Koga's sword, he slashed at me even faster. My eyes started to get used to it. Finally, I goaded him into overcommitting and broke through his stance. Without a moment's delay, I switched my knife to a normal grip and aimed for Koga's throat.

"Argh?!"

So close. He dodged, retreating right before I got him. But this put space between us and Koga had stumbled backward. I wasn't so weak that I would miss this opportunity. I threw a flash bomb at him. A bright light painted the night sky white.

"Erg, it's blinding," Koga said, groping at his eyes in pain.

"I told you, everything goes."

I aimed at my silver flame. This was the end. The moment my victory was sealed, I felt the hairs on my neck standing up. What was this? I could sense danger. What could it be?

"I told you too—I'm a Longswordsman." Koga, though still apparently in pain, sneered at me. "Dance, *Secret Swordsmanship Tsubame Gaeshi.*"

Operating on instinct, I flew back. In that instant, the steel smokestack in front of me was scored by innumerable invisible blades.

"Is that what you meant by slash attack?!"

It must have been a Longswordsman skill unique to the East—an attack fixed in the air that he could release it at any time. It was a terrifying skill. I had to think of a way to counter it—but stopping to think could be fatal.

"There you are." Koga, still blinded, was suddenly right in front of me, swinging his sword. I instantly held him off with the silver flame, but the intense shot blew me backward.

"Dammit!" There was no roof—or footing—behind me. I quickly turned over like a cat in the sky and aimed my feet at the ground.

"Not yet!"

Koga jumped after me. I was certain of it now—he had a skill that could detect my location even when he was blinded.

Time to do or die. I tried *Stun Howl*.

"Stop!"

Useless! Just as I feared, he was able to resist. I used my silver flame again, matching it to the timing of his sword slash, but the ground was waiting behind me. I hit it hard, losing consciousness...

"Ergh...ow..."

I woke up to a sharp pain. I controlled my breathing and checked the state of my body. I must have done a good job rolling as I hit the ground, because I didn't feel any broken bones. Nor was there blood on my lips, so my internal organs hadn't been damaged either.

But my body felt sluggish and hard to move. It was probably due more to the crash of the battle stimulant wearing off than the crash of my ass to the ground, but regardless...this fight was over.

"I won," Koga said, thrusting his sword at me. "Noel Shtollen, yer amazing. I ne'er thought a rearguard could run me down so much. Yer my worthiest foe."

Praising your defeated foe? Seriously? *Knock it off.* This wasn't a sport. It was just winning or losing a battle. Nothing else mattered.

But most important of all, the fight wasn't over while I still drew breath.

I still had a chance. All I had to do was win him over in conversation and get him to put down his sword. He didn't want to fight me in the first place—if I said the right things, he would probably put down his sword. And even if I couldn't ultimately convince him to spare me, I could at least buy some time.

It was awkward choosing my next words, but it turned out I didn't need to win him over. Koga was already hesitating.

"Why don't you finish the job?" I asked. "I thought you would kill who you were commanded to, no matter who the target was?"

"I-I know that!"

"It's not the first time you've killed. So what's the problem?"

"H-how'm I supposed t'know?! I just..."

"You're a fool..." I forced myself to sit up and grabbed the sword thrust before me. The sharp blade sliced into my palms, but that didn't matter.

"Wh-what are you doin?! Let go!"

"You can't take pity on me!" I cried. "Kill me, kill me now!"

"Wha?!" Koga recoiled at my roar.

"You're a slave! You can't show your enemy mercy! If you let me go now, your master, Albert, will have your head!"

"Th-that..."

"There is nothing in this world more important than your own life! You can't throw your life away for someone else, especially for an enemy!"

What was I even saying? It was absurd. I was making myself sick with this continued farce, but I couldn't hold the words back.

"I..." Koga was confused, both about his own feelings and about my words. But there was nothing I could do about it. He had to resolve that problem on his own.

Then...

"Time's up."

I tossed away the sword and let out a sigh.

"What did you say?"

Koga cocked his head to the side, detected something, and instantly prepared for battle. He looked up, clucked his tongue, and drew his short sword. Before I could blink, we were surrounded by falling sparks that looked like stars in the sky.

"Who is this?!"

In answer, a sharp roundhouse kick hit Koga square in the belly and propelled him across the length of the alley. Then, a white goddess of death stood before me.

"Buzz off," Alma said. "I'm the only one allowed to knock down Noel."

After receiving my *Link* call for backup, Alma had flown here as quick as lightning. It had only been about two minutes. She had probably been sleeping at the inn. She let out a big yawn and cracked her neck.

"I don't know what's going on, but do you need me to kill that?" she asked, pointing her finger at Koga.

It would be easy to order her to kill. But Koga still had value to me. I wanted to let him live if at all possible, but it would be too dangerous to order her to render him defenseless without killing him. Koga was strong. After fighting him, I could tell that he was comparable in strength to Alma.

With my support, she could probably dominate him, but I didn't think I could generate any skills well in my current state. I needed at least thirty minutes to climb out of the hole caused by the battle stim. Even if I used the recovery potion I carried with me, I'd still be weak. The only skill I could use right now was *Link*.

So I gave a short order.

"Kill."

"Okay."

Alma moved close to Koga, turning her knife in her head.

"Are you Noel's friend?" he asked her.

"That's right. So I have to kill you, his enemy."

"Don't. I don' wanna kill a girl."

"That's funny. I'm stronger than you, so saying stuff like that'll just make you look bad later."

"It's the other way around. You couldn't get me even with a surprise attack... I'm a whole lot stronger than you."

"What?!"

It was true that if Alma were stronger, her *Silent Killing* skill would have ended Koga. As it was, though, Koga had absorbed a fatal attack while at a disadvantage, and he was now back on his feet and talking.

But that didn't necessarily mean he was much stronger than her. No matter the situation, the fact remained that she still had *Silent Killing* at her disposal. As far as I could tell, they were evenly matched. Knowing this would be a close fight, I quickly filled Alma in on Koga's abilities via *Link*.

"You're audacious. Don't think I'll let you die easy," Alma said, her voice dripping with bloodthirst. She was angry. *"Accel—quintuple!"*

She took off like a flash, faster than the eye could follow, literally running on the air. She did run straight at Koga, but then zigged, and then zagged, rushing up one alley wall and leaping across the chasm to slide down the opposite wall. She free-ran through the air in three dimensions as if it was child's play.

It was already difficult to follow her with my eyes. Alma, moving every which way at top speed, had become a white blur, both everywhere and nowhere. I was sure that even Koga could no longer see where she was. He was ready to attack and poised to strike, but he couldn't get a bead on her location.

Alma, still toying with Koga, started throwing darts. She was hitting him from every direction, and thanks to *Perfect Throw*, she couldn't miss. She was certainly using her new *Armor Piercing* skill, too. A direct attack would cut right through his armor.

He might be able to block one or two, but he could never swat down a rainstorm of darts, and he could no more dodge them than he could the sun's rays.

So what was he going to do?

"*Crazy Cherry Blossoms.*" Koga's response was just one swing of his sword. I saw the flash of light reflecting off his blade arc through the air, exactly like flowers blooming where they shouldn't.

"You can multiply *Slash Attacks*?!" The moment I cried out, the myriad darts Alma had loosed were met and destroyed by dozens of swordless sword slashes. Dozens more slashes followed, filling the alleyway and threatening to cut Alma.

But this was Alma we were talking about. She twisted in the air, dodging the slash attacks. She kicked off into the air and took flight. Next, she initiated another dart volley, this one from mid-air. Once she was used to his speed, she could get close, and her knife was an advantage Koga had no way to counter.

"*Calm and Serene.*"

Koga activated a new skill. Then he closed his eyes, swung his sword, and blocked every strike.

"What was that?!" Alma cried out in surprise.

Although startled, she kept at it, stabbing and thrusting. She should have had an overwhelming advantage in close-quarters combat. But Koga showed no signs of faltering.

He'd said the words "calm and serene." Did he have to close his eyes to activate the skill? It explained how he could still best me even after I'd blinded him with a flash bomb.

Judging by what I'd seen, it was safe to assume this skill didn't just enhance his senses, but also greatly increased his speed. I could see a disadvantage—no peripheral vision, no chance to spot enemies from afar, but within range of his sword, he was all but unbeatable.

Alma wasn't giving up. They were parrying and thrusting, attacking and countering. I'd never seen such monstrous abilities from C-Ranked fighters. The alley was full of sparks from their weapons meeting, and the walls echoed with the ringing sound of steel on steel. I lost count of how many times their blades had clashed.

My mouth filled with blood. Without realizing it, I had been clenching my teeth too hard. "Dammit...why can't I be as strong as them?"

My heart filled with frustrated envy. I knew there was no point in bemoaning what I couldn't change, but when I saw this overwhelming difference in talent, it hurt. I wanted to tear off my own head.

"If only I were a Warrior like Grandpa, then I would be as strong as them..."

My grandpa had told me that he would make me the strongest Seeker, even though I was but a Talker. I was proud of the harsh training I'd undergone and of my achievements so far. But there was always more. There were heights I could never reach as a Talker—as a buffer.

"I knew it... My thinking was correct."

I stood up shakily. Watching these two fight each other had led me to an epiphany. I felt relief, but also felt the fire in my soul grow stronger and hotter.

I would no longer waver. I would no longer mourn. There was only one path for me.

"I will conquer the strongest to become the strongest."

The long battle before me was reaching its climax. They had moved on from skills that just grazed the other in a never-ending battle to drawing upon their limit breaks.

"I admit it. You are strong. I'm no longer concerned with winning—I will make sure to kill you,"

Alma cut her own finger with her knife and collected the blood in the gullet of her blade.

Scout skill: *Blood Poison*. This skill produced deadly poison from her own blood. She had given up on close-quarters combat and planned to secure her victory by using poison.

"I don' think of you as a girl no more either. I'll kill you." Koga sheathed his sword and crouched down low. He was surely going to activate another skill. The aura of intimidation surrounding him grew more intense. Who knew what limit of skills this Easterner might have?

This was bad. At this rate, the battle would end with two corpses. I reloaded my silver flame and fired a shot in the air. It wasn't a magic bullet, just a flare, loud and bright. The loud sound cut through their focus and they both looked at me, wide-eyed.

"Wh-what?" said Alma.

"Huh?" said Koga.

"The battle is over. The military police are on their way." As I said this, Alma's hair stood on end in anger.

"No way! We haven't finished the fight!"

"Shut up. Are you going to disobey me? I said that this battle is over."

"B-but!"

"I thought I told you to shut up."

"Tsk..."

It looked like *Peer Support* had worked. Alma settled down and sheathed her knife, shaking her head all the while.

"Koga, you get out of here. You don't want the military police to catch you," I said.

"I don't like doin' as you say...but you're right," Koga said, turning on his heel. I called out after him.

"Wait a second. I have something to tell you."

"Yeah?"

Koga stopped and turned to look at me. I smiled and continued, "My motto is: pay them back a thousand times over."

"Huh? What did you say?!"

"So tell Albert this: I'm going to take out the Gambino family. If he doesn't want that, then he better come and take my head off himself."

"I see. You've had quite the day," Laios said, taking Koga's report after he returned to the mansion. Albert wasn't home. He'd be back two days later.

Koga didn't bother relaying Noel's message. Those words had

just been a bluff. There was no way a Seeker could take out the Gambino family.

"I'll let the boss know what happened," Laios said. "You rest." He gently patted Koga on the shoulder and then left. The big man could be so genuine, it was hard to believe he was a criminal. Both his underlings and the other families saw him as a young talent.

It was all thanks to Laios's efforts that the Gambino family had been able to maintain any appearance of functionality. Without Laios, the family would have fallen apart. However, considering Albert's pride and recklessness, perhaps that would have been for the best. Laios was an honorable man, but his competence had resulted in the pain of many.

"Ironic..."

Koga returned to his room and collapsed on his bed. He was exhausted. But he wouldn't be able to fall asleep easily.

"Noel Stollen..."

Now there was an interesting man. Koga had met many types of people in his life, but none like Noel. He was strong, cunning, had a strong sense of pride, and was brilliant to boot.

"Maybe he could..."

In his mind, he knew it was impossible. But maybe, just maybe, Noel was the one who could take down the Gambino family. Noel was so intense, Koga wanted to believe in him. He was intense like a raging fire—with a soul that burned.

Koga looked at his fist and smiled.

"I wanna fight 'im again."

†

The evening Albert came back, he called Koga to his room.

"Koga, I heard you failed at your mission?"

"Yes...I apologize for my weakness," he said, bowing deeply. Albert didn't acknowledge the apology, but he smiled like he was enjoying himself.

"Ah ha ha, Koga you're so serious. Don't worry about it. I mean, we're talking about a Seeker. The mayor of Mintz Village requested it, so I had to send you, but I never promised him you'd *succeed*."

"O-oh..."

"We've fulfilled our obligation to the mayor, right?" Albert asked. "So you don't need to worry about it at all. It's fine! Relax, Koga."

"U-understood... Thank you very much..."

Koga was still suspicious, but if Albert really intended to let him off the hook, that was great news. He let out a sigh of relief... and Albert continued, as if he'd been waiting for Koga to relax.

"But you know, you didn't follow your master's orders. And that's a separate issue, don't you think? You *do* need to take responsibility for that."

"Huh?"

Koga's heart skipped a beat at this surprise attack. He remembered the mayor of Mintz Village, who had ended up dying from his injuries.

"What must I do to take responsibility?"

"Well, just this once, you needn't do anything. Someone else will take responsibility for you."

"For me?"

Koga tilted his head to the side, confused, while Albert laughed his creepy laugh.

"Laios, give it to Koga."

"Understood..."

Laios, who was standing by Albert's side, brought out a wrapped box. Koga took the box, not knowing what to do with it. "What is this?"

"Go on, open it."

"O-oh. Understood."

Koga opened the box as he was told. Then—

"Agggh!" he screamed, tossing the box away. A badly damaged human head rolled out of the box onto the floor. Koga knew that face. It was the halfling Miguel, his former master.

"Oh, that was a wonderful scream. It was worth the trouble of preparing the surprise."

"S-surprise...?"

"Make sure to thank him. Miguel took responsibility for your failure, Koga. Joint liability, don't you know?"

"B-but..."

"Oh, but understand this, there's no one left to take responsibility for you next time. You'd best make sure not to fail again."

At least Miguel hadn't been skinned alive—though judging by the rictus of agony on his face, he'd suffered just as much.

"I will not fail again..."

"Oh, yes, yes. You're so serious, Koga. I'm sure you'll do great. Now run off. I'll call you when I have another job for you to do."

"Yes..."

Koga turned on his heel and put his hand to the doorknob. But he stopped himself there.

"I forgot to tell you... Noel gave me a message for you."

"A message? For me?"

Koga turned to look Albert right in the eyes. "He said, 'I'm going to take out the Gambino family. If he doesn't want that, then he better come and take my head off himself.'"

"Oh..." Veins bulged in Albert's temples. He was clearly furious. "He said that, did he? Or are you spinning a tale like our dear late mayor did?"

"It's true. He said it."

"I see. I see, I see..."

Albert seemed to ponder the message carefully, nodding repeatedly to himself. Clearly, Noel's words had struck a nerve, leaving him burning like a lit fuse.

"That Seeker has crossed the line! I'll kill him!" Now boiling over with rage, Albert stabbed his knife deep into his desk. "Laios, gather our men right away! We'll find him and tear him limb from limb!"

"Well, that was completely unnecessary," Laios said to Koga in the hallway, angry and irritated. "Why did you tell the boss about the Seeker's bluff? Were you that frustrated about failing at your task?"

"I'm sorry... But that's not why..."

"Then what?"

"That guy...Noel Stollen is amazing..."

"What?"

"His class is the weakest of 'em all, but he's crazy strong... He must've busted his ass to get that strong. But even with all that work, he'll never stand a chance against talented guys from tough classes," Koga said. "And still, his eyes were sparklin'. He has this fire in him, like he'll never lose to anyone... He's somethin' else, really. So I thought I'd at least pass on his message."

It was hard to put his thoughts into words. But everything he had said was true. Koga hung his head, embarrassed at his poor speaking skills.

"I see." Laios stopped and looked hard at Koga's face. "Did you fall in love with him?"

"Huh? No, no! I'm not like that!" Koga said with a furious shake of his head.

Laios laughed. "Heh heh, I know. That's not what I meant. But it's true you felt something strongly for Noel, right?"

"Well, yeah...but it's not a positive feelin'. If I felt that kinda way 'bout Noel, I wouldn't've said a word."

"Maybe you want to test him? To see if he's the real thing?"

"Th-that..." Koga stammered, unable to find the right words.

"You may not understand it now, but you will someday. What it truly means for a man to fall for another man."

"Oh... That ever happen to you, boss?"

"Yes... Long ago." Laios looked off sadly in the distance.

†

That night, Alma and I ate together at The Orc's Club. It was unpleasantly loud outside. Someone was bellowing for another's attention.

"The Gambino family?!"

The door to the tavern was kicked open. In walked six normal-looking men, led by an unhealthy-looking blond fellow.

"Four Rank B. One Rank A. There are more outside, all armed," Alma whispered the results of her battle analysis to me. Koga wasn't there. It was possible he was with the reserve group outside. I didn't know about the four Rank Bs, but I had researched the A-Rank man before. The Gambinos' second-in-command: Laios, powerful Monk class.

And the skinny blond man at the head of the pack was the Gambino boss, Albert Gambino. Albert didn't have a battle-type class himself, but he was still the head of a gang. He probably liked dragging his strongest henchmen around by the collar.

He made his way to our table, barking orders at his men.

"So you're Noel Stollen. You look like a girl."

Albert sat down at our table. Without another word, he started swigging from our dinner wine, then twisted his face in an unpleasant expression.

"This wine is terrible. If you have to drink this cheap garbage, you must be struggling as a Seeker. Or maybe you're just a guppy? Oh, right. You were betrayed by your party and can't work any-more, right? My condolences."

So he had done his research too. Albert looked proud of him-self, like a child using big words he had just learned.

"And you are Albert Gambino, head of the Gambino subfamily," I said. "My, my. Sitting at someone's table and drinking their wine without permission. Did no one teach you any manners? People say you're a mad dog, but they must really mean *wild* dog."

"What did you say?!"

"Oh, come now. Don't get so mad just because you fanned the flames and I fanned them back. We're in public, you know—do you really want to show everyone just how petty the boss of the Gambino family, which serves directly under the great Luciano family, can be?" I asked. "You know that will harm the Lucianos' reputation, too."

Gambino's lips were quivering in anger, but he kept himself from exploding.

"Well, that's fine. Say what you want," he said, a dangerous smile on his face. "I just came to talk to you today, since it seems you've quite the attitude. What was it you said? 'If you want my head, come get it yourself'? So here I am."

I scoffed at him.

"Rushing out to see me just because I said to? Tsk, it's like we're young lovers. I can almost see you wagging your little tail in joy."

"You're done rattling on now! I'll see you out front!"

"I believe you're the one rattling on. Can't you see? I'm in the middle of a meal. If you want something from me, you can wait outside until I'm done eating...like the loyal dog you are."

"You bastard!"

Completely out of patience, Gambino pulled the knife he had hidden in his pocket.

"That's enough. I'll take care of you here. Get ready. I'm going to cut so many holes in your face, you'll be able to pour wine into it from any direction," he said, pointing the knife at me.

But he was interrupted by a brazen voice.

"Mr. Gambino, you'll have to stop your shenanigans in this tavern right there."

A giant of a man stood up. It was Logan, from the King of Dukes.

"Huh? Who are you?"

"I don't know what happened between you and Noel, but you can't fight in here. You have your men, and we Seekers have ours. If word gets out that we let the mob have their way with us, no one's going to want to hire us. And if *that* happens, we'd starve to death."

As if in solidarity with Logan, most of the Seekers in the tavern stood up, weapons in hand. Albert flinched at this unexpected development.

"D-do you know who I am?!"

"We know. But we don't care who we're up against when it comes to defending our honor."

"Wh-what?! You're all dead! Boys, kill all these idiots!"

Now enraged beyond reason, Albert kicked his chair over and sprang to his feet. His underlings fell in behind him—save for Laios, at the front of the pack, who took a step forward and whispered, "Boss, we can wipe these Seekers out, no problem. With the gap in our power, the fight would be over in an instant. But how would we explain it to the Luciano don?"

"Wh-what?"

"We're already on thin ice because of the drug issue. And Seekers are government contractors. The Lucianos won't keep turning a blind eye to our activities if we're caught picking fights with Seekers too. A single individual, perhaps—but to kill this many Seekers, in such a public setting? Neither the Lucianos nor the crown would let that slide. It would be the end of us."

"E-erg, w-well..."

"If you still wish to proceed, just say the word. Your wish is our command. We will obey you unto our very deaths," Laios said.

"Ergh, b-but..." Albert had a look of agony on his face. The man might be crazy, but he was still part of an organization. I snickered at how quickly, after all that big talk, he'd caved at the mention of the main family and the national government.

"Ah ha ha ha. You're hilarious, Albert Gambino!"

"Wh-what did you say?!"

"You try to play the big bad wolf, but really, you're really just a stooge. A leader with neither brains nor charisma is a useless piece of shit. All you can do is rage like a mad dog, breaking rules in service of your selfish desires, until you've squandered all your family's money and are left with nothing. That's as far as someone like you can go."

"You little shit!" The agitated Albert grabbed me by the collar. I motioned for Alma, who was ready to eliminate him, to stay back. Instead, I laughed so hard and loud that I thought my face might split open.

"What?! What's so funny?!"

"You shouldn't get so angry. Think about your heart rate!"

"Huh? What are you talking about?"

"That wine you drank from without asking," I said, "was poisoned."

"Wh-what?" Albert let go of me and moved back a few steps. "Ha, ha ha ha. You got me there for a minute, but poison? You lie! I drank *your* wine! You would never poison your own wine!"

"You're right, it was my wine. But that doesn't mean I was actually drinking it, right? I just had it out so you would drink it."

"There's no way you knew I'd come here!" he said.

"I did. I'm the one who told you to come for my head, remember? If you're going to look for a Seeker, the first place to look would be a Seeker tavern. Isn't that right?"

"B-but you had no guarantee that I would drink it!"

"That's correct. But it's laughably easy to spike a bottle of wine with poison every day. Barely an inconvenience at all. I had no guarantee you'd show up, much less drink it—but if you did, then I'd win. And if you didn't, it's no skin off my back. And it looks like I won this time. Do you understand now, boy?"

"Argh, urp... Bleeech!"

Albert stuck his finger down his throat, trying desperately to vomit up the wine he'd drunk.

"That's a waste. It's already entered your bloodstream, thanks to all your carrying on. You're going to die."

"No! A doctor! Quick, a doctor! You, take me to the doctor immediately! Aggh!"

Screaming like a terrified little girl, Albert fled the tavern at full speed, taking his underlings with him.

Correction: not all of his underlings. Laios remained behind.

"That was a brilliant story," he said. "I almost believed it myself. You really are a Talker."

"Story? I just told the truth."

"Don't play dumb." Laios sat down, and without hesitation, emptied the rest of the bottle Albert had drunk from. "Mmm, that's good. Simple, with a clean flavor."

"I'm stunned. I told you it was poisoned. Are you suicidal?"

Laios smiled broadly at me. "Koga was right about you. There's determination in your eyes. They're manly eyes."

"What?"

"I hear you're aiming to be the greatest Seeker of all time. Someone like that wouldn't poison anyone in a public place in front of witnesses. You'd arrange to have him assassinated instead," Laios said confidently.

He was probably at least partly guessing, but he was right. I hadn't poisoned the wine.

"You're right," I said. "But why didn't you tell Albert that?"

"I don't want the family to be torn apart by his antics," Laios said.

"I see. Good enough reason," I said. "So how can I help you?"

"I'll let you live. I'll release the men waiting outside. And you will leave the capital. If you leave, the boss won't cross a line."

"What if I say no?"

"Then I'll kill you right here," Laios said, gesturing at the table-top between us.

For a moment, Laios gave the illusion of his body swelling up, filling the whole room like a giant. He was ready to kill. In that moment, I felt like he could defeat everyone in the tavern, even if we all attacked at once.

"I understand. I'll leave the capital. Are you happy now?"

"Yeah, you're a good boy. A boy like you will find success wherever you go." Laios stood up and called out to the other Seekers. "I'm sorry for any problems we caused you! As an apology, all of your drinks are on me! Please imbibe to your heart's content!"

He'd brought the situation deftly under control, then taken his leave like a gentleman. So that was the Gambino second-in-command, huh? Albert's predecessor must have been a great man indeed. It was the only thing that could explain Laios's loyalty.

When I thought about how he must feel inside, I pitied him.

"Let's go."

"Okay."

When Alma and I stood, we were met with cold stares all around. It was only natural. Seekers who do nothing but attract trouble are a plague on their colleagues, and thanks to my selling Lloyd and Tanya off as slaves, and now this, The Orc's Club was no longer a safe haven.

Well, I was already prepared to play the bad guy. I didn't care if the C-Rank rabble hated me, since clearly, none of them were classy enough to help us.

Logan met us at the door. "Are you really leaving the capital?" he asked.

"I made a promise," I said. "My career as a Seeker is over. It's terribly disappointing."

Logan scoffed and pinched my cheek, nearly lifting me out of my boots. "Out with it. You're not exactly the believable type."

I didn't answer. All I did was give him a one-cheeked smile and a light punch on the shoulder on my way out.

None of Gambino's men were waiting outside The Orc's Club. Laios was indeed a man of his word.

Once we were alone, Alma's face flushed with excitement. "That was amazing! All of it happened just the way you said it would, Noel!"

"It's too early to get excited. We've merely sown some seeds—the real show is yet to start."

"I know. We'll leave tonight and return in one week."

"Yeah, that's the plan. Let's rendezvous back here in seven days' time," I said. "What are you going to do until then, Alma? Hide in another city?"

"I'll go to the mountains and hone my reaction time. I'm going to kill that Asian man for sure next time."

"Understood." I nodded, but I knew there would be no rematch. They were equal in skill. Another battle between the two would leave me with two superlative fighters to bury. I couldn't allow that to happen.

"Okay, then, see you in one week," she said.

"Right, one week."

Alma and I bumped fists and went our separate ways.

Finally alone, I walked the dark road and muttered my secret ambition to myself.

"Gambino family, I'm going to swallow you whole."

4 The King's Vessel

NOEL AND HIS FRIEND returned to the imperial capital one week after the incident at The Orc's Club. When word reached Albert, he summoned his hard men immediately to the residential quarter managed by the Gambino family. Next, he ordered the crowded neighborhood evacuated. The Gambino crew knocked on doors, helping people pack their things. No matter what happened here, there would be no bystanders and no witnesses.

The moon was hidden by thick clouds that night. Noel's team, who'd been rounded up and brought to one of the empty homes in the area, were surrounded by a wall of the toughest fighters the Gambino family could field. Not even a fly could squeeze through their defenses.

Koga had been summoned as well, despite how conflicted he felt about the situation. Everything would come to an end on this night—that much was clear. The battle set to take place was overwhelmingly unfair. The odds were stacked in favor of one side.

THE MOST NOTORIOUS "TALKER" RUNS THE WORLD'S GREATEST CLAN

With victory guaranteed, Albert was licking his chops in anticipation of the horror show he was about to host. He laughed out loud in triumph. "Ha ha ha ha. The idiots! They could have just kept away, but no! They decided to come sneaking back! They can't possibly think I'd let them off the hook, can they? You're goners! You're going to die here! Hee ha ha ha!"

Noel shrugged his shoulders. "What a vulgar laugh. You really were poorly raised. Even with your parents' assets to flaunt, you're not fooling anyone!"

"I love an impudent prisoner. It's music to my ears. You two— I'll start by breaking all your legs and arms. I won't kill you quickly. The night is long, and I plan to enjoy every minute of it."

Albert cracked his knuckles and snapped his fingers. The Gambino soldiers all attacked at once—or at least, that was what Albert expected them to do.

"Huh? Can't you hear me? Go on!"

Albert stamped his foot impatiently and bellowed his command again. But not a single man moved. Koga didn't either.

"Wh-what is going on?! Don't just stand there, you fools! What are you playing at?!" Albert looked around frantically. "Laios, *what* is the meaning of this?"

Laios, supposedly his faithful follower, didn't answer, but only released a deep sigh.

"Wh-what is this...? Just what the hell is going on here?" Albert was dumbstruck, the color draining from his face. The only response he got was the quiet city night. Then, cruel laughter echoed through the air.

"Ha ha ha! What a wonderful clown you are, Albert Gambino!"

"Wh-what?! No, it can't be. You did this?!"

In answer, Noel just laughed at the crescent moon in the sky.

Yes, this was an overwhelmingly unfair fight—a foregone conclusion designed and put into motion by Noel Stollen, Talker. It was not Albert and his phalanx of thugs but, in fact, Noel who held all the cards here. Noel, who had only one ally.

But how could he have done such a thing?

Koga recalled the day's events in order.

It had been one week since Noel left the capital city, and Albert, humiliated and incensed, was frantically trying to ascertain his whereabouts. He sent men out searching, but none of them could find a trace of the young Seeker...because Laios, Albert's own right-hand man, had issued secret orders to not report it if they did find Noel.

Koga, who hadn't been there, wasn't sure what had happened at The Orc's Club. All he knew was that Laios seemed set against capturing Noel, and the Gambino men liked Laios far more than they did the boss. It wasn't always apparent, but Laios's orders were routinely prioritized over Albert's. Simply put, as long as Noel stayed away from the capital, he was safe.

Not part of the search teams, Koga concentrated on fulfilling the tasks assigned to him directly by Albert every day. He had, in fact, just completed a job.

"Koga, you really are something," a Gambino man who'd been on the job with him said admiringly. "That guy was strong too, but you took him down in an instant. I couldn't believe my eyes."

Their target that day had been a squatter helping himself to a Gambino property. The man, a former underground fighter, had been a B-Ranked Gladiator. But he didn't stand a chance against Koga.

"I'm hungry. Laios said he'd pay, so let's eat."

Albert might've been a madman, but the mobsters led by Laios were mostly good guys. To be more accurate, it was the ones who'd joined up before Albert became boss who were good guys. The new recruits were all as deranged as Albert, and their antics damaged the Gambino family's reputation more with every passing day.

"Oh, there you two are." Laios waved as they entered the designated restaurant. The family had reserved a number of tables. Gambino family members were already seated throughout the place, eating and drinking. Koga also sat down and started shoveling food into his mouth.

"Koga, have you gotten used to your work?" Laios asked.

Koga nodded vaguely. "Ah...well, somewhat," he said between bites.

"I see. That's good to hear. You are but a slave, but you're talented. If you keep up the good work, I'll talk to the boss about rescinding your Oath of Subordination. You could earn your freedom."

"R-really?!" Koga had never dared to hope for such a thing. He'd dreamt about freedom many times, but he had given up on it long ago. Now he may be granted it. Koga felt like doing a little dance.

"Mmm. I don't ever lie. I promise that you will be free. When you are free, would you enter an official agreement of brotherhood?"

"You mean...join the Gambino family?"

"Of course, it would be your choice. If you want to do something else, then you should. But if you decide to join the family, I will make sure you're taken care of for the rest of your life," Laios said.

Koga wasn't sure what to do. The criminal life wasn't so bad. Besides, even if he won his freedom, the only thing he was good at was swinging his sword. It would be nice to always know where his next meal was coming from. He hated Albert, but he respected Laios. He thought he could stay if he were working under this man.

While he was pondering his future, he remembered Noel's face. He wondered what Noel was doing now. Would he really never return to the capital? Once he started down that train of thought, he couldn't think of anything else.

"Are you thinking about Noel?"

Feeling like Laios could read his mind, Koga suddenly stood up straighter. "N-no, I wasn't..."

"Hmph, you don't need to hide it. He was exactly as you said. Even though he was young, he had those eyes. What you really want is to work under him, right?"

"I..." Koga didn't know how to answer. Suddenly, the table shook violently.

"Laios! I can't take it anymore! How much longer do we have to obey that madman?!"

The outburst came from a drunk Gambino mobster who was clearly upset—tears running down his face, his expression frustrated. In his hand, he held a bamboo dragonfly.

"The kid I had to take care of today was holding this the entire time. He was just a child and I had to do that to him... No flesh-and-blood human would ever bump off a little kid... But under him...what can I do...?" He was sniveling, shedding real tears. "You just have to do something."

"Settle down. We can talk later. This is not something to discuss in front of other customers—"

"I can't settle down! I joined the Gambino family because I loved the old man. If I knew I'd have to obey this madman, I'd never have walked this path!"

"I said, *settle down*! Which word did you not understand?" Laios bellowed.

The very walls shook. Everyone shut up. Even the forks and knives stopped clinking.

"It's true..." Laios said, calm again. "The boss has been somewhat egregious lately. But that doesn't mean his soldiers can start slacking off. You joined the family of your own free will, and those are the rules."

"B-but..."

"I know. I'll talk to the boss. Now will you let it go for today? Please." Laios stayed in his seat but bowed his head deeply to his underlings.

"I-I got it! Please lift your head!" When the second-in-command went so far as to bow his head to them, the henchmen could no longer grumble. This ended the discussion for now. But even Koga, the newcomer, could tell the peace was only superficial. The man who'd spoken out wasn't the only disenchanted mobster here.

Then they heard an unpleasant voice jeering at the situation.

"Hey now, what's this, a fight? It's not good to fight among friends."

Everyone present grew tense as soon as they recognized that voice.

"Noel Stollen, what are you doing here?" Noel, who had supposedly left the capital a week earlier, was now standing calmly before Koga and directly across from Laios. His eyes rested on the toy that the sobbing soldier was holding, but he immediately looked back at Laios.

For a long moment, he and Laios simply took each other in. Laios looked perturbed, but he kept his cool, as befitted the family's second-in-command. "What are you doing here? I told you to leave the capital."

"And as promised, I left. For a week. I had a great vacation and feel refreshed."

"A vacation? Do you understand the gravity of what you're doing?" Laios grew angry, but Noel smiled, looking relaxed.

"You're the one who needs to settle down. I'm not trying to stir up trouble here. I just wanted to bring you your souvenir from my vacation." Noel pulled a piece of old parchment from

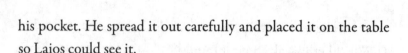

his pocket. He spread it out carefully and placed it on the table so Laios could see it.

"This parchment is my souvenir? What is... What?!" Laios scanned the paper, and his eyes grew wide with astonishment.

"What? What's it say on there?"

Made curious by Laois' reaction, the other mobsters gathered around the table. Koga joined them too. Laois panicked as they surrounded him. "Y-you fools! Mind your own business! Get outta here!"

But it was too late.

"I-it can't be..."

"Seriously...?"

"We've been duped...?"

"What the hell is this...?"

Every one of the soldiers were astonished and disappointed, and their anger was evident in their words. Even Koga, who wasn't an official family member, understood their pain so well, it hurt him too. The information on this piece of paper...was a bomb. One with immeasurable destructive power.

"Are you pleased?"

"I hope you're prepared for the consequences of this," Laios said.

"That's not right, Capo. There's something else you need to do before you threaten me." Noel motioned with his chin to the soldiers surrounding Laios.

"Laios, did you know about this?" asked the mobster who'd just been crying over the current state of things.

"No...this is the first I've heard tell of it."

"I see. I believe you. But we can't let this go. This is vile!"

"Wait! Let's think about it calmly!"

"What is there to think about?" the man said. "Isn't the boss the bastard son of the previous boss?! Then why's he got some other man's name on his birth certificate?"

That was the bomb Noel had brought back to the capital. The government kept a mandatory register of families, so every citizen was required to possess a birth certificate. Since these birth certificates were strictly protected, Noel had had to employ various means to procure the original copy of Albert's.

Normally, the birth certificate of a child born out of wedlock was submitted with the father's name left blank. However, there was clearly a father's name written on Albert's birth certificate. And it wasn't the name of the previous Gambino don.

In other words, Albert was born to parents who were legally married.

The document didn't appear to have been forged—and even if it had been, every mobster in the family knew the names on it were likely correct. Koga had only heard stories of the previous boss, but he had been a great man, completely unlike Albert. The Gambino men had always harbored doubts about Albert's parentage. In that sense, it might be more accurate to say the birth certificate was more of a detonator than a bomb.

"The previous don of the Gambino family was an honorable man who cared for others," Noel said plainly. "He earned a reputation as the Robin Hood of his time. However, he did like the ladies. He had mistresses all over the country, and Albert's mother was once one of those women. She later married another man and had Albert with him, but her new husband abused the boy, so Albert's mother appealed to her former lover, the old boss."

"Could it be...?"

"Absolutely. His mother said to the boss, 'This is your child. I want your help.'"

"Th-the old man believed her?"

"No, I'm sure he didn't. The previous boss was shooting blanks."

The spectators stiffened at this new truth that Noel divulged.

"He was unable to father children. But he was a good man, so he granted her request. Maybe he wanted an heir," Noel said. "Anyway, the young Albert was entrusted to an acquaintance whom the boss trusted. Later, Albert's mother died—murder-suicide. Tragic stuff."

"H-how did you find out about all this?" one of the soldiers asked. "You didn't know the old man."

"There's an excellent information broker in the capital. I had his help. To verify the truth of this information he turned up, I traveled to Albert's hometown and made inquiries. That's how I got hold of his birth certificate." Noel said.

"So it's not exactly certain that Albert wasn't the old man's bastard..."

"So what?" Laios, who'd been listening quietly, chose this time to speak up. "Even if they share no blood, they're still parent and child. The previous boss recognized Albert as his heir in his dying hour. Nothing else is necessary."

He was right, but the fact remained that people held blood

relationships in high esteem. The reason Albert was recognized as the Gambino boss was because he was believed to be the son of the former don. If that proved to be a fiction, then his underlings' loyalty would be severely undermined.

"You say that, but doesn't knowing this," Noel said, pointing to the paper, "make it hard to stay loyal to him the same way you have been?"

"It's not your decision to make. Is that all?" Laios asked, cracking his knuckles and standing up from his chair. It was clear beyond a shadow of doubt that he planned to kill Noel. For a moment, Koga's hand almost strayed to his sword.

"That's right. It's not my decision to make. It's the decision of your men. And I can help."

"Help...?"

Noel was good. By presenting the information in this manner, he gave Laios no choice but to listen to him. He'd walked right into the midst of what should have been hostile territory, and yet, his clever tongue was running the show.

"Here's my proposal..."

The murderous urge faded from Laios's face as he listened to Noel's idea. Then he laughed.

"It is a good idea. But do you really think I'll get on board?"

"You will. Let me tell you why."

Noel stood up and whispered in Laios's ear, causing his face to twist.

That was the moment Laios fell.

He would no longer serve Albert Gambino. And where Laois

went, the other mobsters followed. They followed Laios because he had earned their respect and loyalty, and they had only ever served Albert because they feared Laios's wrath.

Back in the present moment, Laios finally spoke. "There are two things I'd like to ask you, Boss."

"Wh-what is it?"

"First, you are not the true-born son of the previous leader, correct?"

"Wh-what are you saying?!"

"Second, you poisoned him to make it appear he died of illness, didn't you? You wanted to ensure your place as successor before another candidate appeared."

"A-are you stupid? Just what are you trying to say?" Albert's panicked reaction suggested that it was all true.

"I see... So it is true..." Laios let out a deep sigh. Then his expression turned stern. "Albert, we will no longer follow you."

"What?! What do you mean?"

"You have no morals. You are a sociopath. We will not serve such a despicable man."

"Stop this immediately! The old man named me as his successor—you have to respect that!"

"Says the man who murdered him. There really is no saving you... But there is some truth to what you say. So you will have a chance to prove your mettle," Laios said, pointing at Noel. "You will fight him in a duel. If you win, we will recognize you as the official Gambino boss."

"A-a duel?!"

"You don't need to fight. You can choose someone to represent you. Select anyone here. Whomever you choose will fight to the utmost of their ability."

This was Noel's proposal: offer Albert a chance to prove his mettle in single combat. It was a strategy that targeted only Albert, while simultaneously allowing Noel to get a whole army—the Gambino family—off his back. On the Gambinos' part, this would serve as a good opportunity for them to gauge Albert's worth.

Once Laios had learned the truth about their last boss's death and lost all faith in Albert, there had been no reason for him to refuse.

"Why should I? I am Albert Gambino! I don't need to listen to anything you say!" Albert howled desperately. But eventually, his eyes started to cloud over with resignation. Nothing he could say would change the situation he was in. Even a child could understand that.

"Take your own life. It's shameful to be in the same family as you," said someone in a casual yet disgusted singsong tone. When they all turned to see who had spoken, they saw a fop in gaudy purple clothing, surrounded by several extremely large men.

"I-Impossible... Finocchio?"

"Oh, are we on a first-name basis, then? Please address me as *Miss* Finocchio. We may be in the same family, but you still need to respect your superiors."

"Wh-what are you doing here?"

"What am I doing? Well, I came to serve as witness for the duel, of course."

"Witness?!"

Few things were as satisfactory as taking a buffoon who thought he was smart and proving to him just what a fool he really was. Albert, already stunned that his own underlings would betray him, seemed so terrified by Finocchio's appearance that he was struggling to draw breath.

✝

I was the one who'd summoned Finocchio here, asking him to serve as witness to the duel.

As a subfamily of the Lucianos, the Gambinos were technically Finocchio's allies. But the two families sometimes found themselves competing with each other in the business arena too. When he heard he could crush them with no risk to himself, Finocchio happily agreed to witness the spectacle.

More importantly, the Gambinos were also sullying the main family's reputation with their stimulant dealings. The Lucianos had been turning a blind eye, due to their esteem for the previous boss, but the truth was that they wanted to take care of the Gambinos as soon as possible. By serving as witness, Finocchio could claim the Gambinos' downfall as his own achievement, so there was really no reason for him to refuse.

And so, as I knew he would, Finocchio agreed to both of my proposals. The first was that he would pay me a reward of fifty million fil if I succeeded in ousting Albert. The role of Gambino boss would automatically transfer to Laios—though naturally, Finocchio would use this duel as an excuse to bring the subfamily directly under his own management. The annual income of the Gambino family was approximately three billion fil. How could Finocchio pass up the chance to secure that in exchange for a mere fifty million?

I could probably have asked for more, but I had no desire to antagonize Finocchio. Even if he did agree to inflated terms, I'd end up being in his debt, rather than this being a one-time transaction. Being in debt to the mob is never a good idea, and so I'd stopped at fifty million.

"I-I see...fine!" Albert erroneously concluded, pointing his finger at Finocchio. "So you're the mastermind, you mad clown! You pulled all the strings to entrap me!"

Finocchio heaved a deep sigh at being accused of something he hadn't done.

"No, you idiot. I haven't done anything. It was Noel, right over there, who entrapped you. He has you dancing in the palm of his hand."

"No, I don't believe it! That dumb child couldn't entrap the likes of me!"

"Oh, no? And yet, here we all are. You're a fool," Finocchio said coldly. "Anyway, I have a brothel to check in on later, so I can't stay here all day. Hurry up and choose a representative. I mean, you're welcome to fight yourself if you want to. At least it'll all be over quickly then."

"I didn't agree to a duel! You can't just decide everyth—"

"It's far too late to for you to spew garbage at me, you piece of shit! If you're part of this family, then you must be prepared to defend your position at any time! Are you prepared for the consequences if you keep running your mouth?" Finocchio thundered, his attitude suddenly fierce.

Albert was trembling with fear. "D-dammit!" He hung his head and nodded, finally giving up.

"Fine... I will duel. But you make me a promise. If my representative wins, you will recognize me as the boss of the Gambino family forever more."

"Fine with me. Not only that, I'll even ask the Luciano boss to forgive you for taking your minions to a Seeker-only tavern."

"What?"

"That was a mistake," Finocchio said. "You threatened to fight all the Seekers for no reason, then let Noel trick you into fleeing the tavern, crying like a little baby. The boss is furious."

"Erg..."

Albert clenched his teeth in frustration. Keeping his temper in check, albeit just barely, he turned to his underlings to select a fighter. After a moment, he pointed to one man.

"Koga! You will fight for me!"

It was exactly as I expected. Albert undoubtedly wanted to choose Laios, but he could no longer trust him. If Laios took a dive, it would all be over. The only person he could trust now was Koga, who was bound to him by the Oath of Subordination.

Koga answered Albert's call and stood in front of us.

"You were right, Noel, he chose the Eastern man. Now I can kill him," Alma said, bloodthirsty again. But I had no intention of giving her a rematch.

I grabbed Alma by the nape of the neck before she could go forth and pulled her back.

"Agh?! Wh-what are you doing, Noel?!"

"Sorry. I'll take care of him."

"Huh?! What are you saying?! You can't beat him! You saw him, you know it!"

She was right. I couldn't beat him in a normal fight. But if I planned to be the greatest Seeker of all time, I couldn't leave any stains on my record.

"When we're done, I'll buy you lunch. So just be patient and wait."

"You're going to die before lunch, Noel!"

"Do you really think so?"

"Everyone thinks so!" Alma said.

"That's your inexperience talking."

"Huh? Wait a second!"

I pushed the unconvinced Alma aside and downed a battle stimulant as I walked to stand before Koga. I felt bad for her, but this duel needed to be me versus Albert's chosen representative.

I would settle things with Koga.

"Third time's the charm, huh?"

It began to rain. My hair was dripping wet as we stood face-to-face, and I laughed. Koga smiled back, looking happy. His fighting spirit had been renewed. The feeling that I was outclassed was much stronger than before, and my senses were sharpened like a blade.

"Well, you sure look ready," I said. "You don't mind being forced to fight for a guy like Albert? Winning won't bring you any glory."

"Who cares 'bout that stuff? I'm just happy to fight you."

"You have high expectations for someone you've already beat."

"You already lost an' still came back for more. Even someone dumb as me understands you got somethin' up your sleeve. Right? I can't wait."

"You're smarter than your master. That must mean you know I won't be holding back. You better come at me ready to kill."

I would no longer waver. *Third time's the charm.*

Koga left his sword sheathed and crouched down low. This was the move he used when fighting with Alma. When I left the capital, I'd researched the Longswordsman class at the Appraiser Association and learned this was a move required to initiate a skill.

Longswordsman skill: *Iai Flash*. This skill increased the attack speed and power by five times upon drawing a sword. If I carelessly got too close to him, he would cut me in two without any special moves.

But it didn't merit fear. I had already planted the seeds I needed.

"Since this is our last time fighting each other, I have some good news I wish to share with you before we start."

"What? Tell me."

"You can use orange peels to scrub out tough grease stains."

"H-huh? Wh-what does that mean?" Koga tilted his head to the side for a moment—and I rushed him.

We were already standing close to each other. My distraction worked, delaying his reaction just a notch. And that wasn't all. Koga, wary that I had a strategy in place, stiffened up as he saw me rush him. He understood that a man who could set up Albert Gambino for destruction in one week's time would never challenge an opponent to whom he'd previously lost unless he had a plan.

Those were the seeds I'd sown. I would bind Koga with his own subconscious thoughts.

The requirements to initiate *Iai Flash* were unsheathing the sword and swinging it once. Because of my rush, Koga completely missed his window to initiate it. Even if he were to draw his sword now, he couldn't initiate the skill before I was up in melee with him.

But Koga was flexible. Once he realized I would be right in front of him before he could draw his sword, he immediately switched hands and drew his shorter sword about halfway from its sheath. He was going to hit me with the hilt to create some space.

He was good. I'd planned to keep him from completely drawing the sword by pressing down on the pommel with my hand, but that wasn't going to work anymore. Changing my plans, I crouched down low. When Koga charged me, I guarded my neck and head with my right arm.

"I'll have your arm!"

He spun around and cut me all the way down to the bone of my right arm. Thanks to the battle stim, I felt no pain. I constricted my muscle, holding the blade in place.

"What are you—?!" Koga opened his eyes wide in surprise. I punched him right in the jaw with my left hand, shutting his mouth.

The punch had rattled him. He wasn't unconscious, but he faltered, bending backward from the impact. I went in for a follow-up, this time with my legs.

One of the hand-to-hand combat tricks my grandpa—Overdeath—taught me was a skill to cause cardiac arrhythmia by punching the opponent in the chest. However, when the opponent is of a higher rank than you, a mere punch doesn't carry enough force to do the job. That was why Overdeath had developed a different technique specially for me.

I jumped and flipped over in midair, using the momentum from the flip to kick Koga right in his armored chest. This move, designed by Overdeath, was the secret trump card of the kind of hand-to-hand combat that didn't rely on class skills. It was called—

"Roaring Thunder."

The instant the flip-torqued kick hits, it creates a sound like thunder. It carries the force of a punch multiplied several times, and it makes the target's heart stop immediately.

"Agh...ha..."

Koga collapsed.

He was an opponent I could never beat if I fought fair. But as long as I had time to prepare, there was no opponent I couldn't beat.

This was the path I had to walk until the end.

I faced Koga and remained on guard, taking a deep breath. *Ruthlessness.* Even after defeating an enemy, I remain ready for battle.

Finally, Finocchio called out in a high voice, "Huzzah! The winner is Noel Stollen!"

The crowd erupted in deafening cheers at the declaration.

†

"Noel, you really are stupid."

After the duel was over, I went to an empty private house to rest my body. The rain was beating down on the windows. My right arm, nearly sliced off by Koga, was recovering thanks to the potion. As long as I rested, it should be back to normal by the next day.

"Noel, you really are stupid."

The rebound from the battle stimulant was less severe than I expected. However, that meant my body was starting to build up a tolerance to it, so it wouldn't be as effective the next time I used it.

"Noel, you really are stupid," Alma said.

"Shut up. You don't need to say it a third time."

Alma ignored that, pinning me with an angry stare.

"If you'd let me fight, you wouldn't be suffering from such serious injuries. You're really stupid."

"Ah...but I won, so what's the problem?"

"That's not the issue. I'm on your team. It's my job to fight. Your role is commander, right? Don't steal my role in the party."

It was rare for her to sound so serious. I felt a little guilty.

"Sorry. I won't do it again."

"Really? Do you promise?"

"I promise. I swear it on my grandfather."

"In that case, I believe you." Alma's face softened and she laughed gently. "From now on, you will rely on me, bro."

"I told you, you are not my sis—oh, whatever." I was tired. Like, really sleepy. Maybe I should take a nap.

"By the way, Albert ran away."

"What?" My exhaustion evaporated. "What do you mean he ran away?!"

"When you won and everyone whooped it up, he used the distraction to run away."

"Not good," I said.

"It's fine. The Gambino family is out looking for him. They'll find him quickly."

I listened to Alma, one hand on my chest. "I see. Well, that's good. Chelsea will be able to rest easier too."

"Who's Chelsea?"

"It's nothing. Forget it."

Just then there was a knock on the door. "Who is it?" I called out.

"Laios. Can I come in?"

Alma and I looked at each other.

"It's fine," I answered. "Come in."

Laios came into the house and gave me a broad smile. "That was an amazing fight. You are a real man."

"Well, thank you."

"I'm sorry for the problems we caused you."

"Don't worry about it. Albert is gone. That's a relief."

"I see... If you're ever in trouble, come to me. The Gambino family will fight for you."

"I don't need the help of an organized crime family."

Using the mob was one thing, but I didn't want to be indebted to them. A single misstep could change the balance of power, leaving me in a position where they could exploit me.

"Ha ha ha. That's correct." Laios turned away. He kept talking, his back now turned to us. "You've got real balls, kid. Reminds me of someone I used to admire. Thank you, Noel Stollen. I will forever be grateful for that."

With that, he left.

The next person to enter was Finocchio. "Oh, there you are, little Noel! I want to talk to you about something."

I just wanted to rest, but apparently, everyone wanted an audience right now. I couldn't exactly turn Finocchio away. It was I who called him to be the witness, after all.

"What is it? Please make it short."

"I know that. I have plans anyway. But I want to talk to you alone, so would you mind leaving, young lady?"

"Fine..."

I signaled with my eyes and Alma left the room.

"What is it?"

"I hate beating around the bush, so I'll just say it," Finocchio said. "Noel, join our family. I'll be good to you. You could even lead the Gambinos. The boys would accept you as their leader."

"You want me to be an underboss?" I was caught off guard. His suggestion felt so far from my reality that I burst out laughing. "Ha ha ha, are you serious? I'm sixteen years old. A child. A brat."

"Age is irrelevant. What matters is that you have balls. The same applies to Seekers, right?"

"Well, yes. But I already turned you down before."

"That's why I'm asking again."

"My answer will never change."

"Why not?" he asked.

"Because it won't."

Finocchio's shoulders slumped. "I see that you have your mind made up."

"Sorry."

"It's fine. I expected you to say no." Finocchio stood up straight and he smiled at me. "Hey, Noel, do you know what my class is?"

"All I know is that it's a combat type," I said.

"Well, I'll tell you. My class is Scout. I'm an A-Ranked Punisher. My direct battle capabilities are inferior to a vanguard class, but I have mastered various special skills."

"Oh..."

"Some of those skills are tremendously entertaining. I can even use them to put on quite the show. Are you ready? Watch me."

Finocchio hummed to himself as he pulled a handkerchief out of his pocket. He made some exaggerated movements and then dropped the handkerchief over his empty palm.

"Tralala, tralala. There! Now, don't blink! One, two, three! Abracadabra!"

He whipped the handkerchief away, revealing a red object that I didn't recognize in his hand. At first glance, it resembled a fruit, but it was too grotesquely shaped to be a fruit. Also, it was beating...

"What do you think this is? Why, it's little Noel's heart."

My hands went straight to my chest.

"There's...no beat."

I should have had a heartbeat. But I couldn't feel one at all. I broke out in a sweat, but then told myself to calm down. If my heart really was gone, then I would be dead. So was this an illusion? Talkers can resist mental manipulation, but Finocchio was A-Rank and I was but a C, so he could perhaps still beguile me.

But I knew in my gut that this was no illusion.

"It's amazing that you can so calmly assess your situation." he said.

"What...did you do?"

"This is the *Judgment* skill. I can initiate it once you refuse a request from me twice in a row. It allows me to forcibly pluck your heart from your chest."

"An insta-death skill for hand-to-hand combat... But I'm still alive."

"That's because you are in close proximity to me. Once you stray more than five meters away from me, or when I crush this heart, you will die. Your life is literally in my hands," Finocchio said.

He smiled, gently stroking my heart. There was no pain, but I felt a chill pass through my body, followed by nausea.

"Noel, you're a little...well, more than a little. You're remarkable. It's hard to believe you are only sixteen. Call it feminine intuition, if you like." He winked at me. "But you will bring disaster to the Luciano family someday. I am sure of it."

"So you want to flick me off the chessboard while I'm still a pawn?"

"That's right. But I'm not the devil. I'll give you one more chance," he said. "Little Noel, become a Luciano brother. If you do, you may keep your life."

"I see. That's very kind of you..."

My mind raced, thinking of a way to overcome this situation. I could barely move, thanks to the battle I'd just fought. Even if I were in full health, I could never outrun an A-Ranked opponent. Should I call Alma using *Link*? But Alma couldn't beat Finocchio either. Should I ask her to call for Laios? They were both A-Ranked. He might be able to render Finocchio ineffective.

But if I escalated the situation, Finocchio would simply crush my heart like an overripe fruit. The purple fop wasn't stupid enough to allow someone else to get involved. So what could I do? Should I cave to Finocchio's threats?

"Hmph, unbelievable." I forced myself to stand up and started shuffling toward Finocchio.

"Do you think you can take your heart back? I don't think I need to tell you that that's impossible, with the difference in our skill. Even if you do retrieve it from me, and that's a one-in-ten-million shot, it's hopeless. Your heart will not return to your chest unless I dispel the skill."

"Finocchio Barzini, you are correct."

"Huh? What are you talking about?"

Finocchio cocked his head to the side and I walked closer.

"I will be the greatest Seeker of them all someday. And then, I will never lay a hand on the Luciano family, no matter what. So if you want to kill me, do it now."

"W-wait! Don't get so close to me! If I drop your heart, you'll die! Do you understand that?!"

"You're gonna kill me, right? So do it. Kill me."

I moved another step closer.

"But don't forget. The second you kill me, you will lose any dignity you may hold as head of the Barzinis, subfamily of the Lucianos."

"What do you mean?"

"Kill the dangerous ones while they're still weak. That's the smart thing to do. Survival of the fittest and all that. But it's not the *manly* thing to do, is it? To put it another way, you're scared. You have my heart, but do you have any balls? Answer me, Finocchio."

"Y-you...in a situation like this..." Finocchio's face quivered with anger and embarrassment. He was a head taller than me, but I stared him down, not budging.

"I am the king of *me*. No one will hold me back."

"Erg, y-you..."

In that moment, Finocchio took a step back. He looked like he couldn't believe he had.

"I-I lost...a game of chicken...?" Finocchio was dumbfounded but then finally started laughing out loud. "Ah ha ha ha! Little Noel, you look so scary! It's a joke, a joke! I wouldn't kill you, little Noel. There we go—show's over!"

When he turned over the hand that held my heart, I felt it begin to beat within my chest again. Proof that I was alive. The *thump-thump* of my heart beat through every corner of my body.

"I'm sorry to scare you. I'll be going now. Buh-bye!" As Finocchio faced the door to leave, he muttered, "Words once spoken cannot be taken back, you spoiled brat. After beating me at chicken, you'd better make it to the top, or you will pay."

"Naturally. You just be quiet and watch."

†

Finocchio opened a purple umbrella with a flowery frill and walked silently in the pouring rain. Behind him, a giant body-guard sighed and opened his mouth to speak.

"Miss Boss, was that all right?"

"Huh? What?"

"Noel. If you let him go, won't he be a problem later?"

"Who knows? Que sera, sera." Finocchio sulked, then stopped, shoulders slumping. "Maybe...I should have done something?"

"You should have. He'll definitely be a problem later," the bodyguard opined.

"You're right... At least if my instinct is correct..."

"Do you want to go back and kill him now?"

"Impossible—that would be far too embarrassing!" Despite his reasoning, Finocchio couldn't bring himself to kill Noel. However, his bodyguard seemed more amused than disappointed in his boss for that.

"Miss Boss, is Noel Stollen really such a great man?"

Finocchio got a sour look on his face. "Well, he has guts for his age, and he's a great *young* man... Even though he's really very weak, he works harder than anyone, so it makes you want to root for him... B-but! I have no interest in boys with faces so pretty, you don't know if they have a dick or not! I prefer handsome older men!"

"Miss Boss..."

"Wh-what?"

"It's love. That's wonderful."

"Huh?! What are you saying?! I'll kill you! I would never fall in love with a brat like that! I-I'm docking you one month's pay!"

Just as his voice was getting loud, another Barzini henchman showed up.

"Miss Boss, Albert has been apprehended. Come and see."

Albert, covered in mud from head to toe, looked like he'd been dug out of a ditch. He was a shadow of his former tyrannical self, reduced to an abused puppy shaking from fear.

"My, my, Albert. You certainly have made a mess of yourself."

"F-Finocchio!"

"You mean *Miss* Finocchio? Oh well. We're not related anymore, so I guess it doesn't matter."

"H-help me! I don't want to die!"

Finocchio looked at him, cold as ice. "A man who doesn't flinch even when his heart or parts are being squeezed in an iron grip is a man among men. On the other hand, garbage with neither parts nor pride to defend is no man at all... Do you really want to live so badly?"

"I want to live! I'll do anything if you save me!" cried Albert.

"Okay, then. I'll save you."

"R-really?!"

"Yes, that's fine."

Finocchio's face lit up with an ominous smile. "I'll keep you in my pigpen."

"P-pigpen?"

"Yes, my pigpen. I'll cut off your hands and feet so you can walk exactly like a pig. My breeding hogs will have all kinds of fun with you."

"Wh... Wha?!" Albert's brain was shutting down.

"Oh, but pigs are omnivorous, so they might decide to eat you, Albert. If that happens, I'm sorry. You should make sure that the breeding hog takes a liking to you."

"Wh-what are you playing at?! Stop it! Don't touch me! Let me go! Let me gooo! Stoppp!"

Finocchio's henchmen picked up Albert without a word. He struggled and called for help atop their shoulders, but no one responded.

"I hope Sire Piggy will be happy to have a new lover." Finocchio put a hand to his cheek and tilted his head to one side. The twisted smile on his lips was the smile of the mad clown.

†

After the duel, Finocchio transferred fifty million fil to my account. After he'd threatened to murder me, I'd thought he might try and tack some conditions onto the reward payment, but he didn't. In that sense, the fop was true to his word.

I used thirty million of the fifty million fil to buy the *Exorcism* guidebook. The shop owner seemed surprised but also pleased that I'd been able to come up with the money as promised.

I also got the item I'd requested from Finocchio as a bonus. It was a silver ring and a piece of parchment written in blood: Koga's Oath of Subordination.

"I'm your owner now."

I sat in a chair in my room at the Stardrop Inn, my legs crossed, brandishing the paper. There were two people there besides me. One was Alma, looking grumpy, and the other was Koga, expressionless.

"But I'm going to be frank. I don't need a slave."

"Then why'd you take that? Long as you have it, my power's all yours. I can burn or boil for you."

"Don't get cocky just because you're pretty strong. In Seeker terms, you're low down the ladder. A slave's combat skills are no match for the greatest Seekers."

"So whaddya want?"

The only thing I wanted since the day I swore a promise to my grandfather.

"I only have one desire," I said. "I want to be on top. Above all the other Seekers. And for that, I don't need a weak mutt for a pet. I need a fierce wolf."

I handed the parchment and the ring in my hand to Koga.

"Do what you want with these. You are free."

"Free..."

"And now I'll ask you. Are you a feral mutt? Or are you a fierce wolf?"

Koga looked at the Oath of Subordination in his hands. "I've... been used by people my whole life... You say I'm free, but I don't feel it. Like you say, I'm nothin' but a feral mutt. But I know one thing."

When he raised his head, there was a powerful desire shining in his black eyes.

"Noel, I wanna be there to watch you make good on your dreams. If you need a fierce wolf, then that's what I gotta be," he said. "So, please. Lemme join you."

"I approve, Koga Tsukishima, Longswordsman."

The sunlight pouring into the room illuminated the three of us. I'd finally recruited one more member to my party. After all this time spent back at square one, we could finally move forward again. Minute progress toward my goal, but still a sure step forward.

And I *was* sure. With this team, I knew we could someday establish the strongest clan of them all.

"Let's go outside. We will begin synchronized training."

Epilogue

H UGO COPPÉLIA was born the third son of a poor shoe-maker. He was raised in an unhappy home environment, physically abused by his father and brothers, often forced to subsist on nothing but broth.

When Hugo was ten years old, he underwent a free assessment provided by the government and found that he had an aptitude for the Puppeteer class. The assessor was clearly taken aback, but he went on to enthusiastically explain to him what a Puppeteer was.

Puppeteer was a rare dual class. While potential Seekers usually held combat-type or support-type classes, a Puppeteer was an extremely special class that combined the two. When the freshly assessed Hugo tried to activate one of the class skills, a toy soldier appeared before him in an instant. The assessor was even more surprised—Hugo was a prodigy! Very few people could use their innate skills perfectly with no training at all.

That was the moment Hugo first felt like he'd found his place in the world. On his way home from the assessor, he turned left instead of right and ran away from him. He left the town where he'd been born, choosing instead to walk the world in search of his fortune.

Trying to make it on his own as a ten-year-old—and while constantly on the road, at that—was no easy task. Hugo was attacked by thieves in the night, wild animals, and even monsters. He suffered through food poisoning and illness, but overcame it all with the aid of his Puppeteer skills. After making it through many long, hard nights, he began to think he might need to take advantage of his combat abilities by becoming an official Seeker.

He registered and started racking up achievements right away.

But Hugo never joined a party. He never formed any alliances, working only as a temporary hire. In essence, he was a mercenary who happened to do Seeker work. As his reputation as a skilled Seeker grew, a number of parties and clans tried to recruit him, including the strongest clan in the capital, the three-star-regalia Supreme Dragon Team. But Hugo politely refused.

He'd never relied on anyone and didn't plan to start now. He disliked working in groups. The main reason for his refusal, however, was that Hugo didn't plan to work as a Seeker forever.

He had another dream.

By the time Hugo reached his twentieth year, he had saved up a fair sum. He used that money to purchase an atelier in the capital, where he could craft puppets to his heart's content. He didn't want to make doll soldiers that could be used in combat. Hugo dreamed of being a true artist, hand-carving dolls that were meant only to be seen and admired. Thanks to the irrational violence he'd suffered as a child, violence brought him no joy. He was a good fighter but hated conflict. His career as a Seeker had been only a means to an end.

Finally realizing his dream, Hugo set enthusiastically to work making dolls. His finished products flew off the shelves. No matter how many dolls he made, there was always someone willing to buy them. Orders for dolls came in from people of all ages across the capital, and even from people living in faraway nations.

His dolls were loved for their elaborate design, but most of all for the strange charm they carried. Everyone who picked up one of his dolls said the same thing: "When I look at this doll, my heart feels warm. I want to take it home and care for it."

Hugo had never set out to inspire such emotions. Having never known the love of a family himself, he constantly imagined the love for which he yearned. When he poured that love into doll-making, his creations were imbued with his affection for them. Ironic and confusing...but Hugo decided he didn't mind if it made people love his work. It was rare for an artist to be so recognized by society. Most wasted away without anyone knowing them or their work. Hugo had undoubtedly been blessed by the god of art to have met with so much success at such a young age.

However, the god of fate did not care for Hugo quite so much.

One day, Hugo was delivering a doll to the customer who'd commissioned it. He enjoyed meeting his customers, and always delivered dolls personally, rather than by courier, to clients living in the capital.

However, the moment he set foot within his wealthy client's manor, Hugo lost consciousness. When he came to, he found himself on the floor, in a puddle of blood not his own. Before him was the corpse of one of the customer's servants.

The corpse was badly mutilated. Its skin had been peeled off and stuck to the doll he'd brought with him, as if the mannequin had tried to clothe itself in a suit of flesh. Human organs and viscera littered the floor around Hugo. As he lay there, stunned by the extraordinary circumstances he found himself in, the military police showed up. Apparently, someone passing by the manor had heard a scream and reported it.

Hugo was arrested. Naturally, he desperately argued his innocence before police as well as on trial. However, his pleas were futile. After a short hearing, Hugo was sentenced to death. There was no evidence to be found to suggest a suspect other than Hugo, and the judge deemed that making too many dolls had driven the Puppeteer mad, leading him to commit such a violent crime.

News of Hugo's fate spread quickly through the capital. The newspapers picked up the story of the genius doll maker who committed an outrageous crime, and Hugo earned a great many new names, such as "a modern macabre murderer" and "the Bloody Taxidermist."

The prison was dark and dingy. The stone walls and floor were hard and cold. There was no bed, just some straw in a corner and a bucket for bodily excretions.

Hugo Coppélia sat in a corner of this cell. The boy once revered for his beauty was no longer recognizable. His hair and beard had grown, and his body was thin and weak. The rags he wore made him look more like a ghoul than a drifter. Two years had passed since his trial, and in truth, Hugo had been reduced to little more than a husk of himself. He'd lost all will to live, no longer so much as stirring when a fly landed on his face.

The only reason he hadn't been executed yet was because the Appraiser Association was studying his class for research purposes. However, their two-year project would soon be at an end. When that happened, Hugo's time would be up.

"Number 103! Wake up! You have a visitor!"

The guard opened the door to his cell and barked, "Stand up!"

The guard forced him up. The guard checked the collar around Hugo's neck carefully. The collar was made of beast leather—it would drain the MP if its wearer attempted to initiate a skill.

"Okay, no problem with the collar. Let's go!" Hugo's hands were bound in front of him. The guard pulled him along. The visitor room was divided in two by a thick glass-and-steel partition. His visitor was already sitting on the other side of it.

"Five minutes, starting now! Don't cause any problems!"

The guard positioned himself in the corner of the room, nodding for Hugo to proceed. Hugo let out a sigh and sat before his visitor.

"You again... Noel Stollen."

Noel gave him a friendly smile. "Hugo, you've lost more weight. I know the food here is leftover pig slop, but you have to eat more. You can't die on me."

"Because you're going to get me out of here and put me on your team?"

"That's right!" Noel answered cheerfully.

Hugo sighed again. This was the third time Noel had come to visit. Before that, he'd written him letters. He had one agenda: to set Hugo free and recruit him to join Blue Beyond.

"I keep telling you that's impossible. My sentence has already been decided. The authoritarian Department of Justice would never reverse their own verdict."

"There's plenty of ways to deal with them," Noel declared confidently. Hugo couldn't bring himself to laugh at him, even though he'd just told him what he wanted was impossible. The fact that Noel could get access to visit a prisoner on death row meant that he had found a weak spot in the system.

It didn't mean, however, that Hugo was ready to believe everything Noel was telling him.

"You don't trust me."

"Why would I? I know you're special. But it's still impossible for you to secure my release."

"You shouldn't dismiss me so easily," Noel said. "I've already made all the necessary preparations for your release. Why don't I show you what I'm capable of?"

He snapped his fingers abruptly. A side door opened and a guard came running in—a man famous for unjustly beating the prisoners. Hugo had been beaten by him many times.

"D-did you call, Mr. Noel?!"

"Tea."

"U-understood. I'll bring it right away!"

The guard ran off and came back with a tray holding a cup of tea. "I'm so sorry to make you wait! Here is your tea."

"Mm. Thanks. That's all. Leave."

"Right! If you need anything else!"

The guard bowed graciously and left the room. Noel drank his tea daintily, pinky extended. Hugo was taken aback.

"It's good tea. My tax fil at work, I suppose."

"I can't believe it... Did you threaten that guard?"

"Not *that* one." Noel looked at the guard standing on Hugo's side of the room, and the man went pale, his teeth beginning to chatter. "Every guard in this prison will do as I say. Every single one of them."

"How did you do that?"

"Trade secret."

Hugo didn't really get it, but whatever Noel had on these men must have been serious. Maybe there really was a chance he could get out of here. But the thought brought him no joy. He lacked the will to even desire that anymore.

"What's wrong? Aren't you happy?"

"If you get me out of here, I would be happy. But unfortunately, I can't join your team."

"Why?"

"First of all, I hate Seeker work. And most of all, it's been too long. Even if I did join your team, I wouldn't be able to help at all."

"Just give it a chance. You just have to train to get your old form back," Noel said.

"You...don't be ridiculous. But the fact is that if you do get me out of here, I will owe you a debt I can never repay. That's why I want you to allow me to pay you back in another way."

"Another way?" Noel scoffed, crossing his arms and looking displeased. "Well, we can talk about that some other time. Today, I have a favor to ask."

"A favor? Of me? Like this?"

"I'm going to establish a clan soon. But my current party name has bad associations, so I plan to rename it upon forming the clan. So my question is this: got any bright ideas?"

"Why are you asking me?" Hugo said. "Think of one yourself."

"But you're the artist. I thought you would have some good ideas."

"You're trying to make me the clan's godfather by having me name it, right? So I'll have a soft spot for it?"

"You got me. Is that a bad thing?"

Hugo frowned at the brazen, shameless boy before him. "I'm not thinking of a clan name for you."

"Why? That's so mean."

"You're like a snake..." Hugo said. "You're not just crafty and ruthless; you get close to your prey and then swallow them whole. It's horrifying."

"Me, a snake?" Noel raised an eyebrow, seemingly miffed, but then turned contemplative. "Hmm, a snake. That's not bad. Hmm... Not bad."

"What are you muttering about?"

"You gave me a good idea. Thank you, Hugo." For some reason, Noel was smiling with genuine gratitude. He tilted his head to the side and stood up. "I'm going to go. Incidentally, if you agree to join my group now, I'll make sure you get better food. How about it?"

"Mind your own business."

"Fine. I'll be back. Be well."

After Noel left, Hugo was returned to his cell. He chuckled to himself in the dark. "Heh heh, he really is a ridiculous boy."

Laughing made his dry lips crack, and they started bleeding. When was the last time he had laughed like that? The numbness encasing his emotions was beginning to fade.

"So I guess I'm going to be a Seeker again..."

SIDE STORY

The Strongest and Most Notorious Seeker

T HERE WAS ONCE a Seeker who was feared as the strongest and the most notorious of them all.

His name was Brandon Stollen. He reached the apex of the Warrior class, the EX-Ranked Destroyer, when he was still young. The battle-axe he wielded with both of his muscled arms was the epitome of destruction. He could turn a mountain to dust and split an ocean in two with a single blow. He was also sly as a snake, and vindictive to boot. When he faced a foe stronger than him, he did anything and everything necessary to definitively win in the end.

That was why he was dubbed Overdeath.

Brandon belonged to the clan that held the top regalia spot at the time, Bloodsword Federation, and served as the forward team leader. No matter how dire the battle, he always led the clan to victory. His path to being an undefeated hero was paved with the bodies of beasts, drenched in streams of their blood. The people both revered and dreaded him for his heroic deeds.

But no matter how many victories Brandon accumulated, he never knew peace. When he wasn't fighting beasts, he drowned himself in alcohol, women, and gambling. If he had beef with someone, whether they be mobsters or royals, he always made sure they paid. The problem was clear to anyone with eyes: Brandon was a twisted man, and the reason he'd come to be that way was rooted in the circumstances of his birth.

Brandon had been born the bastard son of a certain aristocrat. Taken from his mother as a small child, he was raised by his strict father for the purpose of devotedly serving his older brother, the rightful heir. His father physically abused him under the guise of "education," as did his older brother and stepmother.

But Brandon endured the abuse, as his father had promised to support his mother in return. She had injured her leg in an accident, leaving her unable to work.

Luckily, Brandon was born strong. By the time he was twelve, he was already larger than most adults, and he was so talented that even Seeker instructors refused to spar with him. His family grew more and more afraid of him as he matured.

Soon, nobody could control him.

Then one day, he received a letter from the neighboring tenant of the house he'd lived in with his mother as a child. The letter contained news of his mother's death. She had taken a job in a run-down factory, and industrial pollution on the line had destroyed her lungs.

Brandon felt like the ground had crumbled below his feet.

He plummeted into a deep pit of despair, surrounded by anger and hatred that eventually swelled to consume him.

His father had lied to him. He had never intended to care for Brandon's mother. When Brandon confronted him, his father initially pretended to be bemused. But it wasn't long before he let out a wicked laugh and admitted the truth.

"You fool. What does a useless woman's death have to do with you?" the man jeered.

Before Brandon knew it, he was beating his father to death. His hands were bathed in the blood that flowed ceaselessly from the now-headless stump of his father's neck. The convulsing corpse writhed in a sea of blood like a fish on a cutting board, which Brandon found ridiculously absurd.

His brother and stepmother heard the commotion and came running with guards. They surrounded the boy, guns drawn and swords unsheathed.

But Brandon just laughed. "You think you can kill me with those?"

It was all over in an instant. Brandon crushed everyone like hot grapes in his fist. His brother and stepmother died at his hands that night, joining his father in hell. Brandon burned down the mansion and never looked back. He discarded his father's name and instead went by Stollen, his late mother's surname.

That was over twenty years ago. Although Brandon continued to amass achievements, he indulged evermore in momentary pleasures. His allies were worried about his daily debaucheries, but he would listen to no one.

Brandon was free. He had attained the highest of ranks. He could even defeat beast lords on his own. But even with all his power, he could not fill the black hole in his heart.

Maybe that was why *her* presence felt so bright.

His aimless travels had led him to cross paths with a certain young lady. She was beautiful, and even though Brandon had bedded many women, he fell in love with this one at first sight.

She was in her mid-twenties. Her white-gold hair was like the sun, and she had bright, emerald-green eyes. Her skin was white as snow. Her face was slender, with a well-formed nose. She was short of stature, and her beauty made look dainty but not weak at all. She was called Clarice, and she lived and worked as a seamstress in the downtown area of the imperial capital, managing a storefront she had inherited from her parents.

Brandon wanted to make Clarice his. However, in his experience, it wasn't easy to win a woman like her. She had many suitors among the sons of merchants and aristocrats, but none could get her to look their way. Thus, Brandon carefully researched Clarice and the type of man she would prefer before he started to approach her. However...

"Brandon Stollen, I know you well," she told him. "I'm flattered by your attention, but I'm sorry, I could never love someone who lives for violence as you do."

Brandon was hurt by his own reputation, rejected upon first meeting. He still didn't give up and frequented her store, but Clarice never yielded.

Naturally, Brandon's pride was hurt. He had no choice but to give up on pursuing her. His allies made fun of him for his first failure with a woman, but carrying on after Clarice would have been naught but vanity. As a womanizer, Brandon knew that too.

And yet, some people in the world never notice their own folly.

By pure coincidence, on his way home from gambling, he happened to pass Clarice's house and heard a piercing shriek. He ran toward the noise and saw Clarice being carried off by multiple men.

The ringleader was one of the men who had been courting Clarice. The son of an aristocrat who couldn't bring himself to give up on her. He'd devised a plan to rape her, and he'd flashed some money around to gain the assistance of a local band of hooligans.

Immediately understanding the situation, Brandon felt an intense rage that even he couldn't understand. The anger took over his body, and in an instant, he had knocked out the hooligans and seized the aristocrat's son by the throat. Suddenly, the man's face looked just like Brandon's father's. His father had also attacked and raped his mother. Then when he'd tired of her, he tossed her away.

Brandon lifted his right fist to smash the aristocrat's head in. But the second he was about to throw the punch, Clarice embraced Brandon's right arm.

"Please stop!"

"Let go! I need to kill this garbage!"

Brandon tried to shake Clarice off, but she wasn't going to let go so easily. He had no choice but to squeeze the aristocrat's neck with the other hand and drop him.

"He's just unconscious. The military police will take care of the rest. Are you happy now?" Brandon told her.

Clarice finally let go of his arm.

"Thank you very much for saving me. I will be forever grateful," she told him, eyes lowered.

"I was just passing by. You don't need to be so formal. But...why did you stop me? You do know what they would have done to you had I not been passing by? Don't you hate this man?" Brandon pointed to the aristocrat on the ground. But Clarice shook her head quietly.

"I hate him. But that doesn't mean you need to commit a crime."

"Huh? So you stopped me for my sake, not his?"

Clarice nodded. Brandon was dumbfounded. He feared nothing. He had plenty of ways to keep people quiet, were he suspected of murdering an aristocrat. But Brandon couldn't laugh at her. All he could do was turn away from her face.

Clarice's hand stroked his cheek gently.

"Why are you crying?"

Flustered, Brandon touched his own cheek. It was wet. He was crying and hadn't even realized it. He was baffled.

Clarice looked up at him, tears in her eyes too. "You wanted to save someone else too, didn't you?"

Brandon clutched his chest, as if to tear out his own heart. She was right. Brandon had really wanted to save his mother. But it was too late for that.

Brandon became friends with Clarice and they started to get

to know each other. He had shown her his vulnerable side, and she appreciated that nearly as much as she appreciated him saving her from her suitor.

Though she had grown up a simple shop girl, Clarice was whip-smart and had a good sense of humor. This was Brandon's first experience of simply being *friends* with a member of the opposite sex, and it was both strangely refreshing and satisfying.

After a year of this, Clarice told him she was closing the shop. "I haven't been feeling well lately..." she explained. She could no longer work as she had and she would rather sell the shop than have it fail under her faltering stewardship.

Clarice had a weak heart. Neither medicine nor surgery could heal it. She knew well that she didn't have much time left.

"What will you do after closing down shop?" Brandon asked.

Clarice laughed awkwardly. "I don't know... What should I do?"

Brandon knew that Clarice had already half abandoned herself to despair. He wanted to reach out to her. He wanted to ask her to be with him, to tell her that loved her with all his heart...as far more than a friend.

But he didn't think Clarice would agree to it. She had rejected all her suitors because she knew she didn't have long left to live. Brandon could imagine her rejecting him if he proposed.

In that case, it would be better for both of them to spend their days happy and for him to support her as a friend until the end. He made himself accept that.

But fate was about to shake things up, and in the worst way.

Far from the capital, the beast lord Valiant had emerged from the Void. The Abyss that had formed around it had an abyssal depth of 13.

Valiant was one of the ten greatest beast lords, a dragon so gargantuan that it covered the sky. It boasted incalculable strength, its true name was Krysta, and it believed itself to be god of both the sky and the sea.

The Abyss expanded around Krysta like an omnidirectional tsunami, engulfing and destroying three nations in as many weeks. The empire mustered all its forces to fight this threat. The military and regalia-owning clans were sent into the most desperate battle humanity would ever know.

Brandon's clan, Bloodsword Federation, played a major role in the world's salvation. However, even with the strength of the empire's most powerful clan and hero brought to bear against it, Krysta did not go down easily.

The battle lasted for a week, and many of his allies lost their lives. Even Brandon, who feared nothing, almost broke many times under Krysta's frightful power.

But Brandon never gave up. His pride, his love for his allies and those who had fallen, and most of all, what he wanted to tell Clarice kept him going.

The curtain to this hellish, drawn-out battle fell after one fatal stroke. Brandon's battle-axe finally split Krysta's skull in half. When the massive body that blotted out the very sky collapsed to the ground, everyone cried out in excitement over the victory.

However, the hero who contributed to the victory more than

anyone dodged the hands of his allies, ignored the voices calling for him, and traveled back to the capital at top speed. When he arrived, he located Clarice in a subterranean shelter.

Brandon hugged the confused Clarice and cried out, "I won! I have slain the greatest of beasts! I was so frightened. I thought I would never see you again. I was so scared, from the bottom of my heart!"

He stepped back from Clarice and looked at her, so overjoyed he'd lived to see her again that he could barely contain himself. Clarice smiled gently and softly touched Brandon's cheeks.

"You're crying again. You really are a crybaby," she said, tears in her own eyes as well. Brandon could see the deep relief in her eyes and the affection she felt for him. He knew exactly what he wanted to tell her.

"Clarice, I want to live for you." Brandon had his mind made up. He continued, "Will you live for me too?"

✝

"The weather is so nice…"

An old man sat on a stump in a clearing within a lush, green forest. His face was tired and creased with deep wrinkles, evidence of his age.

His name was Brandon Stollen. While he'd once been a great hero, thirty-five years had passed since he saved the world. Now he was sixty-seven years old, still strong and healthy, though the power he'd wielded in his prime was long gone.

A butterfly landed on his faithful and ever-present companion—his old battle-axe.

"Hmph, I wonder how much longer," Brandon muttered to himself as he stroked his white beard. Little birds sang and a squirrel groomed itself among the many branches of the trees around him.

The bright sunlight was warm. Brandon was having trouble keeping his eyes open. He let out a big yawn and all the animals fled at once.

"Oh, it's coming this way."

Brandon turned back toward the forest, seeing a bandit running pell-mell his way. The man's eyes were bloodshot, his face painted with tears and snot. He looked as though he was fleeing from some terrible monster.

"Old man! Run away!"

The crazed man approached Brandon, swinging his sword. He was running so fast, he couldn't even control his own body enough to avoid colliding with Brandon.

"I guess I have no choice."

Brandon picked up his battle-axe—and the next instant, the bandit fell face-first onto the forest floor. There was a throwing knife sticking out of the back of his head. The man convulsed a bit, then was still.

"It's over."

A child giggled in the distance. Then, a young boy emerged from the forest. This boy, who bore a startling resemblance to Clarice, was named Noel. He would be fourteen this year.

He was Brandon's grandson.

"Third time is boring. I'm used to hunting bandits now."

Noel smiled as he walked up to his grandfather and plucked his knife from the bandit's head. He then cut off the bandit's ear and put it in the leather bag on his waist. The bag was already bursting with trophies—the ears of twenty different men, proof that he had defeated them.

It was Brandon who'd ordered Noel to exterminate the bandits as part of the lad's Seeker training. The first time had been rough. The second had gone smoothly, and this, his third mission, had been a cakewalk. He wanted to praise his grandson for his improvement, but instead, he hardened himself and raised his voice. "Idiot! This one almost got away. What are you bragging about?!"

Noel scoffed at his grandfather. "No, he didn't. I *let* him run. I need to learn how to kill enemies who sense that their end is nigh and try to flee."

"And now you're making excuses..." It sounded like a lie, but the fact remained that Noel *had* made the kill. Arguing the point further would be pointless. "Fine. I'll accept it."

Brandon shrugged—then, in the blink of an eye, faced Noel and threw a punch faster than the eye could see. Noel easily dodged the attack, got up close to Brandon, and held a knife to his throat.

"Heh heh. Well done." Brandon smiled happily, patting Noel hard on the head. "That's my boy! You've done well for such a young lad!"

"Hey, stop messing up my hair!" Noel scowled and jumped away from his grandfather. "I'll be an adult next year! How long are you going to treat me like a child?!"

"Hmph, that's only what the law says. It wasn't so long ago I had to take you to the bathroom because you were afraid of ghosts."

"Wha?! When was that, you senile old man!"

"Who are you calling senile, fool student of mine?!"

They bickered, each giving as good as they got, and the dispute soon turned physical. Noel was strong, but Brandon was still overwhelmingly stronger, eventually landing a merciless blow that put Noel down hard, the wind knocked out of him.

"Ahh, ahh...so hard..."

"Of course it is, idiot. No matter how strong you think you are, the difference in our ranks—and even more importantly, our classes—means you'll never beat me."

Noel was a Talker, and so had no direct-damage-dealing combat skills. Brandon's training regime, both physical and mental, was designed to give him a fighting chance despite the weak nature of his class. He'd shared all his tactical and strategic knowledge with Noel, with the result that, although Noel was still a child, and a Talker at that, he could face off against medium-level foes and acquit himself well. He could also fight most beasts, though he'd never taken them down alone, of course.

"Noel, are you sure you really don't need me to write a letter of introduction?" Brandon asked as he sat on the stump again.

Noel sat up. "It's okay, I'll figure it out. I don't plan on joining someone else's party."

"So you'll start your own from scratch? Well, that's a good idea too. You are the grandson of Overdeath. No matter what path you take to get there, you can become the strongest Seeker."

The unfortunate truth was that Noel's class wasn't exactly a powerful one. However, he possessed the most important talent required of a Seeker—the will to win at all costs, and to never admit defeat.

"Noel—" Brandon was about to say something, but stopped himself.

He could see his late wife in Noel's face again. Noel resembled Brandon, Brandon's daughter, and her husband, but most of all, he looked like Clarice. He especially resembled her when he was angry, so much so that it reminded Brandon of their domestic quarrels. Clarice had also been a Talker, though her actual profession was that of a seamstress.

He wanted to tell Noel that he could always ask his grandfather for help if he needed it. His beloved wife had died in childbirth, and the daughter he'd raised all by himself had died alongside his son-in-law in an accident. Noel was the only family Brandon had left. He wanted to stay by the kid's side and protect him, no matter what.

But even Overdeath would die someday. Someday, he'd have to leave Noel behind. And so there was only one thing he could say to him now:

"You better become a man whom no one looks down on."

Experience all that SEVEN SEAS has to offer!